Death and Other Lovers

By Jo Bannister

Death
and Other Lovers

JO BANNISTER

A CRIME CLUB BOOK
DOUBLEDAY
New York   London   Toronto   Sydney   Auckland

A Crime Club Book
PUBLISHED BY DOUBLEDAY
a division of Bantam Doubleday Dell Publishing Group, Inc.
666 Fifth Avenue, New York, New York 10103

DOUBLEDAY and the portrayal of a man
with a gun are trademarks of Doubleday,
a division of Bantam Doubleday Dell
Publishing Group, Inc.

Library of Congress Cataloging-in-Publication Data

Bannister, Jo.
Death and other lovers / Jo Bannister. — 1st ed.
p. cm.
I. Title.
PR6052.A497D4   1991
823'.914—dc20   90-45165
                                                      CIP

ISBN 0-385-41652-0
Copyright © 1991 by Jo Bannister
All Rights Reserved
Printed in the United States of America
April 1991
First Edition

I charm thy life
From the weapons of strife,
From stone and from wood,
From fire and from flood,
From the serpent's tooth
And the beasts of blood.
From Sickness I charm thee,
And Time shall not harm thee;
But Earth, which is mine,
Its fruits shall deny thee;
And Water shall hear me
And know thee, and fly thee;
And the Winds shall not touch thee
When they pass near thee,
And the Dews shall not wet thee
When they fall nigh thee:
And thou shalt seek Death
To release thee, in vain;
Thou shalt live in thy pain
While Kehama shall reign,
With a fire in thy heart,
And a fire in thy brain;
And Sleep shall obey me,
And visit thee never,
And the Curse shall be on thee
For ever and ever.

"The Curse of Kehama"
by Robert Southey
(1774–1843)

Death and Other Lovers

CHAPTER 1

Fire and Flood

1

The fire told him it was time to move out, to move on.

There had been other indications, but he had chosen to ignore them. He was happy where he was, with the woman he was with, and did not want to leave. The scratch-marks on his steel door could have been only an opportunist burglar—one with leather lungs, as Flynn's apartment was five storeys and ten flights of stone steps above the river —and nothing to do with the visitation he had been half-expecting for the last four months. The funny phone calls that seemed like somebody checking to see if the apartment was empty could have been someone's idea of a joke: someone he knew getting drunk in a Fleet Street pub and giggling into the lapels of his trenchcoat at the thought of Flynn having to stop what he was doing at intervals to answer the phone.

About the fire, though, there was no room for doubt. The fire was arson, deliberate, premeditated, well-planned, well-executed arson, and it had been designed to destroy his darkroom and his home and maybe him too. It had come within an ace of killing Laura.

Perhaps they had not expected to find her there. It was only these last few days that she had been living here: before that, when Flynn went out the apartment was empty. If they had laid their plans a week ago they might not have known about the woman.

But they had seen her when she saw them, when she answered the door to them: two men, one in his twenties, one in his forties, of Middle Eastern appearance.

In the brief time he had known her they had exchanged more inti-macies than confidences, and he had not yet told her why he had to be wary of people of Middle Eastern appearance. In bed she had exclaimed over the scars on his back, but he had been too preoccupied then to tell her how he got them.

Even so, she had lived in the world long enough to know better than to open the door of an isolated apartment atop an empty warehouse to two men without first ensuring that the chain was in place.

It delayed them not a moment. The younger of the two produced long-handled shears from behind his back which nipped through the chain like nipping off a hang-nail. Then, still quite calmly, they shoved the door wide with enough force to knock her against the wall. Half stunned, she slipped down to the carpet.

The younger one watched her. The older made directly for the darkroom; thirty seconds later he returned and they left. They took the key from the wooden inner door, locking her in. She picked herself up off the floor and stumbled to the phone, and while she was dialling the darkroom exploded.

She owed her life to a hole in Flynn's pocket. Even had she the presence of mind to go on dialling, the best fire crew in London could not have reached her before the chemical-fed flames did.

But Flynn looked on camera-bags rather as overgrown handbags and would as soon have carried one as the other. Instead he piled lenses, filters and films into the marsupial pockets of an old combat jacket and slung the camera round his neck. But one of his pockets had a hole in it, and a zoom lens in its leather drum had squeezed through and bounced down half the steps outside the British Museum before he could catch it. It might be undamaged, but he did not want to take that risk with important photographs until he had examined it thoroughly on the bench and tested it. He went home for a replacement, and a safety-pin.

The darkroom had no windows so there was no tell-tale smoke to alert him as he parked on the wharf and ambled towards the building. But as he reached the ground floor entrance, the one that was left open to accommodate the comings and goings of a community of winos who lived in the derelict lower levels, there was a sudden crash of sound above him and, startled, he shot his gaze upward in time to see his bedroom window sail through the morning in a million sparkling fragments that caught the pale sun as they cascaded towards the river. Behind them billowed thick, roiling smoke and a gout of flame.

He yelled only, "Laura!" in horror and dread, the cry wrenched from him as if by torture; then he had flung aside the door and was racing up the stone flights as fast as his long limbs and his young man's strength would carry him.

On a corner he lurched into Derek the senior wino. Derek must have had another name once, probably another profession, but these were the only ones he acknowledged now. Flynn gripped his mouldering lapels and panted into his stubbly vacant face, "A fire. At my place. Get everybody out."

"Out?" Derek did not often go out. The last time was for a Crisis at Christmas reunion.

"Out!" Flynn flung him aside and attacked the next flight of steps. By now the smell was percolating down through the building, a thick acrid smell with chemical overtones which were familiar but which he could not identify. There were all sorts in the darkroom, some of them flammable, some of them toxic. If it was like this here, what was it like in the apartment?

Sheer physical exertion saved him from cowardice. Getting up these stairs left him neither the time nor the energy to dwell on what waited for him. All he knew, or cared, was that he had left Laura in the apartment—actually, still in his bed—when he went out two hours ago and so far as he could guess she would be there still. If the blast that took the window out had gutted the place, or if Laura had gone back to sleep, in all probability he was busting a gut for nothing but the chance to die in the same inferno.

Going up the last flight he could not get enough air to feed his clamouring lungs, and his heart raced and leapt crazily in his chest in the effort to push round whatever oxygen was in his blood. The sound of it filled his ears. He could not be sure if the fire had stolen all the air, or if it had more to do with the ten flights of steps.

The steel door barred his way. When he turned the corner and saw it through sweat-blinded eyes he thought, in a moment of utter despair, that he had left his keys in the car. But of course he had not: the car would not have been there when he went back. They were in his pocket—one without a hole—and he fumbled fitting them to the appropriate locks.

Then the five-yard passage lit only by the naked top-light that burned night and day. The smoke was visible here, the smell overpowering. He could see it wreathing lazily under the inner door. He knew he should feel the wood to see if it was hot inside. He knew that if he did and it was he would not dare open it and Laura would die within a few feet, maybe within inches, of him. He blanked his mind, turned the key—luckily its twin was not in the lock on the other side—and threw the door open, flinching as he did so in expectation of the dragon's breath of searing flame that would belch at him, crackling his skin, boiling his eyes.

There was flame inside, and thick biting smoke, but not against the door. The burst window of the bedroom had drawn it from the adjacent darkroom and it was spreading out slowly into the living area. He hoped the livingroom window would hold out. If they got a through-draught in here . . .

He shut the door behind him. The smoke made it hard to see. "Laura?" He got a mouthful of the stuff that sent his starved lungs into spasm. He doubled up, coughing until he tasted blood. All the time the smoke was thickening. Flames hung like a curtain, roared like Niagara, across the open door of the bedroom. He could not see her. If she was in there . . . ?

She had given him flowers, the day she moved in here. No-one had ever given him flowers before. He had to go out specially and buy a vase. If the tall glass flute he chose was not ideally suited to the frothy mass of chrysanthemums, Laura smiled and said nothing. The flowers were lasting well.

Now he tore them out of the vase and shoved his handkerchief deep into the earthy-smelling water. With that over his face he could breathe—a little, maybe enough—without the fumes turning his lungs inside out.

He had been in here maybe twenty seconds and still had not found Laura. There was a limit to how long he could stay: if the blaze flashed over it would kill him, but no more surely than if the air ran out of oxygen or filled up with toxic fumes. The time he had was a matter not of minutes but of moments. He had to find Laura, if she was here and still alive; and if she was not, establish the fact and get out while he still had a lining to his lungs.

Keeping low, breathing the mingled smells of chemicals and chrysanthemum water, he moved along the wall. Smoke filled the upper half of the long room but for a few seconds yet he could still see under it. She was not behind either of the big couches set in the corner; not in the well between them; not among the forest of chair legs and table legs where ceiling-high bookshelves defined an arbitrary diningroom. She was not here. Had she been in bed still? The insides of him

shrank. Nothing could have survived in there, the very wallpaper must
be ablaze. He could not go in to make sure. Nobody could have gone
in there. The thing was not possible. Surely to God he did not have to
die to prove it?

The kitchen? The bathroom was already a lost cause, filled with
impenetrable smoke more deadly than the fire, but the kitchen was
across the hall from the darkroom and the bedroom. If she had got in
there and shut the door, and used tap-water to damp down her
clothes, she could be safe—safer than him. He stumbled across the
open space in the middle of the apartment, yawning before him like a
football field though he had never found it too big before, and tried the
kitchen door.

She pulled him inside, slammed it behind them. Her eyes were
enormous white saucers in her long black face. But she did not appear
to be hurt, either by smoke or by fire; though he was not sure what
burns on a black skin looked like.

"Thank Christ!" He clutched her to him, feeling the tremble of her
long body against his own. Abruptly he pushed her away. "We have to
get out of here."

Her sculpted nostrils flared at him. "I'm not going out there—!"

"It's all right. We can make it, but we have to go now."

"Mickey!" Her eyes pleaded with him more eloquently than her
voice, shrill and husky with smoke and fear.

"There's no other way." He was struggling to stay calm, for both
their sakes, but the panic he could keep out of his words and even
mostly out of his voice was still audible in the elevated meter of his
breathing. It might have been exertion, or the smoke, but it was not
and—at least to him—it did not even sound like it. "It's all right,
Laura, I promise you. I came up that way only a few seconds ago. If we
go now there's no problem—we'll be outside in half a minute."

"Mickey, I can't go out there!"

"You have to." He turned both taps full on, dumped towels and tea-
cloths under the flow. Then he used a jug to pour water over the long
djellaba that was all she wore. The shock of the water hitting her drew
from her a little breathy scream. He baptised himself in the same way.
"Once we reach the steel door we can shut it off. The air stinks but
there's no fire."

Or had not been half a minute before. The roar outside was louder
now. If the livingroom had filled with flame, or if the smoke had

reached down from the ceiling, could they survive even the few seconds it would take them to reach the door? If it came to that, would they be better knocking out the kitchen window and jumping for the river? There was a narrow walk round the front of the building; they should have no difficulty clearing that, but it was a fall of five storeys into a river often thick with debris. Moreover, when the tide went out the water barely covered the silt below the long disused warehouse.

He tried desperately to remember the state of the tide but could not, nor could he judge it from here. He thought it was a bigger risk than the fire.

He pulled the towels from the sink, wrapped them round Laura's head and hands. He could do nothing practical about her bare feet. "When that door opens, we're committed. You keep hold of me, and you keep moving."

When the door opened he thought he had made a terrible mistake. Flames leapt in the doorway. Laura's hidden face screamed in his shoulder. But mostly it was the movement of air which had made it flare up. The curtains were on fire now, the two couches smouldering, but the centre of the long room remained essentially free of fire, though the black boiling smoke was reaching down further from the ceiling every moment.

Flynn had filled his lungs with the last clean air from the kitchen and doused his handkerchief again before tying it over his face. Now he hurdled through the frame of fire, dragging Laura with him.

For a moment she was a dead weight resisting him; then she found courage from somewhere and she was running with him, letting him guide her but relying on his strength not at all. There was one bad moment when Flynn found the coffee-table in front of him and hurdled it, forgetting that Laura would not see it in time to do likewise. But somehow she did see it, or sense it, and got one bare foot on its polished surface, and the tug of Flynn's hand and her own momentum carried her safely over, and then they were at the door.

Flynn reached for the handle and yelped, snatching back his hand. The mounting heat in the apartment had made the brass fitting hot enough to burn him. Before he could steel himself to grasp it anyway, Laura had one of her swathed hands on it and it was open.

Fresh air fanning into the room fed the fire. They heard the roar behind them as the flames balled and burst, and the explosion of glass as the livingroom window flew out, but they saw nothing because they were running, heads down, backs bent, for the first real promise of safety which was the steel door.

When they got there Flynn slammed it, shutting in the flames, and leaned against it, his chest heaving as if something had to give. But the safety they had reached was a temporary one at best: there was almost nothing here for them to breathe. They picked themselves up and proceeded, still quickly but no longer at that breakneck pace, down through the building.

On the last flight of steps they met Derek. Flynn had his breath back by now, enough to ask, "Is everybody out?"

"Out," Derek agreed vaguely; "yes."

Flynn shook him by the shoulders. "Are you sure?"

The wrecked man drew himself up with dignity. "Of course I'm sure. Else I wouldn't be leaving, would I?"

The first fire-engine arrived as they spilled out onto the wharf. The fresh air hit Flynn like a slap. His hands were shaking. Thinking, because he was still holding her, that it was Laura who trembled, he took off his jacket and put it round her shoulders.

The firemen leapt from their appliance—which to firemen means a fire-engine and to most other people a truss—and began unspooling hose-reels. The officer in charge ran his practised eye along the assembled ranks of winos with growing despair. When he came to Flynn he breathed an audible sigh of relief. "You. Is there anyone still inside?"

"Not where the fire is." He explained about the chemicals and the steel door. "And as far as I know, not in the rest of the building."

One team trained a hose on the bedroom window belching red flame and black smoke above them. Another moved into the building and up the stairs, taking Flynn's keys with them.

A police car arrived, another fire-engine and an ambulance. For the first time properly, Flynn looked at the tall straight woman beside him. "Are you all right?"

Long slender hands swept the hair back from her face. It stood out round her head in a mass of dense curls like a black halo. Her eyes were laced with red and tears, but she smiled and nodded. "You?"

"Yeah, sure." He was not, not quite. The door handle had burned the palm of one hand; burning matter in the air had left its mark on the back of the other, on one cheek and a shoulder. None of it needed more than first aid or promised more than an uncomfortable night. He would lose more sleep when he discovered the irreparable damage to his jacket, that was not so much a garment as a security blanket.

But reaction or relief or something set a nerve twitching behind his knee, then the muscle went momentarily to jelly and he sat down abruptly on the doorstep. Then the ambulance men moved up with their oxygen, and after that the policemen moved up with their questions.

2

When Laura told the police what had happened, Flynn turned very white. He had had no chance to hear it before and had assumed that the fire was some kind of a freak accident. He reckoned to be careful with his chemicals and equipment, but anyone could make a mistake or be plain unlucky. The idea of men breaking into his apartment, starting a fire and deliberately locking his woman in with it chilled him to his very soul. And more, not less, because he felt he should have expected it.

For seven years he had worked as a news photographer. In that comparatively short time—shorter if you subtracted the months he had spent hors de combat—he had become one of the top names in the field: partly for the quality of his images, which were strange and violent and disturbing and lingered on the mind long after the headlines had passed on, but partly too for his reputation for capturing these arresting images by sticking his neck out further than was common or wise.

This was not the first time someone had had a go at him. He had displeased a lot of violent, corrupt and unscrupulous people in seven years. He had been threatened, he had been hurt because of it. He expected that, tried to watch his back for it. But this he had never expected, and he thought now that he should have done.

They adjourned to the police station. Laura—they had found her some more suitable clothes—made her statement, then they set her to work with a PhotoFit expert. Meanwhile Inspector Ford, who had clearly received some surprising information about Flynn via his computer, sat him down with a mug of coffee and eyed him speculatively.

"We have requests from two foreign police forces to keep an eye on you."

Flynn was too drained, mentally and physically, to manage much of a reaction. "Only two?"

"A friendly eye," explained the Inspector, "a protective eye, but an eye for all that."

Flynn's tired gaze found him through the steam. "So where were you this morning?"

Ford sighed. "Keeping a less friendly eye on a lot of other people. What can I tell you?—we can't mount a twenty-four-hour guard on people for years at a time. It was a good job you got back when you did."

Flame bloomed again in Flynn's eyes and he shuddered. "It was a bloody miracle."

"So who might hate you this much, Mr. Flynn?"

Flynn thought for a moment. "Alphabetically or chronologically?"

He had had "I'll get you for this" hurled at him more times than he could remember. Mostly it was rhetoric, spat out by people who would not have known how to set about making him pay even if they had stayed mad long enough to want to. Mostly the people who had the money, the clout and the reason to vent their serious displeasure on him also had the sense not to warn him first.

But this was no spur-of-the-moment retaliation, a flung fist, a drawn knife, even a car grinding him into the brick wall of a dark alley. It was colder than that, more calculating. If they had wanted to burn him they would not have waited until mid-morning when his car was gone. They wanted to burn something dear to him instead, and not just his home. Four days Laura had been here with him. Before that there had been nobody he would have grieved over. So they had waited and watched.

Four names he could think of, four men who might have hated him that much, and that coldly, that they would watch for months or years until he had something he cared about and then destroy it. Obregon, Loriston, Wylie and Fahad; not necessarily in that order.

He saw from Ford's face that none of the names were new to him. Still he asked, "Who are they? What did you do to them?"

Flynn shrugged. "I took their photographs."

Without question, Tomas Obregon was the most evil of the four. He was probably the most evil man Flynn had ever met; also one of the most urbane, cultured, charming. The walls of his white house in

Florida were covered with mostly modern masters: Picasso, van Gogh, Salvador Dali, Modigliani. He supported a youth theatre in Miami, a writers' commune in Nassau, several orphanages and a resettlement programme for Cuban exiles. He paid his taxes, and his big white car obeyed speed limits.

But the money for the car, and the paintings, and the house, and the assorted orphans and exiles and writers, came from the drug trade. Tomas Obregon was one of the top half-dozen drug barons in the world, and everyone in that world knew it. The difficulty lay in proving it. The U.S. Drug Enforcement Administration had tried. Some of their agents had died trying, but it was no easier to prove him a murderer.

It was not so much that Flynn had succeeded where the FBI had failed, more that he could do things which it could not, and achieve his effect with mere careful suggestion where the FBI required hard evidence that would stand up in a court of law.

Thus began a brilliant, bizarre campaign that over a period of five months shredded the apparently impervious cloak of respectability Obregon had spent fifteen years weaving; a campaign that made no allegations against Obregon, that only once mentioned him by name; a campaign spread through a dozen newspapers in as many cities.

The first photograph appeared in all the papers, to the considerable if short-lived gratification of its subject. It showed Mr. Obregon stepping out of his distinctive long white car to attend the opening night of the Miami youth theatre that bore his name. It was a very pleasant photograph, if a shade tame by Mickey Flynn's standards, and the kindly mien of the dapper middle-aged Hispanic, the stylish opulence of his favourite car and the happy pride of the multi-coloured ragamuffins welcoming their patron ensured it a prominence that perhaps its content alone could not have justified.

The second photograph was also taken in Miami, a dramatic study of the docks made one thunderous early morning with the heavy clouds picked up by a moody filter. Three-quarters of the frame was filled by the high flaring bow of a Panamanian freighter, her name *Cartagena* in rusty white letters at top right, behind her the Miami skyline. Bottom left, parked on the quay by the freighter's gangway, was a long white car. The picture carried Flynn's by-line and some cosy caption about day beginning early for those who work on the Miami waterfront.

Elsewhere on the page, connected by nothing more substantial than coincidence, was a paragraph about the *Cartagena* being allowed to proceed on her passage from Miami to Norfolk, Virginia, after being delayed by a customs search.

The third photograph showed a great panorama of fall coming to the wooded mountains of Pennsylvania. It was in colour, which was hardly more archetypal Flynn than the Wonders of Nature style of photography but which showed the autumn growing down the sides of the hills from the scalped peaks, through as many shades of red and yellow and auburn and umber as there were leaves on the myriad trees, to meet the green of late summer in the valley. Behind the peaks the sky was that particular pale, intense blue that comes with the first cold.

From edge to edge the picture must have captured four miles and two thousand feet of Allegheny Mountain land, and in all that vast expanse there was only one indication of human intrusion. Halfway up the mountain, visible through the thinning boughs, ran a road and on the road, nose to nose, tiny as toys from a Christmas cracker, were two cars. One was long and white. The other had steer horns on the grill.

And elsewhere on the page was a reference to the arrest, on charges of drug trafficking, of a Philadelphia businessman whose sole interest was hitherto believed to be beef cattle and whose stocky figure, Stetson hat and horn-bedecked limousine were a familiar sight at state fairs the length and breadth of the country.

By now those most closely involved, and a good many others besides, were alert to the game being played and watching for its next move with feelings ranging from glee to black fury, depending on the degree and nature of their involvement. They were not kept waiting long.

In New York Flynn photographed the long white car outside a lawyer's office. The ostensible subject of the picture was some street theatre. On the same page was news that the lawyer had been retained to defend two men accused of breaking legs in a dispute over who should sell what drugs on which street corner.

In Washington Flynn photographed the long white car in traffic alongside a delivery van for a major, and wholly respectable, pharmaceuticals outlet. Both vehicles had been held up for the parade that was the alleged focus of the picture. But the placement of the caption describing it had necessitated cropping most of the van's side panel including its owners' names. Only the word "druggist" hung over the top of the white car like an accusation.

Then Obregon took his two young nephews to a flying display. He had his car parked as centrally as a generous tip could ensure, and adjacent to a static display of veteran planes. If he noticed that one of them had its propellers on the trailing edges of the wings he thought nothing of it until Flynn's photograph of the plane, the white car clearly visible in the background, appeared under the headline PUSHER.

Tomas Obregon was not the man to take all this lying down. But even the high-powered help he could afford found it difficult to formulate a tenable complaint. A series of unconnected newspapers had published a series of unconnected photographs on divers topics, in which the assiduous reader armed with a magnifying glass might spot in the background a car which might possibly be Mr. Obregon's. So? There was no suggestion, in words or pictures, that the vehicle was anywhere it should not have been, or doing anything it should not have been doing. Was Mr. Obregon denying that he had been to a flying display? Was there libel potential in indicating that he had driven through a Pennsylvanian wood?

Obregon might not have restricted himself to legal remedies, nor probably to breaking legs; but about that time the snowball Flynn had so carefully shaped and set rolling began to develop a momentum of its own. Things that had been secret were now public knowledge, the stuff of jokes. One New York cartoonist began to include a white car, vanishingly small but still quite distinct, in the background of his sketches. Embarrassment at past failures led to a political will to deal with Obregon which had previously been lacking. A new determination and a new priority, together with new funds, entered a renewed investigation of Tomas Obregon.

And at just that time Obregon gave up his house in Florida and shipped his paintings, and his car, to a property he owned in Barranquilla, across the Caribbean in Colombia, out of reach of U.S. law. It was not the best end that Flynn had hoped for when he began his crusade, but nor was it the worst. Crimes had been acknowledged, and even if the criminal had escaped justice for now, his time might yet come. All the rewards of his crime, except for the money, were forfeit: the respect he had enjoyed, the status. The youth theatre closed down and the orphanages changed their names.

And for a little while Mickey Flynn was as careful as he knew how to be. But there was no hint of retaliation, no sign that Obregon deigned to acknowledge his existence. Until one morning the post brought him an envelope plastered with South American stamps. There was no letter inside, only a small cartoon. It showed a graveyard, and a stone cross from the shoulders of which hung a camera, and in the background driving away was a long white car.

Flynn framed the cartoon and hung it in his bathroom.

Peter Loriston was not an evil man. He was not even a dishonest one, although following the scandal that led to his resigning his seat at Westminster he was perceived almost universally as not merely dishonest but corrupt.

As the Honorable Member for Chingley South and a junior minister at the Ministry of Defence, Loriston made three serious mistakes in the course of one heady week that turned him from one of the government's young lions into one of its banana skins.

The first mistake he would probably have been forgiven, since it was merely cheating on his wife and there was ample parliamentary precedent for that. The second, which was lying to the House, was much more serious, but even that he might have got away with if he had refrained from providing proof of the rumours that ran at the speed of an inspired leak through the corridors of power. The real mistake he made, the fatal one, the one that clinched it and made him overnight into a politician with a great future behind him, was being photographed on a yacht with the daughter of the man to whose company Loriston's ministry had just awarded a fat contract.

There was only one way the press, the public and particularly Her Majesty's Loyal Opposition were going to read that. Like the name of the latest soap-opera starlet, suddenly the cry "Corruption!" was on everyone's lips. Hadn't Peter Loriston, MP, been in a position to influence the award of this important defence contract? Hadn't the choice of Coxton Electronics been a controversial one? Hadn't Mr. Loriston assured the House, in the most direct and unambiguous terms, that neither he nor anyone else involved in allocating the contract had any association with Coxtons prior to or other than their dealings on the current matter?

And then hadn't Mr. Loriston, MP, forty-six-year-old ex-Guards officer, married man and father of two, been photographed aboard a floating gin-palace at anchor in a remote Sardinian bay washed by the wine-dark Tyrrhenian Sea, plainly engaged in an illicit Mediterranean idyll with the twenty-one-year-old daughter of the eponymous head of Coxton Electronics?

Those closest to the affair knew that Loriston's involvement with the girl was a bit of mid-summer madness, a frivolity, nothing more. It had in no way affected the government's business with Coxtons—nor could it have been allowed to, because what Coxtons had to offer was worth a great deal more than one junior minister at the MoD. Unfortunately for Loriston, what Coxtons had to offer was also secret, so that the award of the contract could not be publicly explained and justified.

Besides, the Honorable Member for Chingley South had lied to the House. There was no alternative but the Chiltern Hundreds. That one heady week had cost the ambitious, arrogant, able Mr. Loriston his career, his wife, his home and even, now her father had found out, his bit on the side. A week is indeed a long time in politics.

Flynn had no particular scruples about invading the privacy of a junior minister playing hooky with the daughter of a defence contractor, but nor did he consider the photograph one of the highlights of his professional career. He would not have included the embittered but probably still essentially honest Mr. Loriston on his list of Men Most Likely except for one thing. He rather thought Mr. Loriston had tried to kill him once before.

It was hard to be sure. It might have been only a moment's carelessness. It might have been a rather vicious joke devised to extract a small revenge for the damage Flynn had done him. But Flynn had seen his face in the split-second before he was leaping for his life, and it was his firm and abiding impression that Loriston was in absolute earnest.

Nine months had passed since their previous encounter, through a telephoto lens off the coast of Sardinia. Flynn had hardly thought of Loriston in that time. Now here he was on the public relations staff of a firm of architects showing him round the shell of a Wapping warehouse they were converting into a vertical village using startlingly modern technology that Flynn wanted to photograph.

They exchanged cool greetings and made no allusion to their earlier confrontation, but Loriston had neither forgiven nor forgotten. It showed in the stiff squareness of his broad shoulders, the almost gladiatorial way he moved round Flynn. Of course, he had been a soldier.

Flynn was not interested in Loriston. He was interested in the monster machines, in the play of structures hung over London at church-spire level, in the stark surreal views he hoped to see from the roof. Height had always fascinated him.

A rigger took them up as far as was safe. Flynn wanted to go higher. The rigger objected but Loriston saw no problem and, leaving his coat across a beam, began to climb. They scaled steel for another storey. Loriston pointed out the views downriver towards the Thames Barrier and up it towards St. Paul's. Flynn grafted himself to a girder by casually crooking one long leg round it and unshipped the camera he carried round his neck.

It was then that he saw Loriston looking at him. A moment later a cry of alarm and warning above him took his gaze racing up in time to see the grab of a crane opening to drop its contents of broken masonry and mortar dust into a skip below.

Looking back he was not sure that, if he had stayed where he was, rooted to the girder like ivy to an oak, the debris would have hit him. It might have poured straight past. Leaping back from the girder with no clear idea where he would find another was probably more dangerous than staying put, and he was lucky to have escaped with nothing worse than a racing heart and a lost filter. But in his own mind he was sure of one thing. Loriston had hoped the roaring debris would tear him from the face of the building and smash him to bloody pulp in the skip thirty feet below.

Even in his own mind, Flynn had never been able to decide whether Michael Wylie was an evil man or not. What he did was certainly illegal in the places where he did it, but in those places it was not always safe to equate illegality with wrongdoing. Besides, when Wylie was successful, very often the laws were changed. As history is written by victors, there were places where Wylie was regarded as a hero of the liberation and others where his life stood forfeit for revolutionary insurgency. Often these places stood cheek by jowl on the map, alternating like squares on a chess-board.

Wylie was a mercenary. War was his trade. He had learned it as an American soldier in the closing phase of the Vietnam adventure, had refined it in covert operations in South American jungles, had finally faced the choice of serving in the make-believe world of a peace-time army or getting out and finding some real battles to fight. Once he had thought of it in those terms it was no contest. Now he ran his own army.

Of the four men who might seek his death, Wylie was the only one Flynn reckoned to know in any degree personally. It might have been the shared nationality, or the three months he spent with Wylie's group in Africa which gave him the chance to talk to this tough, hard, infinitely professional man as he had not with the others. But there was another element too, and Flynn suspected that it was something as much in him as in Wylie. They had things in common, not so much experiences as attitudes. The way they worked, the way they lived, were not that dissimilar.

A casual observer would not have seen it. There were thirteen years, a generation, between them, the compact, intense violent-hearted man and the long-limbed footloose photographer with his kind eyes and his wicked grin. Wylie dealt in death, Flynn strictly in dollars. Flynn swore constantly and foully and it meant nothing. Wylie almost never raised his voice, but his displeasure was so abrasive it flayed the skin and drew blood.

But Flynn sensed what, having no particular skill with words, he could not describe: that he and Wylie were fellow-travellers on the same current of time and events, exiles mostly by choice with no allegiances and no master under a god neither of them believed in. Both sold their services where need, inclination and an ability to pay were conjoined. Neither paid even lip-service to the conventional morality that condemned them, yet neither was without a morality of his own. Flynn would not sell his camera, and found that Wylie would not sell his guns, where only the money was attractive. Wylie was a man who made almost a religion of being unlikeable; but Flynn liked him and found much to admire in him, and came finally to respect him, which was harder.

At the end of his time with Wylie, Flynn returned to London. They had arranged that he would publish nothing until the opening shots had been fired in the small war which Wylie was preparing for. It was always Flynn's intention to abide by that. But when news came through of a fire-fight on the border between government forces and alleged ivory poachers, Flynn assumed it was the signal he was waiting for and called the magazine he had sold the pictures to and told them to print.

Before the first copies reached London he knew he had made a mistake, that the alleged poachers were poachers indeed and Wylie was still manoeuvring his forces into position. The next he heard Wylie had been taken prisoner.

For ten days Flynn dwelt in an agony of guilt and horrid imaginings. He had spent long enough with the mercenaries to have learned something about this particular cashew republic, and what he had learned left him with no illusions as to its policy on human rights. That was one reason there were enough disaffected citizens to pay for professional help to overthrow their government.

Then word came out of fighting in the streets of the capital. The revolt had begun, the partisan forces organised and led by the mercenary army under the command of Wylie's lieutenant. The government must have thought itself safe for as long as they had the rebels' leader, and were wrong-footed by the attack, coming long enough after Wylie's capture for them to have relaxed and not long enough for them to have realised that a professional army which puts its own interests before those of the paying customers quickly runs out of paying customers.

By the time the government troops were mobilized the rebels had seized the power-station, the radio-station, the airport and the main armoury. Fighting continued all that day and throughout the night, but it was increasingly a rearguard action by government forces attempting to safeguard a negotiating position for their political masters. But the partisans had scented victory and were not interested in negotiating. Government House fell at dawn on the second day, and all remaining government installations were ceded to them by noon. Including the prison.

When Flynn learned that Wylie had been taken from the prison alive he tried desperately to obtain more information. But he could not get into the country—all flights had been cancelled and land borders closed—and when he tried to contact the new regime all he got was a message from Wylie's lieutenant saying, "Haven't you done enough?"

Flynn never succeeded in speaking to Wylie. He wrote explaining what had happened but had no way of knowing if the letter reached him; certainly Wylie never wrote back. But five months later Wylie was commanding his small army in a promising little war in Central America, and Flynn inferred that he must have recovered from whatever abuse he had received during his ten days of captivity.

But Flynn remained deeply uneasy about how his actions must have seemed to Wylie and his men. Some sins he was quite happy to have attributed to him, but betrayal was not one of them. He had respected Wylie, and would have liked his respect in return. After all that had happened, it seemed an optimistic ambition. Even more, he would have chosen to avoid Wylie's enmity. He suspected that Wylie's enemies slept as lightly and woke as nervously as turkeys in the first three weeks of December.

Then there was Fahad.

Very little of what happened to Fahad's organisation was Flynn's fault, but he doubted if Fahad saw it that way. The Israel Defence Forces had used Flynn, without his knowledge—he was about the last man involved in the operation, on either side, to find out—to infiltrate the Palestinian base Fahad had established in the desert by the Dead Sea.

When the IDF cleared it out, everyone there was either captured or killed. Except Fahad. His bomb expert was serving a life sentence. His chief of staff was dead. An entire intake of PFLP recruits, young Palestinian men and women come to him for training, together with those there to train them, had been lost to the intifada. Jamil Fahad's escape left him a general without an army.

Flynn knew that Fahad had intended to kill him at one time. It would come as no surprise to learn that he still did. The timing was a little odd. It was three years since the episode at Bab el Jihad: if Fahad had wanted vengeance for it, why had he waited so long? Of course, the first year Flynn would have been harder to get at. He was a prosecution witness at trials not only in Israel but also in Holland, and the assorted police involved were keeping a more than just friendly eye on him.

And after that he had moved around a lot. Perhaps Fahad would have tried for him then if he could have found him. New York, Nebraska, Mexico, Peru; the Obregon episode up and down the eastern states; at other times he was in Australia, in the Mediterranean where he caught up with Loriston, and in Africa for three months with Wylie's mercenaries.

He had only been back in England four months. Perhaps this was the first time he had stayed put long enough for Fahad to do something about him. After three years he had thought he was safe enough slowing down. It looked as if he had been wrong.

Inspector Ford gave a long low whistle. He looked impressed but not in the least envious. "You fairly get around, don't you?"

"It seemed like a good idea. Maybe I should have kept it up longer."

"And any of these four could hate you enough to want to—"

"To incinerate my girlfriend. Yes. But I don't know that any of them did."

"Anyone else?"

Flynn considered, shook his head helplessly. "Maybe. Maybe some-one who took something I did more seriously than I thought. But I don't know who."

"OK," said Ford. "Well, we'll get to work on it, see what we can find out." He fingered the intercom. "How's the PhotoFit coming?"

"We've got one decent likeness," said a man's voice. "Shall I bring it in?"

It was more than a decent likeness, it was a picture of a man Flynn knew. He let his eyes close and his head rocked back. Then he drew a deep breath. "Fahad," he said.

3

By the time the police had finished with Flynn and Laura, the Fire Brigade had finished with the apartment so they went back there. Laura was more than uneasy, practically needed dragging up the stairs. Flynn could have left her in the car but he felt in his bones that, even if she never set foot in the place again, she needed to go back once. So he half cajoled, half bullied her into going up with him.

The smell of wet soot was everywhere, so pervasive that even the winos had moved out for the moment. The stone steps were greasy with it. They went carefully to avoid falling. Laura was resigned now to returning, but still her hand clutched Flynn's tightly like an anxious child and on every corner her steps lagged so that he had to tug her gently along in his wake.

The forensic people had locked the steel door when they left. Flynn opened it, hardly knowing what to expect, from some nasty scorching to total devastation.

It was bad enough but it could have been worse. All the furniture was burnt beyond repair, all the windows blown out, the carpets charred in black drifts and soggy all over, some of the floorboards beneath in need of replacement. But structurally the building seemed to have escaped serious damage. The fire-engines had arrived in time to save the roof, and those stout Victorian walls would take more than a little fire to bring them tumbling down. When the insurance came through, the place could be made habitable again.

But not by tonight, or the weekend, or the end of the month; and even if he could have got the work done that quickly Flynn doubted it would have been a good idea. Until the police found Fahad, or at least knew he had left the country, it was only asking for an encore to move back here with Laura.

In fact, he did not think he could go anywhere with Laura now. Not until this thing was resolved. He could not expose her to that kind of danger, that kind of fear. In the wet sooty ruins of his home, with nothing to sit on, he tried to explain.

"The man who came here, the older one. He's been waiting three years for the chance to—hurt me. It isn't coincidence that you'd just moved in here. He must have been watching since I got back, looking for some way of getting at me. It wasn't enough to kill me, he could have done that before now—he wanted to kill someone I care about. If we stay together, wherever we go, however careful we are, he'll try again. We have to split up. Go away; and don't even tell me where you're going."

Laura Wade was a beautiful woman. She was very tall and straight, with long strong expressive hands. She had broad shoulders and narrow hips, and a long slender column of throat that ended under her pointed chin. Her eyes were the shape of almonds, her nose rather long and straight, her lips full, sculpted and mobile. Her skin was the colour and texture of the darkest parts of a seal-point Siamese. Her hair, when it was down, was an electric cloud blue-black around her head, and when she fastened it up it became a tight cap drawn into a braid at the back and underscored the attenuated lines of her skull much as shaving it would have done.

At thirty-three she was a couple of years older than Flynn: the calm, unhurried confidence that came with that maturity, amounting at times almost to a serenity, was one of the things that attracted him to her when they first met ten days ago. Today that confidence had taken a beating, but already the strength of maturity and independence was reasserting itself.

She said, "Are you sure you want to let him win?"

Flynn's eyes flared at her. His eyes were the most attractive thing about him: just brown, plain brown like the hair he could not be bothered to keep trimmed to a sensible length, neither hypnotically large nor wonderfully lustrous; not at all the sort of eyes that get written about in romantic novels. But his eyes were a direct line to his soul, and his soul was a lot nicer than anything else about him suggested.

He was thirty-one now, had been a lot of places and done a lot of things, had known extremes both of failure and success. He had been close to death a few times, and to suicide twice—not even honest, straightforward, head-first-off-a-high-building suicide but the cowardly sort, drink the first time and deliberately courting danger the second. He had suffered pain, and fear, and humiliation; and once he had been considered the best photo-journalist in the world.

So his thirty-one years had left him in no sense a virgin. He had used and been used, and people who knew him a little thought they could see it in his lazy shambling walk, in the cynical twist of his wide mouth even before it broke into its evil grin, in the careless lop-sided shrug of his shoulders.

But they were people who had not known him well enough to look into his eyes, because his eyes gave the lie to that. Somehow the tide of events that had surged past and not infrequently over him had never found its corrosive way into his soul. The notorious self-mocking obscenity of his language did not reflect, as it might have done, some inner cess-pit of despair and disappointment. Somehow his soul had managed to retain a strange innocence, a kind of simplicity, and it was the unexpected glimpse of that which made his eyes so attractive.

But if it came to a straight fight between Flynn's innocence in disguise and Laura's sophistication, it was no contest. He had no defences she could not penetrate. So when his eyes flared she saw the fear behind them, which was for himself as well as for her, and the memory of hurt, and the impotent rage of being hounded from his house and his woman.

"Of course I don't," he snarled. "But what choice do I have? I won't be responsible for Fahad taking out on you what he's got against me."

"Suppose I take that responsibility?"

He shook his head stubbornly. "You don't know what he's like. He wouldn't have started this unless he was prepared to finish it."

"Then we'll run away together."

"I don't want you mixed up in this."

"And I don't want you dying alone!" She broke off and blinked, and waited for her voice to come down a tone or two. Her speaking voice was deep and mellow, the voice of mature sophistication, but she shouted like a fish-wife. "Mickey, I care about you. That's why I moved in here—not to save on hotel bills, or to give me something to do in the evenings when there's nothing on the telly." That drew a quick grin from him and she smiled in return. "I want to be with you. I want us to be together."

He had his hands shoved deep in his trouser pockets. Already he was missing his combat jacket, but even Flynn drew the line at wearing clothes with actual holes in them. "You think I don't?" He was struggling to find words. His emotional vocabulary was less comprehensive and less well exercised than his litany of abuse. He could curse fluently in several languages but found it difficult to express love in his own. "I'd give—anything—I want you, with me, by me. I'd fight him for that, if I could find him. I'd risk what he might do to me. But I won't risk him doing any more to you. Damn it, woman, I think I love you!"

"Well, you've a funny way of showing it," Laura said gruffly, turning away. It was unfair—probably in all the circumstances it was the only way he *could* have shown it—but it still stung. He wanted to reach out and hold her, and let his stinging palm go hang, but held at bay by her resentment he only shoved his hands further into his pockets than before.

What he did not do was let her sway him. It might not be the ideal solution, but for the moment it was the best he could do. With his back against the wall he was capable of almost infinite obstinacy. "We'll get together again sometime. After he's gone, or if the police catch him maybe." He did not have high hopes of that. "I'll give you an address, of a friend of mine. When you're settled, let him know where. Then when it's safe I'll know where to find you."

She shrugged, with a coolness he did not believe she felt. "Sure, Mickey. Unless I've had a better offer by then."

Before they left the apartment Flynn went into the darkroom. This room of all of them was gutted: broken glass and melted plastic and a thick sludge of wet ash heaped together on the floor. Nothing had survived. Laura could not imagine what he was doing. Her brow creased in puzzlement, she watched from the door as he picked his way through the debris to one corner where he folded his long body down like a roosting heron. His fingers brushed at the floor. Then he peeled back the remains of the vinyl and lifted a hinged section of the floorboards to reveal a safe beneath. He opened it with a key from his ring.

"Whatever do you keep in there, the family jewels?"

Flynn grinned. He had no family, and no valuables beside his equipment. "Negatives. The kind of negatives I want to keep, and that people might try to steal. The models who sit for me don't always do so voluntarily."

"Will they have survived the heat?"

The sixty-four-thousand-dollar question. "I'll tell you in a minute." He pulled folders out of the hole, opened them, held the contents up to the light coming through the open door. "Miracles will never cease."

Curiosity moved her closer. "What have you got that someone might want to steal?"

Honesty was not a virtue to which he let himself be held ransom, but somehow he could not lie to her. "Well, nothing much at present. Mostly they're pictures I might be able to sell again, and things I want to keep for old times' sake. I've got the Obregon set in here, and—oh, most of the important stuff from the last couple of years."

Laura was leafing through them with him. "Who's that?"

Flynn looked at the negative, automatically seeing it as it would appear when printed. "That's Hehn. You know, the chemist." Her face remained blank. "The one who won the Sondheim Prize. If I keep it till he wins something else I can sell it again."

"What will you do with these now?"

"Take them with me. I can't leave them here. Besides, there's enough stuff here to pay the bills until I can get working again."

"Where?"

"I don't know. Even if I did, I wouldn't tell you. It's better that way —safer."

"For whom?"

Again he could not lie to her. "For both of us."

She seemed to reach a decision, then straightened up. "All right. I'm going to need some clothes. I'll buy some for you too, and a couple of suitcases. Get together what you can salvage, and I'll see you back here in a couple of hours." She took his wallet: her money was lost with the rest of her belongings.

She had the sense to get him a case big enough to leave room for his files. She said, "Can you drop me some place?"

"I'm not taking the car," said Flynn. "Or only as far as Heathrow. You could keep it, but Fahad will have the number. Tell you what, sell it. It'll give you something to live on until we sort this mess out."

Laura's face had gone still. "You're going to fly? You're going too far to drive?"

"Yes. Please don't ask where."

They had spent too long sorting through their affairs. Now they hit the evening rush-hour. Flynn was driving. "Don't worry, I know a short-cut." He took them a way of wharves and warehouses, through a goods yard, beside a derelict canal.

Flynn was not the only one who knew this way. Coming through the goods yard they picked up the brake-lights of a pale gold Porsche. Coming up from the canal they picked up a police escort.

At first Flynn thought it was him the police wanted and he slowed down, but the car passed him and went in pursuit of the Porsche. When Flynn caught them up both vehicles were stopped, practically blocking the road, and the occupants were getting out. The man in the Porsche, a young black of about twenty-two, was snarling, "Jesus, man, not again?"

The larger of the two policemen said stolidly, "Is this your car, sir?"

"Yes it's my car. It's still my car. It was my car yesterday, and three days ago, and last Sunday afternoon when you asked. I have made no arrangements to transfer its ownership since then."

"I don't believe I've stopped you before, sir."

"Well, if it wasn't you it was some other white cop who don't like to see a black brother doing himself well." He grinned, a sudden feral flash of white with no humour in it. "You all look the same to me."

The policeman's expression never flickered. "Can you show me some documents, sir?"

"Yes, I can show you some documents. I can show you my driving licence and my insurance. I can show you my tax return, proving that I earn about ten times what you do every year. I can show you the sleeve of my latest album, which has a picture of me driving this car on it. And I can show you my diary, with a note of every time I've been stopped, checked and allowed to proceed by you people in the last six months. It makes an interesting statistic."

"No need to be like that, sir," said the policeman, still stolidly, "we're only doing our job. If somebody stole it off you, wouldn't you be grateful if we stopped him?"

"Sure I would." The singer's tone was derogatory. "And if he was white and you stopped him, I'd be more than grateful—I'd be amazed."

Flynn was already getting out of his car, quietly, a camera—the little chain-store job from the glove-compartment—in his hand. He said softly, "There's going to be trouble here. Stay in the car."

Laura stared at him. "How do you know?"

"Stay in the car." Everything about him was suddenly different: his face, his voice, even the way he moved, purposeful and professional and predatory. With cat-like stealth he edged up on the scene developing ahead.

In his exchange with Laura he had missed something of what had been said at the Porsche. Presumably it was more of the same, for now tempers were growing shorter. The singer was shouting. "Now you've got my driving licence and insurance, and I want your number and his number, and if I don't get them I'm going to pick up this yuppie mobile phone and call one cop shop after another until someone admits to owning you two."

Flynn could not swear to precisely what happened next. It was his impression that the driver was reaching inside the Porsche for his car-phone; someone closer might have had reason to suppose it was something more sinister he was being threatened with. So perhaps the policemen were justified in hauling the man out of his car backwards by the belt of his trousers. It was harder to justify them hitting him with their fists until he fell down and then kicking him.

It was the classic photographer's dilemma: whether to record or to intervene, to witness or to participate. Flynn chose, as he usually did, to do his job.

In any event the effect was much the same. The first policeman who glanced up and saw Flynn and his camera barked a warning and they both staggered back, Flynn taking the opportunity to add full-face portraits to the action shots on the film. Then they came towards him purposefully, stepping over the curled-up body of the man on the ground. Flynn took another shot as they came.

Before they had the chance to ask he said, "No, you may not have my camera. If you try to take it I shall bring charges of assault and theft."

They broke their stride, exchanging a glance as if trying to judge if he was bluffing. While they wondered he went on calmly, "If I was not on my way to the airport I would do something about this"—he indicated the young man climbing to his feet—"right now. I may still do something once my own business is attended to. For now what I shall do is tell both you and him how you can find me if you want me. Call any major newspaper and ask for Mickey Flynn. I won't be there, but I'll get the message."

The police car left first, then the Porsche, the driver waving Flynn a grateful salute as he went. Flynn put the camera in his case, then he too drove out of the back street.

At the airport he gave Laura the keys, the documents and a scribbled authority to dispose of the car, then took his case off the back seat. "Well—so long." He was not sorry she did not want to come inside with him. He waited on the pavement until she was out of sight.

All the way here, except for the incident near the canal, he had been wondering what plane to get on. New York was the obvious choice—it was his home town, he knew his way round, could get help there if he needed it. For the same reasons, of course, it would also be obvious to Fahad.

It came down to what he hoped to achieve by running. Just keeping a step ahead of the man hunting him? Shifting the action to where it would not threaten Laura? Was there a way he could get Fahad off his back, or was he only delaying the inevitable once again?

He did not know. Laura's jibe had struck home. Of course he did not want to let Fahad win, drive him from pillar to post until one day he should trap him where he could not run and kill him there. But he did not know what she expected him to do: stand his ground and die there instead, and have her die with him? No police force in the world could protect them indefinitely from a fanatic with time and a sense of grievance on his side.

At least in New York he would not be worrying about Laura. If they met in New York he would be fighting on home ground; he could maybe get hold of a gun and— He sighed. There was a small chill space inside him, a hollowness, an emptiness. He recognised it as fear: the chill, still fear of things for which action offers no remedy. Actually there was nothing he could do, in New York or anywhere else, to make it harder for Fahad to kill him. He could keep running away, that might work for a while yet. But any time he stopped he was going to be right back here: back in the apartment with the roar of flames about his ears, the sear of naked heat on his skin. Fahad was not going to let him go. He was not even going to let him die easily.

At least in New York he could hope that, whatever happened to him, Laura would be safe. On that basis he would fight Fahad for his life. He bought a ticket to the Big Apple; one-way.

There were empty seats on a flight preparing to depart and he took one of them. He warned the security staff about his negatives and they took appropriate care in checking him through. Of course, they knew him, both his face and his name. For a large part of seven years he had been a regular commuter on this route.

Being the last to board, he was expecting the plane to leave as soon as he could find the other half of his seatbelt. But it just kept sitting there, its electrics ticking over desultorily, with occasional slightly tetchy apologies from the flight-deck for the delay. Circumstances beyond their control, they said, which could have meant anything.

Flynn spent the time looking for somewhere to put his long legs and playing the faces game with his fellow passengers. The old man was a famous Hungarian conductor. The teenage boy uncomfortable in his best suit had been bequeathed a controlling interest in a publishing company by his canny Scottish grandmother and was on his way to save the family's honour from a take-over by a soft-porn house. The business-woman with the briefcase was carrying plans for a revolutionary new under-arm deodorant and was being pursued by agents of a rival cosmetics firm.

Actually, he supposed she was nervous about flying. He said, "Don't worry, we're pretty near the back."

She looked at him as if for the first time, with a perplexed and edgy smile. "I'm sorry?" She was an American.

He gave her his grin that sent brave men scampering for trees. "Planes almost never back into mountains."

It may not have been the right thing to say. She disappeared into her briefcase like a Jack Russell down a rabbit-hole.

Finally the waiting ended, not with the little lurch of a tractor taking up the tow but with the opening of the cabin door which had been closed ten minutes before. Two men came aboard and made their way slowly down the length of the plane, their eyes scanning the rows of faces.

From his first glimpse of them Flynn knew two things: that they were policemen, and that they were looking for him. His mind juggled the possibilities. Had they caught Fahad? Dear God, had *he* caught up with Laura? The other prospect was that they wanted to talk about the business with the Porsche.

They spotted him from three rows ahead. "Mr. Flynn? I wonder if we could have a word."

"Is Laura all right?"

"Laura?" The older of the two men frowned. "Who's Laura?" So it was not about her, or the fire.

So it was about the Porsche. Flynn stayed where he was, deliberately not touching his seatbelt. He stretched his legs under the seat in front. "Sure. What can I do for you?"

The man smiled thinly. "Not here. There's an office at the terminal we can use. More private. If you'll come—"

"How much privacy do we need? Say what you have to say, this plane's about to leave."

The policeman breathed heavily. "I'm sorry, Mr. Flynn, I must ask you to accompany me back into the building."

"You got a warrant?"

"Do I need one?"

He went with them. He had no good reason not to. Besides, since they were not going to get their own way on the major issue it was in the interests of press/police relations to allow them this small victory.

They took him to a room where a tray waited with cups and a coffee-pot on the desk. Flynn raised an eyebrow at it. "I don't think the captain will be happy if we settle down to make an evening of this."

The policeman who was doing the talking, who on the short walk here had introduced himself as Inspector Harris, shook his head. "Don't you worry about the captain, sir. He'll do what he's told."

It was about the Porsche. They understood Flynn had witnessed an incident involving a motorist and two uniformed police officers. A complaint had been made and was being investigated. It would be helpful in establishing just what had happened if they could have the film he had shot.

"I'll send you prints, from New York."

They did not want to put him to that much trouble. If he would leave the film with them, they could print what they needed and forward the negatives to him when they were finished. Where was the film?

"In my camera."

And the camera was—?

"In my bag. In the hold. You want to ask the captain to off-load all his baggage while he's waiting?"

Inspector Harris did the thin smile again. He did not think that would be necessary. He thought Flynn's bag could be extricated and the film removed without too much difficulty, given Mr. Flynn's co-operation.

"Damn co-operation," said Flynn tersely, except that he did not say "damn." "You want my film because you don't want those pictures finding their way into the papers. Well, I don't part with my films— not ever—and you have no legal grounds for compelling me to do so. You want to stop me leaving the country with my camera and my film in it, you get a court order. If you're prepared to tell a magistrate why you want it. But you'd better do it now." He was already on his feet and making for the door.

The younger policeman was standing by the door, not exactly obstructing it and not exactly not. The older one did not move from his chair. He folded his hands in his lap. "So you don't feel you can help us, sir."

The way he said it was not quite right. He should have been trying harder, either shouting or wheedling by now. Even the regret in his voice had a certain complacency about it. He would not have liked having to do this, trying to pull some other officers' chestnuts out of the fire; particularly he would not have liked trying and failing; most especially he would not have enjoyed being told where to go by the likes of Mickey Flynn. He just had no business now looking and sounding so god-damned smug.

"Well, if you won't you won't. You don't mind me asking, I hope, sir?" Flynn shook his head silently. He knew there was a punch-line coming, just did not know yet what it was. "Well, that's very decent of you. Sergeant, I think it's time you escorted Mr. Flynn back to his aeroplane."

The sergeant moved away from the door, stepped to the window, parted the Venetian blind with two fingers. "Oh dear, sir," he said woodenly, "I think Mr. Flynn's aeroplane has gone without him."

That was the punch-line. That was what the pantomime had been about—why they had let him board the plane before coming for him. They did not expect him to give them the film. The object of the exercise was to part him from the camera. When his bag arrived unaccompanied in New York someone from security would take charge of it, and before Flynn could get it back it would have suffered some misfortune—an overdose of X-rays, perhaps, a broken zip that left the camera vulnerable to a passing baggage trolley, perhaps nothing more sophisticated than being dropped from a great height. Whichever, the film would be destroyed. The airline would compensate him, of course, unaware that it was not carelessness on the part of its staff that was responsible, but money would not replace what was in that camera. There were his files too. The Sondheim Prize chemist might pose for him again but Obregon would not.

Flynn said a lot of things, none of them printable, as he strode to the window and with the sergeant watched the New York flight in its distinctive livery taxi slowly towards the perimeter, disappear for some moments out of sight behind the airport buildings, then come surging past, accelerating towards take-off speed. The tricky moments between V1 and V2 passed without incident and the great gleaming fish sailed up the sky carrying the roar of its engines out of earshot as it headed north.

"Would you believe that?" said Inspector Harris, hardly bothering to disguise the satisfaction in his broad face and full-bodied voice. "And I asked him to wait. Didn't I, Sergeant? I certainly meant to."

His lip curling savagely, Flynn turned away from the window and back to the Inspector. He dredged his memory for some insults he had not used recently. He said, "If you seriously think you can—"

Still at the window the sergeant said, "Jesus Christ," with such a hollowness of tone that Flynn stopped in mid-diatribe and Inspector Harris got up from his chair and went to see what his colleague was looking at.

It was autumn and the evenings were already drawing in. Dusk was unrolling its slow blanket over England: it was no longer daylight, not yet dark. Lights twinkled palely among the terminal buildings. Cars on the roads were driving mostly on side-lights.

Light like a great pink chrysanthemum bloomed far away over the distant perimeter, hanging high in the quiet air. Others would describe it as a fireball and speak of the deep booming roar as the fuel tanks, full to capacity at the start of the plane's long run, exploded. But no sound reached inside the little office, double-glazed and already ten miles away, and Flynn's abiding impression was of a great flower blossoming halfway down the sky.

After long shocked moments Inspector Harris found a voice, and to his great credit it was a voice without hysteria saying something sensible. "John, you were watching—was that an aircraft?"

The sergeant nodded slowly. The shock that had wiped the expression off his face seemed also to have kicked him temporarily into slow-motion. "An aircraft. The aircraft." At last and with an effort he dragged appalled eyes away from the fading pink light and they found Flynn. "The one we pulled him off."

4

Gilbert Todd was on his way out to dinner when news of the disaster came over the car radio, interrupting a programme on the trout-streams of Scotland. He stopped the car and listened until the news-flash finished. Then he made two calls on the mobile phone, both of them to women. One was to his dinner partner, apologising for the fact that he was going to let her down yet again and wondering if she would risk giving it another try another night. The other, and first, call was to his photographer Leah Shimoni, who lived with a Saluki in a pepper-pot gate-lodge near Windsor. She too had just heard the flash and was about to call him.

The explosion had blown the wings off, but the fuselage had hung together until it had plunged into a water-meadow beside the Thames north of Slough. The impact had dug a deep crater in the soft ground and scattered wreckage over a wide arc on both sides of the river. With the wing-tanks gone there had been no further fire, a fact that might assist the accident investigators who were already on the scene but which had no implications for the survivors. There were no survivors.

There had been two hundred and twenty people, passengers and crew, aboard when Flight 98 left Heathrow. They had all died in the twenty or thirty seconds between the explosion seen by Inspector Harris's sergeant and the collision of the aluminium capsule, invested now its wings were gone with the flight characteristics of a brick, and the planet which spawned it. The bodies of many of them were still inside the wreckage, strapped into the expensively engineered seats which could offer no protection at all from the sudden intercession of the laws of physics a mile above the ground. Others were strewn in a surprisingly neat line along the axis of the crash.

Because there was no fire, and because it was now dark, the scene was illuminated by chains of powerful electric lights. From a distance they looked like fairy-lights picking out a walk beside the river.

From where Todd stood there was nothing whimsical about the scene. The lights, clear-eyed and impersonal as lights in an operating theatre, defined the extent of the devastation. People worked in the midst of it without haste but also without hope. The near-silence was chilling. Todd's job had taken him to the scenes of many disasters, and he had always thought that the agonised and despairing cries of the injured and bereft were the most harrowing part. Now he would have given a month's income to hear someone sobbing with the pain of broken bones.

Back at the airport, in a private area patrolled by priests and Samaritans and other professional compassionates, relatives and friends and lovers of the two hundred and twenty were sobbing with the pain of broken lives. Later some of them would find their way here, to this damp fragrant meadow by the river, and stare with grief and no comprehension at the wreckage of so much. But for now the site was the property of the professionals, Todd among them, and if they grieved they did it silently and without interrupting their work.

The proximity of Heathrow meant the top experts in their fields began arriving on the scene within minutes of the crash. Some of them had seen it, the pink chrysanthemum blooming halfway down the sky. Some of them came in working clothes, some in uniform, a couple like Todd in dinner jackets and several in baggy watching-the-telly cardigans that their wives would be horrified to learn they had gone out in public in.

But time was of the essence, and the urgency diminished only for the medical teams when it transpired that there were no survivors. With identical airframes and engines flying every minute of the day all over the world it was vital to establish what had happened, and whether it could happen again.

No-one said it but everyone there hoped it was a bomb. A bomb cast no doubts over the integrity of the plane, of manufacturing and operating procedures. A bomb would be a disaster that happened in spite of everyone's best efforts, not because of somebody's mistake. No-one would have to decide whether planes should be grounded, which meant all concerned anxiously monitoring the airwaves for the hours it would take to get everything down safely if they decided to, and with even greater anxiety for weeks if they decided not to. In the perhaps blasphemous view of those responsible for making aeroplanes safe, a bomb—planted by someone mad enough to want to and cunning enough to succeed—was an Act of God. It raised the fewest spectres.

Heathrow had been Todd's local airport for many globe-trotting years, and he had written enough about aircraft and flying to paper a jumbo-jet so many of those picking over the site were known to him. By the same token he was known to them and could have expected longer shrift than would have been available to most journalists in such circumstances. But Todd kept his demands on their time light. There was nothing to be gained from haunting these people, still in a state of shock as they began their microscopic examination of the wreckage. He had no deadline to meet: editors who bought his stories looked not for the first but for the most complete account of events. Most of the official information that would appear in the morning papers would come from press releases anyway.

In the course of the next few days he would talk to most or all of them and end up with clear impressions of what could and could not have happened, and how the odds were stacking up on sabotage as against mechanical failure. For the moment, though, it was enough to be here, letting the horror of the thing sink into his soul, watching people who had already done a day's work accept the massive challenge of establishing whether the thousands of people currently airborne in planes like this were in danger of falling out of the sky.

A flicker of light to one side reminded him that Shimoni was getting on with her work too. They marched to the beat of different drummers: these first confused hours, full of horror and heroism and contradiction, that were of scant value to Todd as a serious reporter were priceless to Shimoni in distilling the ethos of tragedy onto film. Later, by daylight, she would photograph specific aspects of the wreckage with specific significances, and those pictures might be more telling and more important. But for ten years people looking back on the disaster would remember it in terms of these first confused, dramatic, chiaroscuro images condensed out of the darkness and the despair.

In the first year they had worked together Todd had worried about taking a young woman into some of the situations his job demanded. The business was too full of people suffering. Hardly a month went by but that he had to look at something he would rather not have seen. Professional pride made him look, just long enough to know what he was writing about. But he was not sure he could have done Shimoni's job, weighing up angles and lighting and carefully focusing and then taking three steady shots; and after that developing the things and printing them. Photography made even fewer concessions to the normal sensibilities than journalism.

But he need not have worried. Shimoni was a lot tougher than she looked: not hard, there are hard photographers in the business but not many good ones, but tough. She had a range of mental, emotional and physical staminas that he had not suspected.

He supposed it was something to do with his age. When he was her age a plucky girl was one who could drive a car, or remount a horse after a bruising fall. The idea of tough women doing difficult, dangerous, dirty jobs as well and as badly as the men they worked with had never occurred to him; and had it done so, he would not have imagined them a little over five feet high, compact going on stocky and, on a good day, quite pretty in a serious sort of way. He would not have imagined them working calmly amid terrible devastation, doing any crying they had to do in private, as he did his.

So he watched Shimoni moving along the perimeter of the crash site, recording the horrors with precision and dedication, and he was proud and impressed and really rather fond of her. As fond, anyway, as was decent for a man of fifty-six and a girl thirty years younger.

It was then, as his eyes skimmed along the front line between darkness and the artificial day created by the fairy-lights, that he saw someone else he knew. At first he jolted to the shock of recognition. Then he doubted, told himself it was too dark, too far away, that the world was full of tall young men and this one did not even have a camera dangling round his neck like a talisman. He could not see the man's face, could not get that clear a view of him at all. Yet something about him was forcefully familiar so that the darkness was no obstacle to recognition.

It was three years since they had parted. It felt both more and less than that. Half of him had expected never to see Flynn again; the other half had taken six months to get used to Flynn not being there when he turned round.

Pitching his voice above the generators he called, "Mickey?" There was no response. The tall stooped figure, round-shouldered as if with hands in pockets, drifted into deep shadow and disappeared. Todd frowned. Could he be mistaken? There was a vagueness, a lack of purpose in the way the man moved that was not typically Flynn—at least, not typical of Flynn on a job. He worked with a restless energy that animated his angular attenuated frame like electricity. Like a child he could keep going as long as the game was worth playing, but five minutes after the final whistle he would be curled up in a chair somewhere fast asleep.

The fact that he seemed not to be working was more puzzling still. It was almost inconceivable that Flynn was here without a camera. He took a camera when he visited his dentist. Still Todd was left wondering why Flynn was wandering around like that and where he had lost his camera rather than whether it was Flynn at all.

Before he was aware of taking a decision Todd was moving obliquely down the side of the low hill he had been watching from towards the shadows where Flynn had disappeared. He was walking quite quickly for a portly fifty-six-year-old reporter. After a moment he began to trot. "Mickey! Wait for me."

Flynn was not going anywhere. Attracted perhaps by a darkness matching that of his spirit, he had stopped in the dense shade cast by a clump of little shock-haired trees standing on the river-bank. His eyes were shut against the mind-numbing horror of an aluminium coffin a hundred and eighty feet long split open and spilling its contents on the grass. But he had looked at it too long already and the image picked out in fairy-lights was printed on the inside of his eyelids.

He did not know what he was doing here. He could not remember how he got here, or why he had felt compelled to come. He had no camera and anyway no inclination to make permanent what he had seen. Someone else could do his job today.

But what should he do? The obvious avenues of prayer and alcohol were closed to him. The sense of loss was as overpowering as it was irrational. A Hungarian conductor, a boy in a suit, a business-woman with a fear of flying—and dear God, how right she had been! But what were they to him? What right had he to mourn their passing? Yet it was a sense of bereavement like vertigo that was tugging at his heart, knocking his perceptions out of focus and making his long body sway.

Todd saw him dark among the dark trees and said his name again, but before he could reach him Flynn's long legs folded and he sank to his knees on the damp earth, sitting back on his heels, his palms flat on his thighs, his head rocked back, his eyes shut. For a moment half the world's suffering seemed reflected in his half-seen face.

Todd hurried to him, anxious and uncomprehending, and uttered possibly the silliest words ever heard at the scene of a major disaster. "Mickey, whatever's the matter?"

In the darkness, the look on his face might have been partly in Todd's imagination. But there was no mistaking the profound shock in his voice that made it run up thin and terribly frail. "Gil? What are you doing here?"

Todd stared at him. "I'm a reporter: where else would I be?" He had been right about the camera too. "Where's your camera?"

Flynn pointed. It seemed an effort.

Todd did not understand. "At the wreck? How come?"

Flynn looked at him for the first time. Moving his head seemed to break whatever spell held him. He blinked and a little animation seeped into the hollow spaces in his eyes. "Not at it. In it. Gil, I was on that plane. Five minutes before it took off I was on it, heading for New York. I'd still have been on it but for a disagreement with the local cops. And Gil—" In the dark his kind eyes were luminous with unshed tears. He could hardly push the words past the grief gathering in his throat. "Oh Christ, Gil, I think this happened because of me."

Shimoni had seen Todd move into the trees and wondered what he was doing. As much as anything for a break from the tension of constantly looking at this, she went to see.

She found them by the sound of Todd's voice—"On your feet, Mickey, we have to do something about this, tell someone"—so she knew, or at any rate guessed, who he was talking to. A sudden unexpected pang of jealousy fluttered under her breastbone. She had never met Flynn, but she had heard all about him—not only from Todd who worked with him for four years but from a dozen different people she had met while working with Todd in the last three. She had seen Flynn's pictures. She had heard about Flynn's awards. She had heard his entire life-story broken down into anecdotes. She had the clear impression, and once or twice had been told to her face though never by Todd, that she was a lot more decorative than Flynn and a lot easier on the ear but she would not be half the photographer he was if she lived to be a hundred.

She could have forgiven Flynn all that. She too thought he was a better photographer than she was. She did not begrudge him the recognition he deserved. What she resented was the place that quite obviously, after a bitter parting and three years of going their own ways, he still occupied in Todd's affections.

Shimoni would have given anything for that kind of relationship with the old man who had seen more of and contributed more to twentieth-century journalism than anyone she had ever met. She knew he was fond of her, that he cared for her as he might for a favourite niece, that he respected her as a person and a colleague. But she would have exchanged all the respect in the world for what she had seen in his eyes, heard even in his anger when he talked about Flynn. That depth of commitment which Flynn had found claustrophobic and rebuffed.

Moving as they did in the same orbit, she had expected to meet Flynn before now. She had wondered idly how they would react to one another, if they would have enough in common to hit it off or if the best that they should aim for was an armed neutrality. She had not expected to feel this sudden animosity towards him.

And the second surprise was that this internationally acclaimed photo-journalist, renowned almost as much for the daring of his exploits as for the brilliance of his published work, the man who conceived and carried out the Obregon campaign and constantly set new standards of boldness, originality and style, should look—stripped of the accolades and the manic grin he wore in photographs—like nothing so much as six-foot-two of lost child, his hair in his face, a suspicious glistening on his cheeks, damp and grass clinging to his trouser legs.

Shimoni's vocabulary could not match Flynn's for offensiveness, in any of her three languages, but in her own quieter way she had a nasty enough mouth when provoked. She demonstrated it now. She looked Flynn up and down with a degree of disfavour apparent despite the dark, then said to Todd, "What's the matter with him? Seen something to upset him, has he?"

Todd was not paying her enough attention to notice the rancour in her voice. "Leah, it's Mickey." As if she knew him. As if that was all the introduction she could possibly need. "I think he's in shock. He was on the plane."

Shimoni looked past him to the twisted jumble of metal and flesh strewn across the water-meadow under the flat glare of the lights. She did not believe it, and made it clear. "Nobody could have survived that," she said flatly.

Todd finally noticed her uncharacteristic hostility and frowned. "No, before it took off—just before. The police—" He broke off. He could tell her later. "Mickey, did you tell them about the fire?"

"Sure I told them." His voice was thin, the accent prominent. "They weren't listening. They told me to get lost or they'd find something to arrest me for. So I came here."

And what he had found here had shaken him to the roots of his soul. Now he was coming out of it he had enough detachment to wonder at the scale of his reaction. He had seen disasters enough before, and if they were different in detail they were all terribly alike in overall effect. Every one of them came down in the end to lists of names, the dead and/or the injured. By tomorrow this one too would be redefining itself in lists of dead and tables of figures for easy assimilation into that custodian of modern history the computer. The fact that his name was scratched from the list in the nick of time was cause for celebration: he did not understand why it had pulled him apart like a cub-reporter at his first road accident.

Todd said, not to him, "I'm going to get him out of here. Then I'll call the police. They'll damn well listen when I tell them."

"Use my place if you like, it's closer." Shimoni freed a key from her ring.

"Are you staying here?"

"A little while. I'll come on when I'm finished."

"What do I do about your dog?"

Shimoni gave him an old-fashioned look. "Offer him a biscuit and he'll come out from under the couch."

In the event it took half the packet to reassure the Saluki that the strange men in his livingroom meant him no harm. Flynn fed them to him, bit by bit, while Todd talked on the telephone, and bit by bit the slender blond dog edged out from under Shimoni's couch. His name was Flute. From the couch he advanced by inches, slim silky paws first and his long slight body low to the carpet, until finally he trusted enough to put his nervous aristocratic nose on Flynn's knee and let Flynn stroke his silk-flagged ears. Flynn had read somewhere that stroking dogs brings your blood pressure down. He may not have known that it does the same for the dog.

Todd made four calls in quick succession: to the incident centre co-ordinating the emergency services, to Inspector Ford who was investigating Flynn's fire, to Inspector Harris who had escorted Flynn off the plane, then the incident centre again. When he had finished he came and sat down, his heavy body sinking uncomfortably low in a chair that was essentially a bean-bag.

"Well, I've got them all talking to one another. They'll send someone round to talk to you in due course. I said we'd be here."

Flynn raised one mobile eyebrow. "Leah *will* be pleased."

Todd frowned. "She did seem a bit out of sorts tonight, didn't she?"

"I wouldn't know." As the horror down the road was beginning to lose its first impact, so Flynn's natural resilience was beginning to make a tentative reappearance. "I know one thing though. She hates my guts."

Todd stared in amazement. "How can she? She doesn't know you."

Flynn barked a laugh that sent the Saluki back under the couch. "With the best will in the world, Gil, it's hard to take that as a compliment."

Todd twitched him half a grin. "You know what I mean."

"Oh yeah."

Todd stood up, not without difficulty, and switched on the television. "I'm going to watch what's coming in on this thing. If you'd rather not, make us some coffee—the kitchen's through there."

"I'm all right," said Flynn; but he was not sure how long it would last when the images started flooding in. As a compromise he made the coffee and watched from the kitchen door.

The broadcast Todd found followed the usual disaster-in-progress format of shocking pictures and not many facts. And the coverage would get worse before it would get better. Tomorrow, when there were still too few facts to make a report, there would be speculation ranging from the informed and therefore guarded to the ignorant and unfettered. There would be interviews with people who had not been on the plane (but might have been) and someone whose house (four miles away) could have been flattened on his eight children if the crash had come a minute later (and a shade to the north). And then some ghoul with more neck than brain would shove a microphone into the face of someone leaving the New York air terminal without the relative she had come to meet and ask how she felt when she heard the news.

Tonight at least viewers would be spared that, if only because there had not yet been time to get it together. For tonight coverage of the tragedy would be limited to pictures of the crash scene from different angles, reassessments of the death-toll and repeated flashes of phone-numbers which people could call to get their worst fears confirmed.

There were no more biscuits, he had fed them all to the dog, so Flynn made some sandwiches. Shimoni had unusual things in her fridge: he selected from them mostly by colour. He put the tray on a trunk that served as a coffee-table and said, "The ones on the left are red. The ones on the right are yellow and green." Then he sat down with a mug in one hand and a yellow and green sandwich in the other and watched the television.

Then he froze rigid. He did not drink the coffee or eat the sandwich. For thirty seconds he scarcely drew breath. His eyes burned with the intensity of his gaze on the screen. He knew he was not mistaken, and after thirty seconds the roving camera picked her up again. "There," he breathed.

Todd heard the shock resurgent in his voice, looked quickly at Flynn then back at the screen. Apart from a crashed airliner he could see nothing amiss. "What? What is it?"

Disjointed words lurched from Flynn as from a man in delirium. "There. Gil! The woman. In red. There!"

"I see her." So he could, but nothing remarkable about her. She was moving along the edge of the site, sometimes on camera, sometimes not; much as a few moments ago he had glimpsed Leah Shimoni. As Flynn had been doing when he found him. "Mickey, what's the matter? Who is she?"

"I don't know." He blinked quickly, as if to lubricate his staring eyes. Perhaps it oiled his brain as well, because he began to make a little sense. At least, the words made sense. "I don't know who she is. But Gil, she was on that plane."

5

Flynn had been promoted. This time he rated a Superintendent.

He told Detective Superintendent Donnelly the whole story—everything he could think of. He started with the fire at his apartment and the man Laura Wade had identified as Jamil Fahad. He explained the grudge Fahad held against him. He recounted his decision to skip London, and the incident he witnessed on the way to the airport. He underlined the fact that he only chose New York as a destination, and therefore that particular plane, on the spot and the spur of the moment.

He boarded, he said, when the flight was already preparing for departure. He only had time to sit down, glance over his fellow passengers and find the second half of his seatbelt before two policemen turned up asking for his help with their enquiries. He related the interview pretty much word for word, also what he thought about it. Then Inspector Harris's sergeant had seen the explosion and he had gone to the window to see the pink chrysanthemum bloom.

His first reaction had been a heartfelt, wholly instinctive delight that the plane had gone down without him. His second had been guilt, twisting up his stomach and his soul, for surviving so arbitrarily where so many had died. And his third reaction was that this was Fahad trying again: that he had followed Flynn to Heathrow and somehow got a bomb on board his plane.

And the person who took it on board was the woman in red, the business-woman with the briefcase. She might well have seemed nervous! At that moment she was sitting in a plane that she knew contained a bomb, presumably looking for a chance to leave without drawing attention to herself. She had already left it late when Flynn spoke to her.

The arrival of the police officers and the small stir they created must have seemed a heaven-sent opportunity, and she slipped off the plane in their wake. Otherwise she would have been reduced to feigning appendicitis or some such, and would have come under immediate suspicion when the aircraft crashed. As it was, only the freak chance of a man who had been sitting beside her surviving to spot her on a roving camera shot came between her and the ultimate security of being believed dead.

"You're sure it was her you saw on the TV?" Superintendent Donnelly was a man in his late forties, not a big man, with grey hair and grey eyes and rather a grey complexion as well, but with some subtle acuteness of personality that suggested rather the blue-grey of steel than the battleship grey of lead.

"I'm sure. I talked to her."

"What did you say?"

Flynn grinned, with more savagery than humour. "That aeroplanes don't back into mountains."

"Can you give me a description?"

She had been about thirty-seven, around five-foot-five, well-built verging on plump. She had curly black shoulder-length hair and dark brown eyes. Her skin had a slightly olive cast. Her accent was Southern with a slight Hispanic edge. She was wearing the red suit, tailored jacket and skirt, over a navy roll-neck blouse with navy court-shoes, and she had a grey briefcase in rigid plastic.

Donnelly gave him a watchful little half-smile. "Mr. Flynn, if you didn't take any notice of her just say so."

Flynn grinned. Todd laughed out loud. He suspected Flynn could have issued a similarly comprehensive description of every woman he had met in the last fifteen years. He liked women—almost all of them, regardless of age or colour or type, or their beauty or physical charm. He liked women the way some people like cats, not for what they might do for him but for the pleasure of their company.

Todd said, "Is he right? Was it a bomb?"

Donnelly retreated a little into the protective shell of professional reticence. "We shalln't know for sure until the people at Farnborough have made a jigsaw out of what's left. But given the fire at Flynn's place, and the woman who ought to be dead but seems to be wandering around outside Slough, I'll be working on that assumption. If we can find the woman she can tell us why she got off the plane. If Farnborough decides it was a mechanical failure or pilot error, she still might have something interesting to say."

"Will you be able to find her?"

Donnelly was a man not given to extravagant gestures. He shrugged economically. "We've a better chance starting now than if you'd thought about it and called us tomorrow. We know where she was half an hour ago and that's worth something." He paused, thinking. "I don't suppose this is a fair question. But you wouldn't have any idea why—if she planted a bomb, or even if she didn't—she should go to the only place that everyone with an interest in the crash would be converging?"

Flynn also shrugged, nowhere near as neatly. The parts of his body always tended towards a certain independence: at times they seemed about to break up a loose alliance and go their separate ways. Except that when you saw his photographs you knew it was an illusion, that where hand, eye and mind were in such accord there was no risk of a separation, however oddly bits of him might behave on occasions.

He said, "Maybe for the same reason I did. It's hard to explain. It's like—as if what happened made them family. It was sheer fluke that I wasn't with them when they died. I felt somehow that I owed them something—mourning, apologies, I don't know. As if I was their heir, or their witness." He did not think he was making much sense so he stopped.

Donnelly understood what he was saying. "That works for you. We know you weren't responsible: you'd have been on the plane if our people hadn't taken you off—in circumstances which they will be called upon to explain before they're very much older," he added grimly. "But if your woman in red deliberately blew up that plane with two hundred and twenty people on board, we have to assume she's a pretty tough lady and not the sort to be overtaken by sudden impulses of self-recrimination. What was she looking for?"

"Proof that I was dead?" There was a rough edge on Flynn's voice. Talking about it had helped a lot, but he was still a man who had seen more than two hundred people die because of something he did.

Donnelly shook his head. "She knew you were alive. If she got off when Harris came aboard, she must have seen them take you back into the terminal. The plane left right after that: there was no chance that you were on it."

Todd voiced what they were all three thinking. "So she let that plane take off carrying a bomb that would kill everyone on board after she knew that the man she'd been sent to kill was already safe on the ground."

"There may once have been a golden age," said Donnelly, "when even hardened criminals would give themselves up rather than risk innocent lives, but it had already ended by the time I joined the police force."

It was a bomb. The accident investigators were sure of it that first night, long before all the pieces had been collected and reassembled in a hangar at Farnborough. The people at Heathrow who saw the explosion knew even before that. Aeroplanes do occasionally fail for structural or mechanical reasons, but they do not usually do it as dramatically as that.

As the investigation continued a picture began to emerge of an explosive device, of moderate rather than massive size, detonating at the after end of the forward baggage hold. The shock-wave had broken through to the inboard starboard wing-tank.

Shimoni got home about midnight. By then she had seen all there was to see. She accepted a mug of fresh coffee then disappeared into her darkroom. Todd thought it might have been natural to show another photographer what she had in the way of equipment and shots, and noticed that she did not.

Flynn did not notice. He was worrying about Laura. "She'll have heard about the crash by now. She has to reckon New York as one of the likelier places I'd go. She knows she left me at Heathrow half an hour before—before it happened. If she calls my place she'll only get the Phone Melted tone. She's no more idea how to find me than I have to find her. We fixed it that way."

"But she can find out if you were on the plane," Todd said reasonably. "The same way anyone else can, by ringing the emergency number."

"She might wonder if there was time to get my name on the list. Hellfire, my name might even *be* on the god-damned list." He paused as that sank in. Then he added, "She might call you."

Todd stared. "Why should she call me?"

Flynn shuffled uncomfortably. "I gave her your number. Well, we needed some way of leaving messages for each other, I didn't think you'd mind. The last thing you said to me in Jerusalem—"

"The last thing I said to you in Jerusalem, after you'd told me to get off your back and buy a cocker spaniel if I wanted something running round after me, was that if we were no longer partners you could make your own bloody arrangements." The indignation in his voice was not genuine, and he smiled slowly at Flynn's expression. "The last but one thing I said was, 'Call me if you need me.'"

Todd stood up, tapped on the darkroom door. "Leah, we're going back to my place. There might be something for Mickey on my answering machine. If Superintendent Donnelly calls, let him know where we are, would you? I'll talk to you tomorrow."

"Yes, sure," said Shimoni through the door. Then, under her breath, "If you've still some use for the second eleven by then."

There was no message from Laura, and Superintendent Donnelly did call. His men had picked up the woman in red. She had left the scene of the crash before a search could be made, but a speculative sweep of late-night cafes in the area found her hunched over a cup of cold coffee in a motorway service station on the M4. The policeman who spotted her knew at once who she was, without having to check through the description he had been given. She was crying.

Her name was Maxine Faber and she was a junior executive with an entertainments consortium in Fort Lauderdale. Her name was on the passenger list, the list of the dead.

At first she claimed Flynn was mistaken, that she had missed the flight. He must have seen her in the departure lounge, not on the plane. While waiting to board she had suddenly felt so ill that she considered it wiser to take a later flight. She was in the washroom when the plane took off, and when the explosion occurred.

She was not sure what she did next. There was a lot of shocked activity in the terminal. For a little while she stayed there but there was nothing she could do to help, she was only in the way, so after a time she went back to the desk where she had returned her hire-car and hired it out again. She really had very little idea what she wanted to do or where she wanted to go, but she was clear on one point: she would not be boarding an aeroplane for a little while.

She headed away from Heathrow and away from London, her thoughts in turmoil, driving on automatic pilot. She found herself being passed by a succession of emergency vehicles and, without really deciding to, followed them. When the scene of the crash came into view, picked out of the darkness by a hundred twinkling lights as if it were a children's party, nausea made her stop the car. Then she walked, aimlessly, drawn to the place where they had died almost as if the two hundred and twenty had been kin, until she was stopped by the barriers. Some time after that she went back to her car and drove away. Donnelly said, "Flynn was never in the departure lounge."

His quiet voice, precise and without inflection, summoned her back from what had become almost a soliloquy. She blinked her large brown eyes. "What?"

"Flynn couldn't have seen you in the departure lounge. The plane was already boarding when he got his ticket: he went straight to the gate and he was the last one aboard. The only place he could have seen you was on the plane."

She began to cry again, bent forward, her curly hair shielding her face. Donnelly waited patiently. By degrees she stopped sobbing and her shoulders stilled; then her face came up, reddened and puffy round the eyes. Her voice was thick and her mouth quivered. "Superintendent, what is it you're accusing me of?"

"I'm not accusing you of anything yet, Miss Faber," he replied, deadpan. "I'm asking you to explain your rather curious and deeply convenient actions. And I'm wondering why you're lying."

"Somebody blew that plane up and you think it was me. You think I killed two hundred and twenty people." Outrage and grief warred in her voice.

He explained patiently. "Airlines do not normally carry baggage for passengers who aren't travelling. As a safety measure. If you change your mind about flying, your luggage is off-loaded. As far as we know only two bags travelled unaccompanied on that flight: Flynn's, because he was taken off the plane by police at the last minute, and yours. I have yet to hear a credible explanation of how you and your bag got parted. We shall sit here—well, you will, I might take a break from time to time—until I do."

There was no need for Flynn to see Faber. She had already admitted most of what he could say about her; it was only a matter of time before she offered a reason, truthful or otherwise, for being on the plane and then leaving it. But Donnelly wanted her to see Flynn. He could not justify taking her to view the corpses: confronting a man who should have been one of them, burned and shattered with the rest, was the next best thing. It might not shake a confession out of her —he was not yet sure what she had to confess—but he thought it would shake something loose.

Todd drove Flynn to the police station exactly as if the last three years had not happened. It was too soon for either of them to have realised it, but the older man had quite automatically taken up again the reins of the younger man's life that had been wrested forcibly from him last time they met. For now, shocked as he was, Flynn was grateful for somewhere to go, some way to get around, someone to do his thinking for him. But when he got his breath back and his feet under him again he would wonder if he would have been wiser to keep the cork in the bottle and manage without the genie's help.

During the last three years Todd had been driven by Shimoni more often than he had been behind the wheel himself. For four years before that Flynn had done most of the driving. The consequence was that Todd drove like an old maid, not only cautiously but cautious in the wrong ways, hesitating halfway across junctions and yielding right-of-way when it caused infinitely more confusion than claiming it. His reverse parking had to be seen to be believed.

So while Flynn appreciated his kindness at driving him across the city at three in the morning, he was not finding it a relaxing experience. He wished he could think of a tactful way of taking the wheel because, even in shock, he was a safer driver than Todd was. Todd took his eyes off the road to talk.

He said, "Did you get much sleep?" and a lamp-post rushed at them threateningly.

Flynn tried not to grab his seatbelt. "Some." He had not. He had lain on his back in the dark room with his eyes wide open, seeing over and over again the seminal scenes of the day projected like slides inside his mind. Laura in the midst of the fire. The people on the plane. The PhotoFit picture of Fahad. The pop-singer in the Porsche. The rosy flowering in the darkening sky beyond Heathrow. The devastation beside the Thames where the big pieces and the little pieces of the destroyed aeroplane had been scattered like barren seed.

And the woman in red. Had she tried to kill him? Had she killed two hundred and twenty people trying to kill him? Why?—because Fahad had paid her? It was not much of a reason. The loss of Bab el Jihad was not very much better, if she was doing it for the Palestinian cause. Fahad had lost a handful dead, rather more imprisoned but still only a fraction of those who had died in the aeroplane. Could he really, after three years, still hate Flynn so much? Enough to burn his apartment, enough to burn his woman, more than enough to kill Flynn—but two hundred and twenty people neither of them knew?

It hardly seemed possible. It did not accord with what he remembered of Fahad. The man was ruthless by any standards, seriously brutal when it suited his life's cause. But on a personal level he had been capable of as much kindness, decency even, as other men. Flynn knew he was also capable of mayhem but was unable to judge whether Fahad would resort to mayhem of this type and on this scale.

Donnelly met them in the foyer and took them to the interview room where Maxine Faber was being watched over expressionlessly by a WPC. Though Todd was not invited, nor was he told to wait at the desk, so he stayed with Flynn—partly because Flynn was still a touch shaky but mostly because Todd was more than a touch nosy. He called it professional curiosity.

Donnelly too noticed that Flynn walked as if he could not feel what was under his feet. "Are you all right?"

"I'm all right," said Flynn; then again, less forcibly, "I'm all right. I'll be even more all right when people stop asking."

The policeman was unconvinced. "While you're here you might as well have a word with our tame doctor."

"What do I need with a doctor?" Flynn's voice snagged like barbed wire. "I wasn't on the god-damned plane. There's nothing wrong with me."

"All the same," Donnelly said imperturbably.

He wanted to say something else to Flynn before introducing him to Maxine Faber, but Flynn's attitude made it pointless. He had wanted to warn Flynn that he would find it difficult. Either this woman had tried to kill him and had involved him in the deaths of two hundred and twenty strangers, or she was like him a freak survivor of an epic tragedy. Perhaps the interview would end without establishing which, but either way the emotions of both of them would be under assault.

What Donnelly was proposing to do was unusual. He expected to be discussed behind a succession of doors; but it would not be the first time and, though sooner or later there would be a last time, he doubted if this would be it. A man with two hundred and twenty murders to investigate was entitled to a certain latitude. It would be different if he was putting Flynn in danger. But this thing seemed to have happened because someone knew exactly who Flynn was, and anyway he had already met Faber. Even if she claimed he had not.

Perhaps nothing would come of it anyway. If Faber had taken money for the contract killing of a man on a crowded airliner by means of an explosive device, probably she had no better nature to appeal to. A woman capable of being moved to remorse by evidence of her guilt would not have gone into that line of business in the first place. But there were other possibilities worth exploring. If she had agreed to do it in a fit of religious fervour—if that tan was due less to the Florida sun and more to Middle Eastern genes, if she were a supporter of the Popular Front for the Liberation of Palestine—perhaps she had not anticipated how it would feel: to kill so many and then to see Flynn alive. If she went for his throat, that was probably how it had been.

Or perhaps she had been persuaded to take the package on board—Semtex, probably, invisible to normal scanners—in the belief that it was something other than a bomb: drugs for instance. The money offered would be good. He could afford to be generous with his promises—Fahad or whoever. She was to be on the plane when the thing went up and never claim the balance of her fee. But in that case, why did she leave the plane?

Donnelly found Todd a seat outside the interview room and, quite firmly, showed him to it. He looked up at Flynn. "All right?" Then he opened the door.

Faber looked up as they went in. She did not need to be reminded who Flynn was. She remembered their conversation. She smiled, too vividly, her lips carmine, her eyes bright with tears in waiting, and said, "Sitting at the back isn't the complete answer."

"I noticed that." Flynn's voice was low, his face grim. Without the manic grin that was his trademark he looked years older; but then, he had nothing to grin about. He believed this woman was responsible for two hundred and twenty deaths and her only regret was that the figure was not two hundred and twenty-one. Hatred welling in his breast like bile, he raised hot, angry eyes to meet her gaze.

And found there a reflection of all the torn and tangled emotions whirling in his own mind: the rage, the grief, the guilt—at surviving, but more at the gut reaction that his life was worth more than all those deaths; the loss of equilibrium, of perspective; the way from time to time, mostly with weariness, the awesome thing slipped from the forefront of his mind, and he wondered where Laura was and what he was going to do next and whether he could fix the apartment, and then it came back at him with the force of a blow and he felt like a murderer.

All these things were in Maxine Faber's eyes too. They were the reason she had been crying in a motorway service area instead of putting miles behind her. She was no more responsible for all those shattered lives than he was, unless in the same involuntary way. Even then her conscience had less to bear, because without her someone else would have been found to carry the device on board, but nothing would have happened without Flynn.

His voice was still low, still gruff, but the rage compressed in it was gone. In its place she almost thought she heard compassion. "Can you tell us what happened?"

So she told him. None of the three of them could have said why she was willing or able to respond to Flynn when an hour of astute, pertinent, perceptive interrogation by Donnelly had brought forth only tears and lies. But a kind of kinship had been created when these two people escaped the death planned for two hundred and twenty-two. It would be with them for the rest of their lives, a communion that no-one else in the world could share in. Donnelly's gamble had paid off. Faber told them what she knew.

She had believed unreservedly that the suitcase with her name on it in the baggage hold contained cocaine. The shipment was on its way from Rotterdam to New York: she took it over in London for the trans-Atlantic leg. She had done the run before and suffered from a minimum of nerves. The anxiety Flynn noted was neither a fear of flying nor a worry about New York customs but a very immediate panic prompted by a casual remark from a passing stewardess that some policemen had asked for the flight to be held so they could talk to someone on board. Naturally she assumed it was her.

What she did next was natural too: she went and hid in the toilet. While there she did perhaps the quickest thinking of her life. Then she opened the door, walked into the galley, helped herself to some remnants of cabin staff uniform she found there, also a sheaf of papers and a clip-board, and when the cabin door opened and the two police-men were working their way down the aisles she walked purposefully to the hatch and left. No-one noticed. At the first cloakroom she came to she lost the clip-board and the uniform, became a civilian again and left the terminal. She was hiring her car when she heard the shocked little gasps that were her first indication of what had happened.

When she realised which plane it was that had crashed, all the conflicting emotions that had surged in Flynn tumbled over her too. What she had told Donnelly about events after that had been the truth: she found herself at the scene, then leaving and driving, then stopping. Then the police picked her up.

So she was a drug courier—a mule. That explained the lies: with her luggage destroyed along with the rest of the plane, only her own words could incriminate her. All she needed was a plausible excuse for not taking the flight and she was in the clear.

Donnelly said, "Does the name Fahad mean anything to you?"

She looked blank. "No."

"Obregon?"

She looked down at her lap. After a moment she looked up again. "There's no point me denying what you can check with a phone call. The firm I work for in Fort Lauderdale: Tomas Obregon owns it."

6

"So what the hell is this?" demanded Flynn, not quietly. "Open season on me?"

"There has to be some mistake," said Todd. A stationary van lurched into the path of his car. "I can imagine all sorts of people wanting to take pot-shots at you, Mickey, but two different ones in the same day? I don't think even you're that unpopular. Your friend Laura: could she have made a mistake?"

Flynn thought about it, shook his head. "I don't see how. She didn't pick him out of a line-up, she put together one of those PhotoFit composites. I recognised it as Fahad."

"Then could you have been mistaken?"

"No way. It was him. I couldn't have made a better picture of him myself."

Todd frowned. For once he avoided looking at Flynn as he spoke. "Mickey, you had a pretty rough time at his hands. It's bound to have left—scars, and probably more in your subconscious than in ways you're aware of. It's possible that you're always going to see him in the shadows. Anyone threatening you may always tend to look like Fahad."

"Just because you're paranoid, it doesn't mean they *aren't* out to get you." They traded a grin, almost like old times. Already the spectre was hanging a little less heavy. Serious again, Flynn went on: "Gil, it was him. It was like he was there in the room with us. Laura had never even heard his name, only saw him the once, but she put together a picture as good as a photograph. It couldn't have been anyone else."

"You didn't see him?"

"I told you, all I saw were flames. And Laura shut up in the kitchen, too scared to make a run for it, waiting to burn. And Derek."

"Derek?"

"Derek the senior wino."

Even senior winos tend not to hang about the same place for three years. Todd had never met him. "Did Derek see them?"

Flynn rolled impatient eyes. "Who knows what Derek saw? Including Derek. He sees things that aren't there. He thinks there's an anaconda living under the floor."

"Did anyone ask him?" Todd knew the problems of getting a cogent story out of a career alcoholic. They were the same as, though greater than, the problems of getting a cogent story out of any eye-witness. He knew from long experience that if he were to ask six good men and true to describe the same incident he would get six detailed, authoritative and wildly divergent accounts. Between noticing different aspects and remembering them imperfectly, their testimony would be chaotically contradictory. Thus their honest descriptions of the same robbery could range from a West Indian armed with a shotgun knocking down a shop-keeper and rifling his till to a white man with a solarium tan armed with a replica handgun waving his fist under the assistant's nose and making his get-away empty-handed after failing to open the till.

Eye-witness testimony, which laymen think incontrovertible, is in fact so seriously unreliable that courts must look for supporting evidence to corroborate even the most honourable of witnesses. But still sometimes it is all there is, and seekers after truth must do what they can with it, understanding its weaknesses and interpreting as best they may where necessary.

All that goes for eye-witness testimony goes ten-fold for wino-witness testimony. But still it may be all there is, and must then be explored for all it is worth. If Derek had seen something, Todd would find out—even if it proved harder to work out exactly what it was he had seen.

Derek had seen nothing. He had not even seen the snake that morning. He had seen Flynn racing up through the building—Flynn had shouted at him, he could not remember why—then a lot of men in yellow trousers arrived and it started raining. All his bedding was wet that night. It was enough to drive a man to sobriety.

They left him pondering the unfairness of life and went to inspect the wreckage of Flynn's apartment. (Even Todd, who was a fundamentalist as regards the English language, accepted that the word "flat" was an inadequate substitute.) It was comprehensive. They stood at the livingroom window, or at least the aperture it left, looking over the river.

Todd cleared his throat. "I don't suppose you need me to tell you no life insurance company would look at you twice."

Flynn gave a little snort that could have been mirth. "Insurance be damned. There's a bookie up the Tottenham Court Road who gives odds on things like the Second Coming and the next pope being a woman, but you try laying money that I'll still be alive by weekend."

"What are we going to do about it?"

Flynn did not comment on it, but he had noticed and appreciated that plural pronoun. He shrugged. It looked like a heron shrugging. "What can I do? I tried ignoring it and damn near got Laura killed. I tried running, and got two hundred and twenty people I didn't know from Adam killed. What's left—fight back? I'd even try that, if I could get near the bastards."

Todd was looking pensive. "We don't have to fight them, at least not yet. All we have to do is talk to them—find out what's going on."

"I *know* what's going on. They're trying to kill me."

"Both of them—Fahad and Obregon? In concert? By turns? I don't believe it, Mickey. Look, the only thing in the world those two men have in common is their dislike of you. A South American drug baron and a Palestinian guerrilla?—they wouldn't be able to find one another even if it occurred to them they might want to. No, this is either one of them or the other. Or—"

"Or what?"

Todd shrugged, broad shoulders rising bear-like up his thick neck. "Or it's someone else again, laying a smoke-screen."

"Oh come on," growled Flynn, "how the hell many people do you think there are with reasons to want me dead?"

"There were four on the list you put together after this." His gaze travelled the gutted room. "Perhaps we should get in touch with all of them, see what they have to say. The one responsible might consider himself safe enough to boast about it. At least then you'd know where you stand."

Steps on the stone stairs surprised both of them. As Todd turned to look he saw Flynn's long body seem to shrink against the smoke-

blackened wall and his eyes flared darkly. He thought, He's afraid—
he's really scared. Then he thought, Of course he's afraid, somebody's
trying to kill him—he might act as if being young and feckless and
earning big money makes you immortal, but actually he's no more
immune to pain and death than I am. In his shoes I'd be scared
shitless.

But it was nothing to be scared of, only Derek panting bronchitically
up the last of the ten flights. He had remembered something. "A man.
Came looking for you. Yesterday, after everybody had gone." The sentences had to fit in with his breathing. "Said if you came back—to give
you this."

It was a business card. Still puffing, Derek held it out in his big
grimy hand. Somehow it had stayed pristine in his custody, as if all his
efforts and whatever sense of responsibility remained to him had been
channelled into keeping it safe. Flynn took it, glanced at it once and
put it in his pocket. He thanked Derek solemnly and Derek beamed
and stumped away.

Todd said, "Who was it?"

Flynn sighed. "Byron Spalding, Deering Pharmaceuticals. He's been
the bane of my life since I photographed their god-damned chemist.
OK, it's nice to win prizes, but it's month-old news now and they're
still looking for copies of the pic—for trade magazines and house
magazines and one for the foyer and one for Auntie Florrie's album for
all I know. They wanted to buy the negative, were quite pissed off
when I told them I don't sell negatives. Almost wish I had now. It was
on the plane, I don't think I'll get much more mileage out of it now."

Todd had thought of writing to the four men who might have grown
tired of waiting for Flynn's funeral. But of course he would think that:
all his life except for the first seventeen years he had defined his place
in the world by what he wrote. He had influenced public opinion and
private values. He had campaigned, and challenged the campaigns of
others. He had taken on the establishment and the sanctity of received
wisdom, and if he had not won every battle he knew he had left his
mark on his adversaries. In the course of nearly forty years as a journalist Todd had seen much that he had written given short shrift, only
to turn up later in the guise of new government thinking or a coura-
geous opposition stance. He had infinite faith in the potency of the
written word.

Flynn belonged to a different generation and a different trade. He grew up on instant food and throw-away ideologies. His idea of an old song was one which had been in the charts for four weeks running; his idea of a classic book was one which was not a TV show first. The Chinese saying "The oxen are slow but the earth is patient" had no appeal for him: the most patience he ever displayed was to wait in a traffic jam without thumping his horn.

Photography too is the ascendency of immediacy over the considered, of appearance over meaning, full of impact and undemanding of intellect. It disdains to explain itself. The photographer, like the Hollywood starlet, is almost entirely concerned with filling the eye. Deeper issues have to be plumbed by some other medium.

So perhaps it was inevitable, a reflection of their different roles in and attitudes to life, that whereas Todd thought of writing to the four men, Flynn proposed going and knocking on their doors.

Todd was aghast. "Well, it'll tell us what we want to know. The one who's trying to kill you is the one who answers the door with a loaded 12-bore."

Flynn was aware of the risk. But doing nothing was also dangerous. Whoever wanted his life enough to destroy a plane full of people would try again and probably soon. If he played it by the book he would end up having it read over him. His best chance of walking away from this was doing something unexpected.

The former MP was a separate case, but the other three were by definition men beyond the reach of law. Each would have been behind bars had it been otherwise. The police could neither touch them nor guarantee to keep them at bay. If the man who tried to kill Laura found her again he would finish the job. Then he would move on: to Todd for sure, and after him to anyone and anything that mattered to Flynn until he was content with the pain inflicted and decided to take his life too.

"There's nothing else I can do, Gil," he said. He was over the horror but despair remained as a thin burr behind his voice. "They've left me nothing else, not even the time to think much about it. I know where to find Obregon and I'm going to see him. If I can I'll build in some edge so he doesn't drop me on the spot; but if I can't, what the hell, I'm only speeding the inevitable and maybe saving us all a lot of trouble. At least this way I'm not going to be responsible for anyone else's death."

"Mickey, you're not responsible for anyone's death. None of this is your fault."

"I don't know. Maybe if I'd been a bit more ready to back off, a bit less keen on going boldly where no photographer had gone before?" He ran his fingers through his hair distractedly. "If Obregon killed two hundred and twenty people because I pushed him over the edge of reason—"

Todd was steadfast, partly because he believed he was right but beyond that because Flynn needed him to be. "If Obregon destroyed that plane, it wasn't because of anything you did to him eighteen months ago but because he is and always was evil, which is why you took him on in the first place. If we're playing the numbers game, set a figure on the lives you saved by moving him along. Add up the misery you prevented.

"Anyway, I don't know. Obregon? I'm not convinced. After these many months why would he suddenly be so angry with you again that nailing you would be worth killing not only two hundred and twenty uninvolved people but also one of his own couriers? Maxine Faber must be worth her weight in gold to him, but he'd have lost her if she hadn't panicked when the police came aboard. Why was it suddenly so urgent?"

"I'll ask him."

"You think he'll give you the chance?"

"Hellfire, Gil, I don't know. Maybe it is crazy." Now Flynn's fingers were shredding the business card Derek had kept so carefully for him. "But I've got to do something, and I can't think what else. He killed two hundred and twenty people—for me—and I have to do something about that."

"All you'll do is die."

Flynn shrugged. "I sure as hell can't live with it."

Todd had said everything he could think of to dissuade him. He thought Flynn was probably throwing his life away for no good purpose, but he had no power to stop him. Once he would have tried, but they were both a little older now. "Colombia, is it? Will you fly?"

"I'll get onto a military flight somehow. I'm not boarding another airliner, or going any place with a lot of people, until this is settled one way or the other."

CHAPTER 2

Beasts of Blood

1

Flynn watched Obregon, carefully, from a distance, for two days before making his move. Partly he was waiting for a set of circumstances that would allow him to approach the man, protected as he was by the power and privilege which his wealth had bought him, and say what he had to say and hear what Obregon had to say in reply, and give him some chance of leaving with his skin intact afterwards.

His other reason for waiting was that once he moved into the open the initiative would pass from him to a man who had already threatened to kill him and was involved somehow, even if he did not know how, in the destruction of Flight 98. Once Obregon knew he was there, he would dictate the pace and probably the outcome. And Flynn was afraid of him.

There had been a time, not all that long ago, when Mickey Flynn had hardly known the meaning of the word. Like the sword Excalibur, his camera had been guide and protector to him, and he had thought in his young man's arrogance that he was close to invulnerable. A bullet in the back during a Dutch riot put him straight. He had recovered completely from the physical effects of that, but not wholly from the psychological ones. Flirting with danger lost much of its charm when he discovered that either his guardian angel had off-days or, more likely, there was no-one up there who cared whether he lived or died. He still took risks as and when necessary, but never again in the absolute confidence that he would get away with them.

Now the prospect of confronting Tomas Obregon on his own ground left him breathless with fear. The stuff clogged his brain like cotton-wool, gathered behind his knees like alcohol, weighed on his shoulders like lead. He had wondered, crouching in shrubbery like jungle, watching Obregon's house—a big white house like the big white car—if a fear that crippling amounted to cowardice. He decided, on the balance of probabilities and judging from the fact that he had got this far, that it was not so much cowardice as the kind of good healthy fear designed to stop people getting themselves into positions like this. But there was no-one, even Todd if he had been here, that he would have discussed it with. Perhaps that was cowardice too.

Finally, after two days, a moment came when he had to either take the chance presented and let events take their course, or admit that he would never get his nerve up enough to do what he had come here for, make a discreet withdrawal and go home. One thing decided him. He had had trouble hitching on a military flight and had no promise of a ride home. The prospect of having to cross the Atlantic on a civil airliner crammed with young boys in new suits and old men with musical beards, and tired women and fretful children, and some bloody nun with a guitar, and wondering what else was in the baggage hold besides baggage, was harder to contemplate than what Obregon might do to him. So he straightened up, brushed the dirt from the knees of his trousers and went to join the party.

Because a party gave him an edge. He knew Obregon would be circulating. With the grounds full of visitors it would be possible to approach the man unimpeded by his staff. Unless they were all very close friends indeed, Obregon would be reluctant to deal with Flynn as he might wish in their presence.

It was not a complete answer, nowhere near enough to guarantee his safety; it was an edge, that was all. If he caught Obregon off his guard, and kept him that way for the fifteen minutes this was going to take, and if Obregon did not crave his blood more than he valued his own reputation, he might be allowed to leave afterwards. Anyway it would be out of Flynn's hands. That would be a relief of a kind.

Even with the leaf-mould removed he was not exactly dressed for a party. Fortunately it was afternoon and fairly informal so he was not as conspicuous as he would have been after sundown. He waited for a moment when Obregon was both alone and surrounded by his guests, then he set off across the cropped green lawn on a collision course with his host.

It was harder than he had expected. The temptation to turn aside in those last half-dozen strides before Obregon spotted him was enormous. Again, only blackmail—the image of the shattered airliner outside Slough, and the other one he would have to buy a ticket for if he left here now—kept him firm to his purpose.

People were milling round so Flynn was quite close before Obregon realised the tall young man in the desert-coloured shirt wanted to talk to him. The play of expressions across his face was interesting. At first the naturally sallow, slightly angular face, its flesh sculpted in satiric lines, was welcoming and open if a shade non-committal because he supposed that even if he could not remember who he was he must have invited this young man, and his purpose and hopefully his identity would become clearer when he spoke.

Then there was a moment of bewilderment as Obregon realised he should know that face—wide across the eyes, pointed in the jaw, the wide mouth, the brown hair that was just long enough to look untidy. Obregon himself was a small man, a little less than average height and slight with it, and perhaps because of that he groomed and dressed himself to the point where immaculate hovered on dandified. So he noticed things like Flynn's hair and had to suppress a shudder at his boots.

He looked again at the long form ambling towards him, and knew it should mean something to him and would do but for the wrongness of the context. This was not a man he expected to see at his home.

At last came recognition and with it, in quick succession, disbelief, indignation, a momentary alarm—his black olive gaze slid out sideways to check the whereabouts of his staff—then mounting anger. Finally, slipping up quietly unnoticed from behind, came a kind of unholy satisfaction.

Flynn stopped in front of him, just far enough away to avoid looming over the smaller man. Far enough, too, that they could speak unheard but any raising of voices would draw attention. He said, "Remember me?"

"Why, Mr. Flynn," said Obregon, his English as painstaking as his attire, "how could I ever forget?"

Something odd had happened to Flynn on his walk across the lawn. It was barely thirty paces from where he had committed himself to the point where he intercepted Obregon, less than that from the last place he seriously considered making a run for it, but somewhere along the way he had shed the crippling awareness of fear. It was not that he was more optimistic now about the outcome. He did not think it was the calm of ultimate despair. He was getting angry. Now he had

Obregon face to face, the outrageousness of the man's behaviour was flooding his veins with fire. Anger is a signal remedy against both fear and pain.

So they were two angry men who faced each other across a yard of expensively maintained Colombian turf.

Obregon said, "I don't remember inviting you to my party, Mr. Flynn. Or are you doing weddings and social functions now?"

"No, I'm still in news," growled Flynn. "Crime, corruption, that kind of thing. Air crashes."

Obregon eyed him keenly. This close—Flynn had never been this close before—there was a world of refined cruelty in the sculpted face. "The London disaster? I heard you were involved. The first list of casualties had your name on it. I thought then, I should *be* so lucky. True enough, the next day they corrected it."

"That must have been a bitter disappointment."

"Oh, it was, Mr. Flynn. It was."

"I hope you hadn't paid up already."

There was no misunderstanding what Flynn meant by that. The barbed humour that had served Obregon while he waited to learn Flynn's purpose here would serve no longer. That was a direct accusation, he had to admit it or deny it or somehow act upon it. There was no room left for fancy footwork. The yard of green grass and sunshine between them grew still with anticipation. Without either of them being aware of it, they were beginning to attract attention.

After a cool minute Obregon said precisely, his tone still light but the anger heavy in his predatory eyes, "However carefully you examine photographs of that crash, Flynn, you won't see my car behind the wreckage."

"Maybe not. But your courier's in some of them."

That seemed to startle Obregon almost as much as the sight of Flynn had done. The creases dropped out of his face and his eyes rounded. "What?"

Flynn laughed, without much humour. "Didn't read that list too carefully, did you? The first one, the one with my name on it—it also had Maxine Faber's."

Tomas Obregon had not got to be a rich and powerful man by showing in his face every notion that passed through his mind. His expression closed like a curtain, like a power-plant shutting down. So

Flynn could have been wrong, but he thought he was telling Obregon something he did not already know.

Obregon said quietly, "I think we'll continue this conversation somewhere more private." He signalled with an authoritative gesture that involved no more than a finger on each hand.

Flynn did not know whether to look behind him or keep his eyes on Obregon. He said, quite loudly, "Me, I'd just as soon keep it public. I mean, there may be people here who don't know what you do for a living, or why you need people like Maxine Faber working for you."

All other conversations in the vicinity had died. Obregon's guests were standing round undecidedly, suspecting that good manners required them to move away and hoping they could put it off until they had heard something juicy. Most of them knew at least approximately the line of business he was in. It had, after all, been rendered common knowledge by Flynn's witty campaign of eighteen months before. But certain echelons of certain societies prosper best by turning a deaf ear to common knowledge and subjugating common good to individual enterprise, so there was still novelty value in hearing Obregon's crimes flung in his teeth as the climax of one of his own garden parties.

Obregon raised his own voice in reply so that his words were clearly audible to those around. His voice was cold, his tone affronted. "Mr. Flynn, you were not invited here, and you have long outstayed any welcome you could have expected. My staff will show you the way out." He terminated the interview abruptly by stalking past Flynn, close enough to brush him aside.

Flynn made a mistake then. Given a moment longer to think, he would not have done—at least, not this one that Obregon had manoeuvred him into. But he was taken aback by the old fox's response, and by his bumping into him like that, and before he could stop himself he had reacted as a man might on being jostled in a pub or a train—he put out his hand to restore the distance between them.

Immediately Obregon staggered back. "How dare you, sir?" he demanded in a voice vibrant with outrage; the members of his staff who had been approaching determinedly now put on a spurt, and Flynn went down as under a ton of falling masonry.

Flynn's consciousness washed in and out like a tide. Sometimes he was aware of voices, sometimes of hands. He was aware that time was passing, but not how much of it. He knew something had happened to him, was not sure what, decided his best policy was probably to sleep it off.

Hands again, pulling him upright. His senses swimming. Explosions of sound and sensation about his face: someone slapping him. A voice, irritable, impatient: "What did you hit him with—a truck?" Flynn knew what the words were without quite knowing what they meant. He blinked his eyes open and mumbled something. It must have been the right thing because they stopped hitting him.

Obregon stood back, watching, his sculpted lip curled in distaste. He was not usually this close to the sharp end of his activities, and it gave him no great pleasure to see a helpless man beaten. Even Flynn. There had been a time when he had lain awake, night after satisfying night, planning the punishments he would inflict on Mickey Flynn when Providence eventually delivered him into his hands. But that was a year ago: he must be mellowing as he grew older; in any event, now Flynn had delivered himself Obregon was not at all sure what he was going to do with him.

Except first. First he was going to find out what Flynn knew about Maxine Faber and the Rotterdam shipment. Had she been on Flight 98?—and if so, how could she have been seen at the crash site? As he grew older, and richer, Obregon had distanced himself a little from the daily workings of his business, and he had not known that Faber had failed to arrive in New York as expected. To find out what Flynn knew, and why Flynn was here, he was prepared to over-ride his new-found delicacy and conduct this interview personally.

Flynn was propped up against the wall, his head on one side, his long limbs slack. The least nudge would have tipped him over. Obregon had never seen him before, knew him only from photographs. He was a little surprised to have recognised him so quickly: awake he looked a fair bit older than those photographs, and a lot harder.

Unconscious he looked much younger, like a beaten child. His lip was split in two places, one eye was blackened, and somebody's ring had left a deep score across his left cheek. The blood had run to his jaw and was only now congealing. His eyelids were hovering at half-mast: there was little sign of intelligence in them yet. Obregon could have wished his people a shade less enthusiastic in defence of his person, but then they were not to know that he had orchestrated the attack on himself precisely so that he could have Flynn hustled away from his guests to where he could talk to him.

Flynn was coming round now but too slowly. His guests would be leaving: he had to see them off.

He apologised smilingly for the disturbance. "These young men of the press—they have no respect! I'm afraid my people were rather rough with him. Well, when he's feeling better maybe I'll pose for his photograph so we can part friends."

Obregon returned to the snooker room where he had left Flynn with the men who had beaten him senseless. He was looking livelier: his eyes were open and his head came up as Obregon entered the room. He moved as if to stand but Obregon's men pushed him back against the wall, firmly but with neither violence nor malice.

Obregon regarded him levelly for some moments. Then he took a cue from the rack, weighing it thoughtfully in his hand. Then he nodded to his men to leave. "I'll call if I want you." The bigger of the two gave Flynn a warning sort of look over his shoulder as he left.

Obregon came and stood over Flynn, resting the butt of the long cue on the floor, one ankle crossed elegantly over the other. Perfectly groomed in his pale grey lightweight suit that could have been silk, with his grey kid shoes crossed one over the other and not a hair out of place on his well-coiffed head, he looked a little like an aging matinee idol and a little like a panther. His voice was light in timbre and he could speak almost negligently and still load the words with meaning and menace.

He said, "You're a bigger man than I am, Mr. Flynn, and a younger one, and now we are alone you may think it a small matter to over-power me and escape the way you came." One shapely eyebrow arched, he waited for Flynn's reply. Flynn made none. Actually that was not what he was thinking.

Then so suddenly that Flynn did not see him begin to move, he snatched the cue up by the business end and brought the heavy butt crashing down on the solid timber frame of the snooker table. The violence of the act was so unexpected, despite what had gone before, and so overt that Flynn could not keep himself from flinching.

The lazy smile that curled Obregon's lip confirmed that that was the desired effect. "That would be a mistake," he said.

Angry at himself for again allowing Obregon to manipulate him, Flynn jerked his face away from the wall. The flock of the expensive wallpaper had left its imprint on his cheek. He growled, "I didn't come here for the privilege of being thumped by your minders and then running away again." He wished his head would stop spinning.

"I wondered about that," admitted Obregon. "I asked myself if I cared why you had come. I decided I did not."

Flynn squinted at him. "Are you telling me you don't know why I'm here?"

Obregon's manner was deprecating. "Mr. Flynn, I'm not telling you anything. I'm waiting to hear what you have to tell me. I'm waiting to see if it's worth anywhere near as much to me as the pleasure of destroying you."

Flynn could not work out if the man was toying with him, for his own amusement or some even less fathomable purpose, or if Obregon was genuinely unaware that he had been implicated in the fate of Flight 98. "You do know Maxine Faber?"

"Of course I know her; of her, anyway. She works for me. At a company of mine in Fort Lauderdale. So?"

"She travels a lot. She carries drugs for you."

Obregon barked a silent laugh at the ceiling. "You're a persistent son-of-a-bitch, Flynn! Twelve months ago I had to leave my home because of your damned insinuations. I swore then that when I got my hands on you I'd rip your lying tongue out."

Flynn's pointed chin came up, his lip curled and brimstone smouldered in his eyes. "Don't waste it on me, Obregon. There's only the two of us here, and I know where your money comes from. I know what kind of work Maxine Faber does for you—and so does the British cop who was there when she told me."

"Told you?" He had succeeded in surprising Obregon. Faber was an experienced courier—not too good to be caught, no-one was that good, but too clever to admit anything and certainly too wise to bring his name into it. "Mr. Flynn, tell me what you came here for."

"I came to ask you a question. I'd have asked it in the garden and then gone away, except that the house fell on me."

"Ask it now."

"Were you responsible for the bomb on Flight 98?"

"I told you already. No."

"You could have been. Your courier was on board. You could have given her a bomb to carry instead of crack. You might have reckoned it was worth losing her to see me scattered across half southern England."

"How could I know you were on the plane?"

"You could have had me followed. From my apartment, after you had the place torched. The two Arabs—Fahad and the other man: God knows how you found them, but they had their own reasons for helping you. But they got it wrong. You wanted me dead and you didn't care who died with me. Faber was in London, and Fahad made the bomb. She thought it was crack, of course. If she hadn't panicked when the police came for me, she'd have died with everyone else."

"I employed two Arabs to burn your apartment? My, didn't I have a busy day! Why Arabs?"

"Because one of them wanted me dead as much as you did."

"That's your answer, then. He blew up the plane. Fahad? He bombed Flight 98."

"And it's coincidence your courier was on the plane?"

"Yes. No-one followed you. Miss Faber would be travelling on a ticket bought weeks in advance: she always does, it looks better that way."

If it was true, it was impossible for Maxine Faber to have carried the bomb on board for the purpose of killing him. "Can you prove that?"

"Miss Faber can undoubtedly prove it to your British policeman. I could probably prove it to you, if I cared to." Obregon's tone dropped a note: something in it reminded Flynn of a cat sharpening its claws on upholstery. "But Mr. Flynn, I have a much more interesting proposition.

"It's like this. If I did what you suggest, it was because I want you dead. I think you will have no difficulty believing that. On the other hand, if I didn't do it, it's in my interests to help discover who did—because others will come to the same conclusion as you, and a businessman who is prepared to blow up his associates soon runs out of people willing to associate with him. So if I did it I'm going to kill you; and if I didn't I'm going to let you leave in the hope that you will discover the real culprit and thus clear my name. Does that sound reasonable to you?"

Flynn did not know what to say. Obregon's voice trickled like slow honey. His manner was infinitely threatening and something like madness glittered in his eyes. Yet there was a kind of inescapable logic to what he said. Finally, fractionally, Flynn nodded.

"Get up, Mr. Flynn."

It took Flynn longer than it should have, and he could not have said how much of the delay was due to his concussion and how much to the fact that he was staring death in the face. He glanced fitfully left and right. But the only door was behind Obregon and certainly guarded from the other side. He got to his feet and stood swaying slightly, the palm of one hand flat against the wall to steady him. He watched Obregon with hollow eyes and hoped that, whatever he intended to do, he would do it before Flynn's shaky knees let him down.

"Turn round. Face the wall."

Flynn did. He put both hands flat against the flock wallpaper and closed his eyes.

The word "Now!" hissed in Obregon's throat, a savage primitive sound, and again the heavy cue in his hands leapt into life, surging in a vicious arc propelled by all the strength and all the bitterness in the small man's wiry frame. It was still accelerating when the loaded butt smashed splinteringly, sickeningly, into bone.

2

Leah Shimoni caught Todd as he was leaving. Another day she would have let him go, saying she would see him again. But she had spent time and nervous energy working up to this. She had spent most of the day and all the drive into town working out what she wanted to say, and how to avoid saying more than she wanted to say once her blood was up, and she thought that if she did not have this out with him now she would burst. His career as well as hers was at issue: it was worth making him late for whatever mercy-mission he was engaged on now.

So when he came to the door with his coat already on and his car-keys in his hand, she faced him out until her small body made his bulky one give way and let her come in. She closed the door firmly behind her.

Todd said, "I hope this isn't going to take long, Leah—"

And she said, "It's going to take as long as it takes, Gil, and it's far and away the most important thing you could be doing tonight so don't start checking your watch."

Todd blinked, surprised at her manner, at the strength of her tone.

Involuntarily, as a reflex action, he checked his watch. "All right. But
—I don't suppose we could do this in the car? I am rather—"

"No," said Shimoni. Everything about her was shouting except for
the pitch of her voice which was ominously low. "We could not do
this in the car."

"All right," he said again, defeated. He put his keys on the hall table
and took his coat off. "What is it, Leah? What's happened?"

"Nothing's bloody happened," she said forcibly. "For the last four
days. I have taken hundreds of photographs of that crash. I have
printed dozens of them. I have done all I can do until you write a
report on the thing. It's four days, Gil! The sodding Sunday supple-
ments will have sorted their coverage out by now! Have you written
anything?"

He had not. She knew he had not. He shrugged uncomfortably.
"I've been busy . . ."

"So have I," she snapped, "printing photographs that are already
past their sell-by date. It's not good enough, Gil. I worked hard on
that. I got good pictures—maybe better than any I've seen printed so
far. But it's yesterday's news already. Even the people who buy our
stuff, who want something better than news-flashes and are prepared
to wait a couple of days for the full story, don't want to be printing this
week what everybody else printed last week. You've let them down,
Gil. You've let me down."

In the last three years Todd had got used to taking criticism from
this pint-sized Israeli girl that he would never have brooked from
Flynn. Partly it was her sex. Partly it was because he held nothing over
her: he had not dragged her out of the gutter, dried her out and given
her something better to do than digging a hole in the Hudson River.
The wide age difference notwithstanding, theirs was essentially a professional partnership between free equals. What Todd had had with
Mickey Flynn had been both more and less than that. He had let Flynn
down more than once. Not in his wildest dreams could he imagine
Flynn storming round here to tax him with it.

He shrugged awkwardly. "I'm sorry, Leah. This is different—personal. Mickey needs my help."

"I need you to do your job!"

He bridled against her anger. "Leah, you know what the situation is.
Somebody's trying to kill him, for God's sake! On top of that, he's
carrying round a load of guilt nobody should have to bear alone. You

want me to stand back and watch it flatten him? I'm not going to do that. Not even for you. Not even for the job."

"Gil, if I thought it would do any good, I wouldn't let you get on with it, I'd help you. I know how you feel about Flynn. Well, that's all right, you were together a long time. But you have a responsibility to me now, and if you can't or won't meet it the least I have the right to expect is that you'll tell me that so I can act accordingly."

He passed a weary hand in front of his eyes. "I'm sorry, I should have called you."

"You're damn *right* you should have called! Four days ago you should have called! I haven't heard from you since you used my house to talk over old times and fed all my biscuits to the dog. I've called you three and four times a day. You're never in. I can't get you on the car-phone. I leave messages on your answering machine but you never call back. What the hell is going on, Gil? Do we still have a partnership, or did that crash in flames too?"

"Damn it, Leah," he snapped then, "you're not being fair. Yes, I've messed you around, I've wasted your time, and I'm sorry. But what else did you expect? The kid's like a son to me, you know that, and for all I know he may be dead now and I just haven't heard yet. No, I'm not going to be much use to you until this is over. I hope you'll bear with me so we can pick up the threads then. But Leah, please—please don't make me choose between my partnership with you and my friendship for Mickey."

"Is it so certain that I'd lose?" she asked bitterly.

"We'd all lose."

She went on staring at him, angry-eyed, for half a minute longer. Then by degrees the anger seeped away. He could not help how he felt. It was unreasonable to expect him to shrug off Flynn's plight: when this was over he would need to feel he had done everything in his power to help him. It was the common duty of friendship. It was no threat to her. Neither, she was coming to realise, was Flynn. A shade ruefully she said, "I suppose I should be flattered you consider it a choice."

They ended up talking in the car after all: hers, as she drove him to his overdue appointment. Even driving through a foreign capital on the wrong side of the road, she was safer behind the wheel than Todd was. And quicker. Todd did not make right-hand turns if he could avoid it.

The small storm seemed to have cleared the air between them. Todd realised he had never explained to Shimoni, not in so many words, about him and Flynn, and he tried to do so now. The darkness in the car, and the street-lamps throwing surreal patterns through the windscreen as they drove, and the fact that Shimoni's eyes were on the traffic and not free to slide his way and embarrass him, made it easier. But still not easy.

When he was writing Todd could reduce the most complex ideas to a form which anyone with a desire to do so could understand. Emotions, however, gave him more trouble, and his own emotions most of all. He had had friends and lovers. He had been married once, briefly; it had ended amicably enough and not a moment too soon for either of them. He had made many enduring professional relationships that gave him respect and something palpably close to affection, and he treasured these—among them the one he had with Shimoni—because to a man with no gift for personal commitment they offered a safe, comfortable compromise between domestic turmoil and loneliness.

Flynn was different. Flynn was the closest thing he had to family.

He had told Shimoni that Flynn was like a son to him, and substantially that was true. He had created Flynn—Flynn the world knew, Flynn the award-winning photographer, Flynn the by-line—not from his seed in the body of a woman but out of a jumble of spare parts dumped in the last stage of dissolution on a bar-stool a stone's throw from the New York waterfront. He was not the first drunk Todd had been accosted by. He was not even the first young drunk, heading for a body-bag as a twenty-fifth birthday present. He had never felt tempted to take one home before. Mostly he asked the barman to find him a seat away from the garbage.

This long after, he had no idea why he had put up with Flynn draped over the bar, breathing alcoholic fumes at him, arguing and bumming drinks. It was true that he needed a photographer, but Flynn was not one and nothing about him suggested that he could become one. He was a lanky, undernourished street-wise hustler with a drink problem and a crazy grin, and sometime this week or the next he would curl up with a bottle of cheap whisky and go under for the third time. But he was not Todd's problem or any of Todd's business.

"Then as I was leaving," said Todd, "he tried to mug me. Can you imagine? It was like being attacked in an alley by a length of well-chewed string. I didn't even have to knock him down—I stood back and he fell down of his own accord."

That had left him with three choices. There seemed no point in calling the police: Flynn posed no threat to anyone. He could have left him in the gutter. Somehow that seemed too easy. Flynn needed a lesson and Todd was in the mood to deliver one, and since he was not in the habit of kicking drunken kids he did the next most vicious thing, which was take him back to the hotel where he was staying and dry him out.

He did not tell Shimoni what that had been like, how Flynn had hurt and cried and begged and how halfway through Todd had hoped he would do them both a favour and die. But afterwards, motivated as much by shame as by charity, he had begun to put the pieces of Mickey Flynn back together, hoping to create a more useful model than the one he had picked apart. That was when the notion of making a press photographer of him had occurred to Todd. He needed a tame photographer almost as much as he needed some way of getting Flynn off his conscience.

"You're too hard on yourself," Shimoni said quietly. It was the first interruption she had made. "You don't have to make excuses for saving a man's life."

Todd nodded slowly. "Yes, he would have ended up on a slab, and therefore I did save his life. I doubt if that entitled me to use him the way I did, then or later. It was a kind of pride. God made man, but Todd made Flynn."

"But not in his own image," murmured Shimoni, and Todd chuckled in the darkness. Seen together they looked like a Government Health Warning on the respective dangers of obesity and anorexia nervosa.

Todd went on, "You know how it finished. After four years of pretending he needed me as much as I needed him, all at once he'd had enough of dancing to the tune of an old fool who talked a lot about Great Journalism but actually couldn't sell his stories without the help of some pretty outstanding photography. I never gave Mickey his due, and after four years he gave me my cards. I was lucky—I found another pretty outstanding photographer, who listens patiently when I talk about Great Journalism and has far too firm a grip on her own life to let me interfere in it. And if Mickey came back tomorrow with his cap in his hand, I'd have to tell him that I'm content with and committed to the partnership I now have.

"But Leah, I still—miss him, I suppose. Even after three years. There's a kind of hole in my soul where he used to live, and I'd got used to thinking it was there for good and now suddenly here he is again, hurting and needing my help again. What can I do? It's like when a marriage is over—mine, anyway: you don't want it back, but you still care enough about the other person to try and keep them safe." He rolled his eyes and his head tipped back against the restraint. "Oh God, I'm not explaining this very well."

Shimoni's voice was low, slightly husky with the accent, with a warmth to it Todd had not expected so that he thought, She *does* know what I'm on about! She said, "You don't owe me any explanations, Gil. You owe me what I'm due under the terms of our partnership, which is the right to know, at a suitable time, what we are and are not working on. You should have called me. I was angry. I'm sorry I shouted."

They came to some traffic lights. Shimoni stopped her car and looked at Todd for the first time since leaving his flat. "Gil—thanks for telling me. About you and Mickey. Some of it I knew, but—anyway. I appreciate your confidence."

He wriggled embarrassed shoulders inside his coat. "You mustn't feel—second choice, second best. Mickey's a bloody good photographer but so are you: I have never for one moment regretted our partnership. This thing with Mickey is—different. Somehow he's etched his initials on my conscience and I think they'll be there until I die." He chuckled. "Even when I don't see him for years; even when I do see him and he immediately starts driving me up the wall. I care what happens to him. Like someone I used to love, or a child grown up and grown away. Family. There," he said then smiling. "Who'd have thought the old man had so much sentiment in him?"

She smiled back, and the lights changed and she returned her eyes to the road. Todd thought he heard her say, "Me," but it might have been a windscreen wiper squeaking.

As they turned the corner she said, "I've two things more to say and then I'll shut up. The first is, don't ever apologise for being nice. It's humanity's greatest sin that we find it easier to talk about our vices than our goodness. And the other is, whatever this address is that you've had me hunting for, we're there."

It was a gentleman's club, much frequented by gentlemen in the trendier types of business. It was the sort of gentleman's club that did not exactly refuse admission to women but did all in its power to make them uncomfortable and reluctant to come again. But Shimoni was about as easy to wither as a brake of camel-thorn, and she stared down the servant who answered the door until he held it wide for her. Then, since she was not wearing a hat or gloves, she gave him her car-keys to hold while she followed Todd to the desk where he was asking for Peter Loriston.

Loriston was a man who had been done a great disservice by nature. It had thwarted his endeavours from his earliest days. Time and again it had prevented him from fulfilling his full potential. It had made men distrust him, and attracted to him the sort of women who could only damage his career. Colleagues had to work hard to take him seriously; the press did not try. Once or twice he had stood poised on the brink of actual greatness when the old curse had reared its head again and left him floundering. Peter Loriston was a seriously handsome man, and he had paid the price of it all his life.

He met them at the lift and showed them to the rooftop conservatory. Like the hall porter he was surprised by Shimoni but he made a better job of hiding it. He ordered drinks for them, revealing as he turned a profile of Greek perfection. He had tried to disguise it with a moustache once, but even the moustache came out beautifully shaped and bright gold. Peter Loriston genuinely hated being that handsome. A less particular man might have neglected himself deliberately, but he would still have been just the ideal few fractions over six feet tall and built like an athlete.

Todd asked for a pint of beer, and it came in a pewter tankard. Shimoni tried to think of something frilly-sounding and settled on a Pink Lady. She had no idea what one was. Neither had the barman. That too came in a pewter tankard.

Loriston leaned back in his chair and smiled handsomely over the single malt in his cut-glass tumbler. "So what is this story you're working on, Mr. Todd? You said on the phone, something about Wren churches and tower-blocks?"

He had. He had said he was writing about those modern buildings that, with the benefit of a century's hindsight, would be considered the architectural gems of their day. He had asked what architects currently working in London considered the flag-ships of their profession.

He had lied. He said with disconcerting candour, "I misled you.

Actually I'm not here to talk about architecture at all. It was just a pretext to see you. Tell me," he went on quickly before Loriston could recover his composure, "have you had a visit from the police in the last few days?"

"The police?" Loriston stared. "No. About what?"

"No. You see," Todd confided, "they think it was Fahad. Or Obregon. Or possibly both. They're probably right. But it occurred to me that, if they're wrong, then it could be you and you might not still be here by the time they get round to asking."

Half a dozen different questions formed in Loriston's clear blue eyes. None of them got past his lips. Finally he managed, "I don't understand. If you're not a reporter, who are you?"

"I'm a reporter, all right," said Todd, swallowing his irritation. Even important people no longer really *read* newspapers. If he had been some twenty-five-year-old blonde TV announcer with a Filofax, a Mot Juste computer and no idea how to drag the truth kicking and screaming out of people who had no wish to tell it, Loriston would have known his name then. Or at least his cup-size. "I'm just not writing about modern buildings. You can tell me about an old building if you like—a warehouse that got burned. No? How about an aeroplane that crashed, then?"

Loriston was either totally bewildered or else a great loss to the stage. But he had not risen to be a government spokesman without learning how to think on his feet. "Mr. Todd, I don't know what you're talking about. The time has come either to tell me or to leave."

"Fair enough," said Todd. "You remember Mickey Flynn."

The bewilderment was replaced not by comprehension but by a black hatred totally independent of it. It was an almost Pavlovian response: he did not need to understand how Flynn fitted into this to react violently to his name. Colour rushed into his cheeks; a vein throbbed at his temple. His classically proportioned nostrils flared and his lip curled. Gouts of flame surged in his eyes. The hand that was not holding his glass actually formed a fist. "Yes. I remember Flynn."

"A few days ago," Todd went on conversationally, as if he had not noticed the effect his last remark had had, "somebody fire-bombed his apartment. He and his girl got out by the skin of their teeth. He decided to leave London and fly to New York. You'll never guess which plane he was booked on."

Loriston's expression was changing again, less abruptly this time, from blank black hatred to an avid interest incorporating a small, indecent glimmer of hope. "You mean he's dead?"

Todd gave that a moment's thought. "I wouldn't stake my pension that he's still alive, but he certainly survived the crash. He missed the plane. What I'd like to know from you, Mr. Loriston, is what you know about (a) the fire at Flynn's warehouse and (b) the bombing of Flight 98."

Loriston had travelled sufficiently far through the unholy succession of blind hatred and vicious optimism to be on his way back to the softly lit conservatory and the smell of damp compost, and with the return of his senses came the awareness that he was being accused of something monstrous. "Bombing?" The word exploded in his mouth. "Me? Are you serious?"

"Deadly serious," Todd affirmed stolidly.

"You think I bombed a plane? That I bombed a plane with—what was it?—two-hundred-odd people on board, in order to kill Flynn?" Quite soon the calumny of that suggestion would provoke in him an anger to dwarf even what he felt about Flynn. But for just a moment yet it was held in check by shock.

The shock of a man unjustly accused of a crime against humanity? Or that of a man discovered in his guilt? Todd wondered. "You had a go at him once before."

Clearly Loriston had thought no-one knew about that, not even Flynn. He had thought it had been accepted as an accident. But he did not deny it. "That was different. Him and me. I didn't push him. But no, it wouldn't have grieved me if he'd leaned out too far."

"Would it have grieved you if he'd burned to death trying to rescue his girl?"

"Actually, no. But I still had nothing to do with it."

"And the plane?"

The anger was beginning to filter through. "This is outrageous."

"When you thought he'd died on that plane, you looked thrilled."

"That's right," Loriston said then, his voice hardening. "For just a moment, before you spoiled it, I thought Christmas had come early. I thought, That's the answer to the question 'Why does God permit such things?' Perhaps somewhere in every crashed plane, every sunken ship, every massacred wagon-train, every Guernica, there's a Mickey Flynn—someone who deserves it enough to make up for no-one else there deserving it at all.

"Thrilled? Yes. I thought, Before that plane crashed there must have been a little time—maybe not long, maybe only a few seconds, but time—when he knew he was going to die. When he knew what was going to happen, and that there was nothing he could do to save himself. When he could see it coming and imagine what it was going to be like—the rending of flesh, the breaking of bones, blood exploding in his eyes and in his brain, fire licking at his body if he lived long enough to feel it.

"And maybe in those few seconds he knew the sheer helpless terror of waiting for an inevitable destruction. God knows how many people he did that to: took what he wanted and left them to await the consequences, robbed of hope and dignity and even the achievements of their past. He ruined me. For the sake of one cheap photograph that wasn't even revealing a vital truth. I served my country honestly and well, and he carved me up for the cash he could make. Oh yes, I was glad to think he was dead. I just hoped he'd lived long enough to know what being a burnt offering feels like."

Todd knew the answer before he asked the question; he felt he had to ask it anyway. "Somebody put a bomb on Flight 98. It seems likely that the target was Mickey Flynn. Did you do it, or have it done?"

Loriston rose to his feet with a sort of slow violence, like a gathering storm. Todd stood too. Shimoni stayed where she was, watching the two big men jousting with words for lances.

The outrage in Loriston's eyes was an almost palpable force, a radiation. He was too angry to shout: he growled. "You've some damn nerve, Todd. You come here, under false pretences, and accuse me of killing two hundred and twenty people. You've no evidence; all you know is that I have reason to wish him dead. Well, I doubt if I'm alone in that.

"The answer to your question is no. I didn't burn his flat and I didn't bomb his plane. Not because I've forgiven what he did to me. Not because I don't want him dead; not even because of the practical difficulties of finding someone with the necessary expertise to do it. The point is, I'm not the sort of man who does that sort of thing.

"Flynn has no need to fear a stab in the back from me. If I take him on, it'll be like last time: just him and me, alone, out of sight, no-one else to get hurt, no-one else to get involved. Not even you. But he'll know. If I decide to pay him back some day, he'll know who and why." He grinned suddenly, savagely. "Duelling is much more my style than mass murder."

It would have suited Todd not to believe him. But Loriston had always been a long shot, and now he had met him Todd could not imagine him acting as he would have had to in order to be guilty of this crime. He sighed. "If I see him again, I'll tell him. I'm sorry you've been troubled. We'll find our own way out."

Shimoni got up then. But she was not quite ready to leave. She stood about five-foot-two, Loriston a little over six feet: somehow she contrived to look down her nose at him. "You blame Flynn for what happened to you? Flynn did nothing but record a moment in time. You are responsible for your actions and the consequences of them. It wasn't a spicy photograph that cost you your career, it was your inability to conduct your personal life in a manner becoming a man entrusted with state affairs. A man who cannot govern himself has no business trying to govern a country.

"You consider yourself victimised because Flynn's photograph stirred up a witch-hunt. You think it was unjustified because you never behaved corruptly. Actually, the issue of corruption hardly enters into it. That photograph revealed you as a man willing to put his own desires above the needs of his colleagues, his government and his country. Your actions were so ill-considered and so arrogant as to prove you unsuitable for authority. A photograph disclosing that was an entirely proper demonstration of public interest over-riding the right to privacy." Then she grinned too, a feral gleam splitting her small watchful face. "You want to meet me with pistols on Hampstead Heath?"

As she drove them back to Kensington, Todd said with admiration and some awe, "When you have a go at someone you really go for the throat, don't you?"

She did not glance round. "Not always. I can't always reach the throat. But there are vulnerable spots lower down."

Todd thought a little longer about what had been said, then sighed. "He really didn't have anything to do with it, did he?"

"No," she agreed. "An arrogant man, a self-centred man, a man of poor judgement and no sense of perspective; but no, not a man who bombs aeroplanes. Perhaps Mickey's had more luck."

Todd shrugged his coat up round his neck. His voice was gruff. "How lucky can you get when you're looking for a man who wants you dead? If he'd been lucky he'd have been stopped at Bogotá airport and deported as an undesirable alien, in which case he'd have been back by now. I don't think it makes much difference whether Obregon bombed Flight 98 or not. When Mickey turns up on his doorstep he's going to do what he's been waiting to do for the last eighteen months."

"You think he'll kill him?"

"I think he'll rip him limb from limb. It wasn't just what he cost Obregon in financial terms, or even in annoyance. He made a fool of the man, and Obregon couldn't stop him. That undermined his credibility in a business which depends on people believing you can and will carry out your threats. Even if Obregon has got over the anger—which is a big if—as a matter of strict commercial necessity he has to be seen collecting his debts. Killing Mickey may be worth millions to him."

"Do you suppose it was him that planted the bomb?"

"I think he's the likeliest contender. He had the motive, the opportunity and the means, and he wouldn't be deterred by the moral implications. Yes, I think probably it was him."

"Then—"

"Yes. I think probably by now he's finished the job."

3

Two more days passed without word from or about Flynn. Shimoni called Todd twice, on different pretexts but mostly to find out how he was, and he called her once to discuss the resumption of normal services.

Superintendent Donnelly called on him—a very angry Superintendent Donnelly who had come straight from Peter Loriston who had failed utterly to be surprised at his name being linked with the loss of Flight 98.

Todd shrugged. "He wasn't involved."

"Perhaps he wasn't. Or perhaps you gave him the time he needed to get his head and his story together enough to lie convincingly."

"He wasn't lying when I talked to him."

"Damn it, you can't know that!"

"Superintendent, I've interviewed as many people in the course of my work as you have, and a lot of them were lying and a lot of them had something to hide. If I couldn't tell when I was being strung along, I'd still be writing dog-show results for the *Todmorden Chronicle.*"

"You had no right to approach him."

"I had every right to approach him. What's more, if I saw any need to do so I'd approach him again. I am ready and eager to assist in your enquiries, Superintendent, because we're on the same side and anyway I am a law-abiding man. But there are more ways of skinning a cat than one, and my profession as well as yours brings guilty men to justice. After four days it was time somebody talked to Loriston and you were clearly too busy."

After that they stopped spitting tacks at one another, split a pot of coffee and talked through what Loriston had and had not said. They agreed there was no more mileage in him and wondered where the real trail led.

"You've heard nothing from Flynn?"

Todd shook his head. "I don't expect to."

"He shouldn't have gone."

"No. But no-one else could. Colombia isn't in your jurisdiction. He needed to know."

"Do we know now? Does it follow, if he's killed Flynn, that he bombed that plane?"

"I wouldn't think so." Todd sighed wearily. It was getting to feel a long time since he had had a proper night's sleep. "Whether he did the plane or not, he was never going to let Mickey leave. I doubt if we'll ever know for sure now."

"And Fahad? Should we still be looking for him?"

"You've *been* looking for him," Todd reminded him, "for at least the last three years. He's on Interpol's terrorist list. It didn't stop him getting into the country, though, and I don't expect it'll stop him getting out again. I don't know what his role in all this was. I doubt you'll ever get the chance to ask him."

Donnelly left then, and Todd took the cups into the kitchen and thought about washing them, and then the doorbell rang and he thought Donnelly must have remembered something else he wanted to say and he answered the door with the battered silver pot, bought in the souk in Marrakech on the occasion of King Hassan II's accession to the throne of Morocco, still in his hand.

Mickey Flynn looked at it and said, "Great idea."

He looked like death warmed up. Under the ragged fringe of his lank brown hair his face was white, except for a smudge of black like coaldust under one eye and a faint rainbow ring around the other. His mouth was swollen out of shape on the side where his lip was split, and a long deep scratch reached from its corner almost to his ear. Also his right hand was encased in plaster, from above his wrist to his fingernails.

For several long seconds Todd's broad face would not make its mind up what it wanted to express. It tried shock, and delight, and amazement, and then a brief detour into concern, then back to delight. His lips rounded on words to start half a dozen different sentences but he got none of them out. He hugged the coffee-pot to him and was glad of something to do with his hands. Finally he managed, "I thought you were dead."

Flynn raised one eyebrow no further than he had to. "Reports were exaggerated."

Todd looked again, taking in the weary stoop of his shoulders and the heavy-lidded eyes as well as the fading bruises and the slightly grubby plaster. "Not by much."

"Jet-lag." He shouldered past Todd, still clutching his coffee-pot in the doorway, and dropped his bag on the floor, and walked to the nearest chair and went down into it without taking his jacket off. Todd thought that if the chair had not been there he might not have made it as far as the sofa. "Can I crash here?" He winced at the unhappy phraseology.

Todd started to grin. He could not help it. He knew it was tactless or worse, and he did not care. He felt like a man witnessing a clash of ideologies between his mother-in-law and a traffic-warden: he did not care how this had happened, he was just happy that it had. Explanations could wait.

He went to make the coffee. Another man might have rinsed the cups under the tap, but Todd did the washing-up while he waited for the pan to heat. When he took the tray into the livingroom Flynn was asleep in the chair.

Todd put the tray down quietly and stood over him, inspecting the damage more closely than he could have done with Flynn awake. It was days old now and, apart from the hand, superficial anyway. He looked exhausted and in need of a change of clothes. For a man who should have been dead a week, he looked wonderful.

Todd phoned Shimoni. When she asked why he was whispering he told her. There was a momentary pause. Then she said, "Gil, I'm so glad," and he had no doubt she meant it.

He thought probably he ought to call Donnelly too, but decided that could wait. Until he got some rest Flynn would not make enough sense to be worth talking to, and it was hard to see what he might have to say that would urgently affect the police investigation. First thing in the morning was time enough. If Flynn would sleep slumped in the chair, Todd could contain his own curiosity until then.

But the click of the phone, or possibly Todd's eyes on him, reached Flynn where he slumbered and Todd watched him struggle awake. His face creased up along the lines that had always been there when he grinned but some time in the last three years had become permanent. The discoloured skin around his eyes contracted in a frown and the meter of his breathing changed, roughening. Then he grunted, blinked his eyes open and was back. "Oh, hello."

Todd smiled. "Who were you expecting—Obregon?"

Flynn's eyes flinched at the name. But he said, "It wasn't him, Gil. The plane. Maxine Faber was carrying crack, not a bomb."

"What happened?"

Flynn told him—about waiting, and then the party. About what he had said to Obregon, and what Obregon had done to him. Very faintly he grinned. "The bastard smashed my camera-hand with a snooker cue. Mustn't know photographers are ambidextrous."

Todd scrutinised the plaster. "Will it be all right?"

"Oh yeah, should be." He was not using any more words than he had to. That, and the drawl that was almost a slur, betrayed the tiredness even more than his eyes. "Got it set in Bogotá. I'll have it X-rayed some time."

"And Obregon—denied it? The plane, I mean?"

Flynn twitched half a grin. "Yeah, sort of. He broke my hand instead of my neck." He explained. "Apparently, speculation that he was responsible for bombing a passenger jet is damaging his good name. If he killed me, nobody'd believe he hadn't tried it before. I reckon he hoped that if he let me go whoever it was would try again and let him off the hook."

"You believed him?"

Flynn had considered the possibility that Obregon had been lying. He could have been. But instinctively, at gut level, Flynn knew it was the truth—if for no better reason than the one Obregon gave when Flynn asked why he should believe a man of so few principles. This was when he was back on the snooker room floor, hunched over his knees and sweating, talking to keep his mind off the strapping the man was now calmly applying to his hand. Obregon had replied simply, "Because it doesn't matter to me whether you believe me or not."

"It's the truth, all right. He knew nothing about it, either the plane or the apartment."

"Neither did Loriston," said Todd. "He was the only one of your four that I knew how to find, so I thought I'd go and see him while I was waiting to hear from you. Donnelly wanted my eyeballs on cocktail sticks, but actually Loriston had nothing to tell either of us. It was news to him that you were involved. But he sent you a message. He said, if he comes after you it'll be pistols at dawn, not a knife in the back."

Flynn regarded his plastered right hand. "Somehow, that's not as reassuring as it might be."

Todd smiled. "Go to bed, Mickey."

"Tell you what," said Flynn, climbing laboriously out of the chair. "I'll go to bed."

In the morning, when twelve hours' sleep had wiped about ten years off Flynn's face, Todd took him to see Donnelly, then took him to see a doctor.

Donnelly listened to his story without interrupting, almost without expression, and at the end had no questions and only one observation. "If you're going to go on behaving like this, you and the Boy Wonder there"—he meant Todd, who could have won prizes for the least probable sight in tights—"it's only a matter of time before whoever started this finishes the job, or someone else finishes it for him."

Flynn smiled at him quite strangely: not his manic grin that made people cross the street, nor his rare gentle smile that made those who thought they knew him think again, but a variant Todd had not seen before and which rather disturbed him. There was a remoteness about it that was not native to Flynn, a kind of indolence, a cynicism, like a man becoming a satire on himself.

He drawled, "That's what I thought. The first time—the fire? Then again when the plane crashed. Even when I went up against Obregon I was still thinking it—you know, that this had to be the time, the luck had to have run out by now. But it hadn't.

"You want to know what I think now? I don't think it matters if they come after me with flame-throwers. I think if they drop a nuclear bomb on London, it'll turn out there's just one safe place to be standing and I'm standing there. I think if they try to hang me the rope will break, and if they throw me off a tall building there'll be a lorry delivering interior spring mattresses stuck in traffic below.

"I think, Superintendent, that I have one of these charmed lives you hear about. People around me drop like flies; buildings burn, planes crash, megalomaniacs grind their heels in a myriad faces, but none of it quite touches me. Somehow all I get is the backwash. Even when I go to sup with the devil, somehow the old guy's got reasons of his own for supplying long spoons.

"So don't worry about me, Superintendent. My life is charmed. Somebody up there likes me. Or else somebody down there is playing silly buggers." The smile glittered like sunlight on a glacier.

The hospital X-rayed Flynn's hand and the doctor studied the results with much lip-pursing and sucking of teeth. Then he admitted the unpalatable truth: that he could not have made a much better job of it himself. He expected the broken bones to knit strongly enough, and though the hand might remain a little misshapen its function should be substantially unimpaired. Lacking a good excuse to intervene in any other way, he shoved a cocktail of assorted antibiotics into Flynn via a hypodermic needle that reminded him of the Alaska pipeline.

When they returned to Todd's flat, the first thing Flynn did was try the answering machine. But there was still no message from Laura Wade.

He could not understand it. "She should have called by now. She was going to call you as soon as she was settled, leave an address for me. She's got to have found some place by now."

Todd had never more than half expected her to contact him and no longer expected it at all. He had hoped Flynn might realise why, but emotion was still clouding his thinking on the subject. Todd sighed. "Mickey, I don't think she's going to call. You can't blame her: not everyone can live the way you do. Somebody tried to kill her, for no better reason than that she was your friend. That must have terrified her—I mean, normal people get really frightened about things like that. I expect she meant to call, but—well, when she found some-where she felt safe, you can't blame her for not wanting to reopen the episode."

Flynn was staring at him. "She wanted to come with me."

"Of course she did. I'm sure she felt about you the way you feel about her. But—hell, Mickey, I'm sorry—you must have seemed like a dangerous addiction that could get her killed. Getting you out of her system was a matter of life and death to her."

He could see Flynn thinking about it. Then he said, "She might at least have checked to see if I was all right." If he sounded a little hurt, he was already growing philosophical.

"It may not have occurred to her you were on that flight. Or maybe it did and she checked with the emergency number."

"My name was on the first list they gave out."

"So maybe she didn't call till later." Or maybe she called right away and was told Flynn was among the dead, and that was why she never contacted Todd: she thought there was no point. Both of them were thinking it; neither of them gave it words. She thought he was dead, and it would take a coincidence of cosmic proportions for Flynn to find her again.

"You don't reckon whoever did this—Fahad, Wylie, whoever—has—?"

"Found her? No. I don't think he'd be interested in her after you split up. And if she had come to any harm, Donnelly would have heard."

Flynn nodded slowly, coming to terms with his loss. "I wish you could have seen her, Gil. She was something."

"I'm sure she was."

At the end of the tape there was a message for Flynn, but it was not from Laura or anyone he wanted to talk to. His face screwed up in dismay. "Oh Jeez no—not him, not again!"

"Who?" Todd had stopped listening when he realised the message was not for him. Now he came and listened again.

A man's voice was saying, "—to hear about the fire at your place. Hope no-one was hurt. Got this number from a policeman. Don't even know if you'll be able to help now.

"Thing is, could really use another copy of that picture of Dr. Hehn. You must think we eat the things. Thing is, he's giving a lecture in Geneva next month—big thing, quite an honour—wants to send them a copy of your picture for the programme. We'd lend them ours but you know what the post's like, wouldn't like to lose it. So—any chance? Be awfully grateful if you could oblige."

"What the *hell,*" said Todd when the tape finished, "was *that?*"

"*That,*" said Flynn, "was our Mr. Spalding from Deering Pharmaceuticals. Our Mr. Spalding handles public relations for the great Dr. Dieter Hehn, prize-winning chemist, incipient deity and narcissist of the first order. I've made so many prints of that bloody photograph, I thought they were papering the bloody building with them."

Todd remembered seeing the picture and being surprised by the byline. "Hardly your usual line of work, is it—beaming portraits of scientific genii?"

Flynn looked sheepish. "It wasn't him I went there to photograph. I wanted the use of their roof, that was all—it overlooks the river."

He had picked up word, at the last possible moment, of a police operation in the London river. A River Police launch with officers of the Drug Squad on board was moving to intercept a yacht heading upstream on a passage from Jersey where she had been moored alongside a powerboat out of Rotterdam. There was no time for him to organise river transport of his own, so he stuffed his biggest telephoto lens in his biggest pocket and looked for a high building with views to the river.

"They were very accommodating. I had half the top floor watching with me, they got quite upset when it looked the action was going to take place up-river. Then the police launch made its move and they all cheered."

Then as he was leaving there had been more sounds of jubilation lower down the building, and Mr. Spalding had ambushed him at the lift with news that their Dr. Hehn had just been notified as the winner of the prestigious Sondheim Prize for chemistry. After the assistance he had received it seemed churlish to leave without taking photographs of the happy chemist posed, all twinkling eyes and dentures, beside the blackboard in his laboratory. Also, of course, he had a market for the picture.

But ever since then Mr. Spalding had been calling at intervals looking for extra prints. Flynn did not feel he could refuse and made him some. Then he made him some more. Then, after a brief respite, he made him another one. By now even Mr. Spalding was getting a little embarrassed and offered to buy the negative; Flynn refused on principle, but that meant printing some more enlargements of the beaming Dr. Hehn. If the negative had not been destroyed in the wreck of Flight 98 Flynn might have been reduced to burning it himself to get Deerings' Mr. Spalding off his back.

The idea of Flynn, whose career had been built on brilliant, dangerous photographs that he had often risked his life to obtain and occasionally risked again to publish, disturbing images that held readers spellbound for a week and later cropped up in textbooks, being haunted to despair by the expensively educated tones of a public relations executive over a jolly snapshot he took as a favour amused Todd. It was a welcome interlude in the grim reality of the past week.

He said, "You could always go round and take another photo of his chemist."

Flynn's glance was eloquent. He knew Todd was laughing at him; any other time he would have joined in. "No. I shall call him, now. I shall tell him the negative was destroyed. I shall tell him all my equipment was destroyed. I shall tell him my camera-hand is in plaster. I shall give him the number of Aiden McNally, who will photograph anything for anyone as long as the price is right. After that, if I hear from him again, I shall go and kick in the headlights of his BMW."

Mr. Spalding was fulsome in his apologies for bothering Flynn yet again, horrified to learn what had happened to his darkroom and his negatives, and grateful for McNally's number. He hoped Flynn would feel free to use Deerings' roof any time that suited him. Flynn did not say so, but he had already decided that if he had to pass within a hundred yards of Deerings' front door again he would wear dark glasses and a false moustache.

"Are you going on with this?" asked Todd.

Flynn knew what he meant. "Yes."

He expected an argument, a reiteration of Donnelly's views couched in less formal language. He was mistaken. "Can I help?"

Flynn avoided looking at him. He did not want Todd to see how grateful he was for the offer, how little persuading he would need to accept it. "No. Thanks."

"I could watch your back."

"There's no need."

"So what the hell is this," growled Todd, "an investigation or a crusade?"

"I don't know what you mean," said Flynn, who knew exactly what he meant.

"You don't want justice for the two hundred and twenty people who died on Flight 98. It's more personal than that. You want revenge on whoever tried to kill you, and cost you your girlfriend. You don't want any help because you want to take him on and beat him at his own game. Just you and him: duelling, like Loriston said. You're crazy."

"Why?" Flynn rounded on him. "Why crazy? If it's the only way I can get him? The police would have found him by now if they were going to. I don't think the police, anybody's police, are capable of dealing with people like Fahad, like Wylie."

"And you think you can?"

"Yes, maybe. I've as good a chance of finding them and a better chance of getting to them."

"Then what?"

"Christ, I don't know. I'm playing by ear."

"Mickey, one of those two men probably killed two hundred and twenty people in an attempt to kill you. All right, you confronted Obregon and got away with it—because Obregon didn't do it and in his own peculiar way he has a certain position to uphold. I got away with talking to Loriston on the same basis—he was always the least likely suspect and anyway what could he do in his own club in the middle of London?

"The same won't apply when you find the other two. One's a mercenary, the other a terrorist—both by definition operate outside the law of any country. Both are wanted men in large parts of the world. Killing you would cost them nothing, not even sleep. Suppose one of them says, 'Yes, it was me.' What will you do then?"

"I keep telling you, I don't know!" Flynn heard himself shouting and stopped, and shoved his good hand so deep into his trouser pocket he could have pulled his sock up. The plastered one would not fit and hung round awkwardly like an embarrassing relative. He went on more quietly, "Gil, I don't have any answers. I know that somehow this thing is about me, and that's all I know. Fahad's involved in it, Laura saw him, but I don't know how deeply. Oh, I can see him burning me out; I can see him burning the apartment with me and maybe even Laura in it. I wouldn't have said he was a vindictive man but there are no gentle terrorists and he's probably killed people who've done him less harm.

"But the plane? I don't know. I can't see him doing that. Maybe, if it was an El Al flight. But that plane was carrying British and U.S. nationals, and the Palestinians are doing all they can to round up support in Britain and the States. It's only opinion in London and Washington that's stopped Israel dealing with the intifada as the hawks in the Knesset would like. I can't see Fahad wanting, or being allowed, to jeopardise Anglo-American sympathy for the Palestinians. Not now; not when they're getting somewhere."

Todd said slowly, "I know what it looks like—what it's looked like all along—but do you think we could have read this wrong? That the fire was Fahad, but the plane wasn't him or anyone else after your blood? I mean, I'm not a great believer in coincidence, but in a way it would make more sense if the two things weren't connected—if the bomb on the plane had nothing to do with you."

Flynn whispered, "I thought of that." He would have given everything he owned, and everything he could borrow, to believe it. The two hundred and twenty people on Flight 98 would still be dead, but no longer for him. It would not affect the grief he felt—still felt, though the practicalities of living one day after another had buried it and begun to grass it over—but it would lift the guilt from him. "You think it's possible? I don't think it's possible. Do you?"

Todd spread large hands in a helpless gesture. "Mickey, I just don't know. None of it makes any sense. Perhaps coincidence is as good a theory as conspiracy. But listen, if that bomb wasn't meant for you, it's even crazier for you to go round renewing old quarrels with people who once wanted you dead. One of them may be unable to resist the temptation, even if he knows no more about Flight 98 than we do. You could die for something as pointless as scratching open an old wound."

"Pointless?" echoed Flynn. Something akin to hope was beginning to flicker like candlelight in his eyes. "Gil, you don't understand. If Wylie didn't do it, and if Fahad did the apartment but not the plane, that lets me off the hook. It means it wasn't me all those people died for. Jeez, Gil, *think* about that."

"I've thought about it. You could end up the happiest corpse in the morgue."

Flynn grinned, his brilliant wolfish grin that made people of a nervous disposition leave by the fire exit. "Come on, you're talking to the guy with the charmed life."

"Then let me help you."

As quickly as it had come the grin was gone. Todd was accustomed to Flynn's eccentricities, but these mercurial flashes of mood troubled him. He knew Flynn had been affected by what had happened. For the first time he wondered how deeply. "No."

"Why *not?*"

"Because—" Todd saw him struggling to put what he felt in the disturbed depths of him into words. He would have helped with that too, if he had known how. Flynn drew a slightly ragged breath and started again. "Gil, look at me. Of what I had ten days ago, all I'm left with is my life and the clothes I stand up in. Everything else, everything that meant something to me—my home, my lady, my darkroom, my equipment, my negatives, my car, even the clothes Laura bought to replace what went in the fire—they're all gone. My charmed life doesn't seem to extend much beyond my own skin. All that's left is me, and you. Gil, I don't want there to be some other damn silly, half-connected incident that leaves only me."

4

For the most part a mercenary soldier conducts his business in the shadows. He has no friends. The people who hired him last year, and were glad to do so because bought guns were all that stood between them and the pit, want nothing more to do with him; and the better the job he did for them, the less anxious they are to see him again. For if their cause succeeded they replaced their enemies and now stand as vulnerable themselves to the assault of a hired army.

Michael Wylie had lost count of the number of times he had been asked to stay on as Commander-in-Chief of a new national force. Partly it was an expression of satisfaction with his work, but mostly it was to prevent him accepting a fresh contract from the people he had just ousted. But Wylie had no interest in gold braid and ostrich plumes, and anyway he had a strict rule about not changing sides in the same conflict within five years of accepting the king's/sheikh's/ Grand Panjandrum's shilling. Except that he worked in Swiss francs.

There were two points at which he had to step out of the shadows: to recruit, and to fight. Once it was time to fight the need for secrecy was over: if Wylie got his men trained, equipped and in position before anyone knew where they were, it did not matter who saw what after that. Given secrecy up to the moment of the first strike, Wylie's men could have their battle won in a matter of hours, and whole wars over in just a few days. Or it could stretch to months, limited only by the amount of money available to buy ammunition.

Recruiting was more of a problem. It could not be done in absolute secrecy. As far as he could Wylie recruited men who had worked for him before, whose strengths and skills he knew and whose discretion he knew he could rely on. Very often they introduced other men with an interest in the work, with the sort of qualities that amounted to mercenary potential, and among them too Wylie could do his recruiting quietly. Men he accepted had a vested interest in preserving the secrecy that protected them all; those he rejected—it was almost always that way, not many men drawn to the job lost their nerve at the last minute—he was careful to leave with the hope of being chosen next time, which was enough to ensure their silence too.

But at some point, if the job was a big one, Wylie had to go beyond personal contacts and let it be known he was in the market for manpower. He left it as late as he could, built in what safeguards he could, but from that point onwards people beyond the circle of those he trusted implicitly knew that he was preparing for action.

So he lived with the prospect that one of the men applying to join him was a spy. He was careful. He did not tell recruits where they would be fighting, only what the job paid. He never discussed politics. Men who wanted to fight out of conviction could volunteer for causes which appealed to them but they had no business being mercenaries.

He never recruited in the same city twice running. He did not advertise his activities. He had core staff, men who worked permanently with him, strategically located to weed out no-hopers and warn him of anyone showing too much interest. Once signed up, men never left the company of their colleagues until the job was done. If they had to tell their mothers they would not be home, they wrote and the letters were checked. If they had to go shopping they went together, each watching the others for the sake of his own safety. It was not fool-proof. It was the best he could do.

When all the precautions had been taken, the time came when Wylie had to set up shop if he was going to have something to sell. Once he did that—announced his presence, however discreetly, and his willingness to do business—he had very little idea or control over who might come through his door.

So when he looked up from the papers on his desk—a wooden board across two trestles in an upstairs room overlooking the port of Tangiers—and the first thing he saw was a plaster cast, he thought Jacquard downstairs had flipped his lid and was sending him cripples now. He said, "I never heard of anybody being invalided *into* an army before."

Then his eyes reached the face above the plaster and he sucked a little breath between his teeth and fell silent. Like everything else about him, his silences were dynamic, alive and crawling with import, not merely an absence of sound.

Mickey Flynn said, "Nobody else's army would consider you fit to fight, Michael."

In circumstances like these, ten seconds with nobody saying anything can feel a very long time. It was time for Wylie to hear and think about that odd hollowness in Flynn's tone that was echoed in the fractionally abnormal wideness of his eyes. Partly it was uncertainty as to the welcome he could expect, which was understandable enough. Partly it was because he had not seen Wylie since before the disaster he was inadvertently responsible for, so he had not seen what happened to Wylie's face. That too was understandable. Wylie had grown used to causing a certain amount of shock. Actually he rather enjoyed it.

The same ten seconds were also time for Flynn to take in the extent of the damage Wylie had sustained as a result of his error. He had lost an eye. A Moshe Dayan patch covered the empty socket. It might have been a kind of reverse vanity, but the deeply puckered scar extending above and below the patch suggested that, with or without a glass stopper, Wylie's left eye was not something people would want to see.

Whatever had taken his eye and left that ragged scar in its place had also torn half his cheek away. The granulation tissue which had replaced it was thick and uneven and incapable of much mobility, so that his expression was as lop-sided as a stroke victim's. It took practice now to read what he was thinking. So Flynn could have been mistaken, but that glint in Wylie's one eye looked like a kind of feral humour.

As his left eye-socket was covered by a black patch, so was his left hand encased in a black glove. Because he was right-handed he was not doing anything with it just now to indicate the extent of his disability. Preternaturally still, it lay on the board among the papers he had been reading and managed to dominate the little whitewashed room. Below the window, open to the breeze, the town sloped away to the sea.

Wylie said, with conviction, "You cannot be serious."

Flynn managed the flicker of a smile. "About joining up, no. About needing to see you, absolutely serious."

The soldier's first thought was for the integrity of his operation. "How did you find me?"

"With difficulty. It's taken me ten days, and I struck lucky at that. I found one of the guys who was with us in . . ." Flynn stammered and could not name the place where his honest mistake had cost Wylie so much. He had to rephrase it. "One of the men who worked for you. He sent me here. He wasn't going to. I persuaded him you'd want to see me."

"You did what?" A coal sparked in Wylie's one eye.

Flynn had forgotten that persuasion means something different to men whose trade is violence. "No, I mean— What do you think, I'm going round hitting professional soldiers with my plaster cast? I asked him and he told me."

"Who was it? I must have a word with him about security some time."

What was it Todd used to say? "No names, no pack-drill. Anyway, you've nothing to worry about. He only sent me here because he expected you to beat my head in."

Wylie leaned back in his chair, leaving his left hand on the desk. He was a man in his forties, with twenty years of this sort of work behind him and, given luck, another ten ahead. He was not a good-looking man, and had not been before his experience in Africa. He was inches shorter than Flynn, a handspan broader, and he was losing his hair. Mostly he wore black—a T-shirt today in deference to the Moroccan heat. Autumn had not reached here yet. The muscles of his arms and torso were square and hard, built by years of physical stress and owing nothing to a home gym. The Mr. Universe panel would not have looked at him twice, but you needed to know nothing at all about him to know not to jostle him in bars. He wore the potential for violence like a cloak, so visible he rarely had to resort to it.

He said, "Is that what you're expecting?" His voice was deep and no longer held more than a trace of the accent he had grown as a steelworker's son in Cleveland, Ohio. Not since the end of the Vietnam

War had he worked in mainly American company, and standard English was better for directing a multi-national, multi-lingual operation.

Flynn shrugged awkwardly. "I don't know what to expect. I had to come anyway."

Wylie had a disconcerting habit of coming right to the point. "Why?"

"There was something I had to ask you. It doesn't matter now—I know the answer." He paused then and his upper lip wrinkled: not with distaste, perhaps with regret. "Michael—I'm sorry about what happened."

Wylie was still leaning back in his chair, watching ambivalently. "I know."

"It was—Jesus Christ, it sounds stupid but it was a mistake. I didn't mean—I didn't *mean* to give you away."

"I know that too." Even the side of his face that could move was devoid of expression, his one eye half-hooded under its lowered lid.

"I thought—what we said, that you were already in action. There was a report of fighting along the border. By the time I found out it wasn't you, it was too late to stop the pictures. If there'd been anything I could have done I'd have done it but—I couldn't even find out what was happening. I couldn't get back—they closed down all the transport. After the government fell I tried again. I got the brush-off from your chief of staff. I knew you were alive, but I couldn't find out—" Embarrassed, he waved his good hand at Wylie's face. "Hell, Michael, you know what I'm saying."

Wylie smiled. It was not a pretty sight. "Sure I do. You wanted to know what they'd done to me and nobody'd tell you."

Flynn flushed. But it was near enough the truth that he could not deny it. "I suppose I wanted to know that you were OK."

"That's why nobody'd talk to you. I wasn't."

"I know." He shrugged again, helplessly. "I'm—"

"Let me guess," interjected Wylie, "you're sorry. Listen, kid. What happened was pure Fortunes of War stuff. Not your fault, not anybody's fault, just bad luck. It happens. Oh, I called you every name under the sun and wished interesting tropical diseases on you, but I didn't blame you. Not then and not since. You want your head beaten in, you'll have to take it someplace else."

Flynn nodded slowly. He hardly knew what to say and anyway for the moment lacked the voice to say it. He had not suspected Wylie of generosity. Or perhaps he was not so much generous as detached, a man who could distinguish between acts and their consequences even when he was himself their victim.

Either way, it was clear he harboured no ill-will towards Flynn. It had been worth the ten days and the miles Flynn had covered to learn that. Quite separately from his feelings about Flight 98, Flynn felt relief like a lightening burden to have made his peace with Wylie.

Wylie said, "So what was it you had to ask me?"

Flynn smiled. "I told you, I already know the answer."

"So tell me the question and the answer."

He could have refused. He could have lied. He considered both and, in view of Wylie's straightness with him, dismissed them. A shade ruefully he said, "I came to ask if you've been trying to kill me."

There were only two or three ways a man could react to a question like that. Again there was that pause of a few seconds before Wylie reacted at all, seconds in which Flynn held his breath. The reconciliation had been good, but it could prove to have been very short.

Wylie ended the waiting by laughing out loud, immoderately. A harsh deep cackle of laughter like defective drains shook his powerful frame and squeezed tears from his eye. He thumped the desk with his gloved hand and still he laughed. Finally the need to breathe intervened and the cackle gave way to a throaty chuckle. "It's a good job you can take photographs, kid," he managed then. "You'd make a rubbish soldier."

The idea of Flynn spending ten days tracking him down and then manoeuvring himself into a private interview in order to ask that was too much for Wylie. "What if I'd said yes and blown your head off?"

"Then I'd have known," said Flynn.

Still chuckling, Wylie shut the office up and took Flynn out to lunch. Lamb stew and couscous, eaten under the awning of a pavement cafe and washed down with mint tea. Flynn had not liked couscous the first time he came to Morocco with Todd, and the recipe had not changed.

Wylie said, "So what's this all about?" and Flynn told him. During the telling Wylie stopped seeing the funny side. He listened, watchful, a black and brooding presence much bigger than the space he took up. When Flynn had finished he said, his voice rough with barely contained anger, "What kind of a bastard do you take me for?"

Transfixed by Wylie's fierce unwinking stare, pinned between the couscous and the sea, Flynn found himself pleading. "Michael, try to understand. *Somebody's* been doing these things. Somebody killed two hundred and twenty people on a plane I should have been on. Somebody fire-bombed my apartment, with my woman in it. Somebody hates me like crazy. All I could think to do was track down people I might have given cause to hate me that much.

"Until just now I didn't know if you wanted my blood or not. I knew you could have organised and carried out something like this. I knew that, when I knew you two years ago, you wouldn't have gone in for that kind of open-ended mayhem. But things happened to you, Michael, that were enough to change anyone. Yes, in all the circumstances I could imagine you becoming—that obsessed by hatred of me. I hoped it wasn't you, but I had to find out."

"And now you know?"

"Oh yes. Your malice takes a subtler form. Like taking a hungry man out to lunch and feeding him sawdust."

Wylie smiled slowly. Then he grinned. "So if it wasn't me, who was it?"

Flynn told him about the short-list, the four names now whittled down to one. "Fahad was always going to be involved one way or another. Laura saw him at the apartment. But somehow I still can't see him doing the plane. A knife in an alley, a bomb in my car, a sniper in an upstairs window—yeah, sure, the guy wants me dead and, like yourself, he's in a line of business that fits him to do something about it. He could have bombed the plane, no question. But I'm not convinced he did. I'd ask him, but I don't know how to find him."

"Sonny," Wylie said heavily, "you keep knocking on trapdoors, sooner or later one of them's going to open."

Flynn shook his head. "I have a charmed life." He had said it so often now he was in danger of believing it. "It should have been Obregon, and even if it hadn't been he should have killed me. But it wasn't and he didn't—only this." He held up the grimy plaster. "I didn't expect it to be Loriston and it wasn't. I hoped it wouldn't be you and it wasn't. Now there's only Fahad. Oh God, Michael, I hope it wasn't Fahad."

Wylie did not understand. "If it wasn't Fahad, who was it?"

Flynn's eyes were a little crazy with hope. "If it wasn't Fahad, who the hell cares? If it wasn't Fahad, it wasn't because of me. It was all a meaningless coincidence—the fire at my place, Obregon's courier being on the plane and then getting off it. Why not? I owe my life to the coincidence of taking the same short-cut as a black kid in a Porsche. There's no law says everything has to connect, you're only entitled to one coincidence every twenty-five thousand miles."

"No," Wylie agreed slowly. "But I mistrust coincidence. Most coincidences are conspiracies that never came to light."

Flynn laughed. "Michael, you're a cynic."

"A man with one eye has to be," Wylie observed obscurely.

After lunch they strolled back up the hill to Wylie's office. There were people waiting to see him so he did not ask Flynn in. They stood in the alley below.

Wylie said, "How will you find Fahad?"

Flynn shook his head. "I wish I knew. I spent ten days looking for you, and the reason I did that was I couldn't think how to start looking for Fahad. If he'd been more accessible I'd have talked to him long enough since."

"Then he'd have killed you."

"Not necessarily. Maybe it wasn't him either—"

"Forget the plane. He burned your apartment. What makes you think he's had a change of heart since then? The rest of us were people who might have had an interest in killing you, but according to you Fahad's already tried it. How are you going to stop him trying again?"

"Why do you say it like that? According to me. Do you think I'm lying?"

Wylie grinned wolfishly. "Kid, we both know you're capable of making mistakes. I don't know, something doesn't hang together here. If Fahad wanted you dead, why call when you were out?—and if he didn't, why call at all? An international terrorist with the police of several countries after him should have more on his mind than playing practical jokes, even vicious ones. And that's all this was. If he wanted you dead, you'd be dead; and if he'd wanted your woman dead, she wouldn't have been picking his picture out of the cops' family album three hours later."

"She didn't. She made up one of those composites—you know, the PhotoFit things. But it was Fahad. It couldn't have been anyone else."

"It was that good a likeness?"

"Sure."

Wylie shook his head. "Well, it shouldn't have been. Those things never look like anybody—the best they can do is rule out a lot of people it couldn't have been."

Flynn was growing impatient. He did not understand what Wylie was driving at. He seemed to be questioning the very few things about the episode that were known facts. Flynn felt the ground shifting under his feet and it made him uneasy and rather querulous. "I don't know what you're *talking* about. What are you saying—that Laura made up a picture of someone who wasn't there?"

Someone with a donkey came up the alley. It was not a very wide alley, but after a glance at Wylie both the man and the donkey gave them a clear berth. Wylie had that effect, even when he was not trying. There was an aura of latent power about the way he moved and, when he was not moving, his very deliberate stillness. He was still now. He said, "Mickey—how well do you know this girl?"

Intimately and hardly at all. He had known her a little over a week. He had known every fold of her body. He had known, when he entered a large building, whether she was inside. He had not known whether she liked musical comedies, or Italian food. He knew the precise shade of every part of her in every light. He did not know when her birthday was.

He tried to say, very matter-of-factly, "I don't believe you said that." But his voice cracked.

5

Superintendent Donnelly regarded the information chattered out by his telex and had no idea what to make of it. A vital clue? A meaningless coincidence? If a clue, then to what? He sought further information, was told no further information was available. If enquiries into a B&E at the East End offices of a small publishing house progressed beyond the stage of showing an intelligent interest for the sake of taxes paid, Superintendent Donnelly would be the first to know.

Alone in his office, ignoring the press of more urgent matters, Donnelly watched the print-out as if he was expecting it to do something. Like Michael Wylie, he did not really believe in coincidence. All the same, he could not begin to guess how this latest fragment might relate to either of the previous episodes, let alone both of them. Finally he picked up the phone.

Todd answered on the second ring.

"Is he there?"

Todd knew very well who the call was for, and thought he knew who it was from. Sometimes, however, he took a stand in the name of common politeness. He said evenly, "Yes, I'm here."

"Flynn," growled Donnelly. "Is Flynn there?" At Todd's interrogative silence he gave his name.

"Oh, it's you, Superintendent," Todd said smoothly. "No, I'm afraid he's not here."

"Are you expecting him back?"

"Not with any confidence."

"Oh God. Is he off on his white horse again?"

"I don't know what you mean," said Todd with dignity. Of course, it was not true.

Donnelly breathed heavily. "All right. Stay where you are, I'm on my way round. Maybe you can make some sense of this." Without further explanation he rang off.

It was an unremarkable little burglary in itself: breaking and entering at an office like a thousand other little London offices that just might have kept enough petty cash in a drawer to be worth the effort of forcing the door. In fact the Pretext operation was slightly more sophisticated than that and had a wall safe, so the petty cash was untouched. The intruder had then turned his attention to the furniture. He had emptied every drawer of every desk and filing cabinet. The contents had been scattered throughout the premises.

Clearing up had taken all day, and only then was the proprietor able to say what was missing. The list included cameras from the darkroom, a lap-top word processor from the office, the tea money from the secretary's desk—and a folder with Mickey Flynn's name on it from the editor's filing cabinet.

Todd stared. "What was in the folder?"

"Nothing. That's the silliest part of the whole silly story. There was nothing in that folder that could have been of use or interest to anyone. Prints of a few photographs that had already appeared in a magazine—low-circulation but widely available. If anybody had wanted a copy they could have bought one for two pounds per issue."

There had to be more to it than that and both men knew it. Nobody breaks into buildings to steal photographs that have already been made public; and nobody stealing cameras and computers would pause long enough to select one file of used photographs out of a cabinetful and make his get-away with it tucked under his arm. It made no sense, and therefore it had not happened that way. There was another element, something they were unaware of or something whose significance they were missing.

Todd said, "Did Pretext have a list of what the photographs were?"

Donnelly nodded. "They went through their back copies for the last couple of years and made up a list of what pictures Flynn had sent them, on what subjects, and when they were published. And no," he added, getting where Todd was going first, "none of them were of Tomas Obregon, Peter Loriston, Michael Wylie or Jamil Fahad."

"Well, they wouldn't be," said Todd. "Hard news isn't really Pretext's area. They print a couple of popular science magazines—by which I mean the science is popular rather than technical; the magazines are only just popular enough to stay in business. They do a nature one called *Preserve* and one with a physics bent called *Context*. They're heavy on photographs with a bit of fairly lightweight prose to help with the layout. Narwhals and novae: that's Pretext."

Donnelly frowned. "I wouldn't have thought Flynn had much interest in either—or in the rates that a three-room marginally solvent publisher could pay."

Todd smiled. "They're not what he made his name with, no. But actually there's almost nothing a good photograph can be made from that Mickey Flynn isn't interested in. After the business in Israel three years ago he went travelling—all right, on the run—and he got to some fairly improbable places. Being Mickey, he photographed anything that moved and a fair number of things that stood still. Some of the suitable ones—the crater lakes at Keli Mutu, electrical storms over the Skeleton Coast, the Great Aletsch Glacier, one of zebra stallions fighting in the Ngorongoro—he sent to Greg Miller at Pretext. Not mainly for what Greg could pay but because he's a friend and the occasional big-name contribution helps him stay solvent. Before he had his own darkroom, Mickey used Greg's. I remember the first film he ever developed there. I kept it for a bookmark: you couldn't have used it for anything else."

"So who steals photographs of zebras?" The ramifications of this case were putting Donnelly under a strain. Three weeks after the crash of Flight 98 the people who had thought him the best man to investigate were tired of being asked if arrests were imminent and wondering if replacing him with a higher-ranking officer would be accepted as a working substitute for progress.

It would not be the first time he had lost top billing, and it was not altogether enviable being the man a nation expected to solve two hundred and twenty murders. But Donnelly liked whenever possible to finish what he started, and it irked him that every time he felt to be getting a perspective on the thing something like a sea-fog came swirling in to cloud the issues again.

"Have you got Greg's list?" Todd's eyes went distant as he studied it, trying to recall the photographs recorded. Some he remembered clearly, others vaguely, some not at all. He might not have seen them all, of course. One name caught his eye. "What, him again?"

Donnelly peered over his shoulder, a task complicated by the fact that Todd was taller and his shoulders broad. "Who?"

Todd tapped the list. "Him. Dr. Dieter Hehn of Deering Pharmaceuticals. Oh, nothing to do with this." He chuckled. "Deerings' personnel department wanted so many copies of the print Mickey was convinced they were papering the boardroom with them. They only stopped nagging him when he told them the negatives were lost in the crash." Then his eyes met Donnelly's speculative grey gaze and his smile turned slowly to a thoughtful frown. "At least, I don't think it's anything to do with this."

"Tell me," said Donnelly.

Their problem in trying to assess the significance of the Deering connection was that, even if Todd's recollection was full and accurate —full and accurate recollections being his trade—they could not know how complete and balanced a picture of his dealings with the firm Flynn's few casual remarks drew. Certainly Flynn had never seen Deerings in a sinister light: they had been useful to him, then a bit of a nuisance, and after the loss of the Hehn negative they had slipped from sight as completely as a major corporation can.

"It must be a coincidence," decided Todd, if doubtfully. "What could they have against Mickey? The only reason he was in their building was to get a photograph from their roof. The only photograph he took inside the building was at their specific request. Why would anyone at Deerings want Mickey dead?"

It was not so much an answer as the sound of a brain working round a jumble of facts much as a sheepdog marshalls sheep. "We may not be altogether safe assuming that murder was the purpose of the exercise," said Donnelly.

Todd stared at him. "You know some way of blowing up an aircraft in flight without killing people?"

Donnelly's expression flickered irritably. "Oh, murder was the inevitable consequence of planting a bomb on Flight 98. But it may not have been the reason for it."

"Explain."

If it struck Donnelly as incongruous to be explaining his train of thought to a reporter, he gave no sign of it. Partly it was because Todd had not achieved all he had, and held onto it for so long, without being both an intelligent man and a responsible one. He did not look a particularly intelligent man, except in the depths of his dark grey eyes, and the very idea of a responsible journalist is so old-fashioned that no policeman younger than Donnelly could have encountered it.

Of the many things Todd had lived long enough to see pass away, he most regretted the respect that was once afforded a serious British journalist in his native land. Now British journalists were respected in Europe, in America and further afield, but at home frequently pretended to play piano in houses of ill repute rather than risk embarrassing their children.

But if Donnelly needed a sounding-board for his thoughts, with the chance of some creative thinking in return, he could have chosen a great deal worse. Todd had neither the face nor the figure usually associated with minds like steel traps, and had not had even when younger. But he was an astute and perceptive man, and if he had a personal interest in this it only honed the edge on his thinking.

So Donnelly explained. "We've been assuming that the bomb was put on the plane to kill Flynn. Suppose it wasn't. Suppose it was put on board to destroy the negatives he was carrying. That might explain why, three weeks after two attacks in one day destroyed virtually everything he owned, there seem to have been no further attempts on his life—but someone has broken into an office and stolen examples of his work."

It had been a terrible thing to contemplate when they had believed that two hundred and twenty people had been sacrificed to a convenient means of murdering one. The idea that someone had murdered them as a convenient means of disposing of some negatives was unbearable. Todd looked at the policeman as if he had made an obscene joke, and could not keep his lip from curling. But he knew it was not a joke, that Donnelly was trying everything he could think of to make sense of what had happened, the bizarre as well as the appalling, because understanding it was a necessary first step towards apprehending the guilty. So Donnelly's speculations were anything but flippant. He was a man with a difficult job to do, and he deserved all the help he could get.

Todd said, "Why should anyone steal photographs that have already been published? What possible secrets can they still contain?"

Donnelly's lip curled too, with frustration and anger. "If Flynn was here we could ask him."

Todd said quietly, "I know he's making life difficult for you but try to understand how he feels. One way or another, even if we don't know quite how or why, this thing seems to have happened because of him. Two hundred and twenty people died, and he wasn't even one of them.

"You're a policeman. It's not inconceivable that at some time you've been responsible for a man's death. Maybe not, maybe you've been lucky. Let me tell you, it's not a great feeling. It doesn't matter that you had no choice, that the man who ended up dead gave you no choice, that he created a situation in which someone was going to die and if it hadn't been him it would have been you or perhaps some innocent third party. So you do what's necessary, or what you believe is necessary, or anyway what he's driven you to, and when he's dead at your feet your first reaction is relief because if you had any doubts that it needed doing you wouldn't have done it.

"But afterwards, when you're no longer in danger and the adrenaline has dried up, and both the relief and the anti-climax that follows have washed over you and drained away, that's when the reaction hits you. You feel so guilty you can't sleep for it. You wish you'd let him kill you. You feel worthless, as if it was something in yourself you destroyed. It taints everything you do, everything you touch. You know, logically, that you did the only possible thing, and if you can make yourself talk about it with anyone else they'll tell you the same. But it doesn't alter how you feel. You feel unclean. You feel like a dead man walking round looking for somewhere to lie down.

"That's how it feels when you're responsible for the death of one evil man. Can you imagine how it feels if two hundred and twenty ordinary men, women and children are dead because of you? It's chewing him up. If he'd sat here waiting for your investigation he'd have gone mad. I mean literally, climbing-the-walls insane. Maybe you think he did go crazy, that only a madman would go chasing round the world hunting out people with a reason to kill him. What he was looking for was catharsis: the cleansing of the flame.

"Now he's pursuing something different: the frail hope that, if none of these men who had a reason to kill him actually tried to, then maybe the destruction of Flight 98 had nothing to do with him after all. Those lost lives belong on somebody else's conscience. If he finds Wylie, and Wylie doesn't kill him, he's going to arrive back here a lot happier than he left.

"And then one of us is going to have to tell him about the break-in at Pretext, and he's going to be right back where he was three weeks ago—staring at smouldering wreckage, smelling burnt flesh and knowing that, somehow, all that was because of him."

Flynn took a taxi from Heathrow. He gave the address of the ware-house. Halfway there he remembered his apartment had been gutted and gave the driver Todd's address instead. He passed Donnelly in the corridor without recognising him.

Todd supposed the bell was Donnelly again, and again he opened the door to find Flynn on his threshold, his long body leaned up against the wall like an abandoned ladder, his face averted. In the split-second of seeing him, even before he had time to be glad, Todd knew that something was terribly wrong. Flynn's face was dark and savage, and at a deeper level despairing, and his long loose-limbed body was rigid with tension.

Todd said nothing. He stood back from the door and Flynn, also silent, wheeled inside. Donnelly was behind him and Todd, eyebrows raised interrogatively, waited for him to pass too before closing it.

In the centre of the livingroom floor Flynn stopped and after a moment turned round. The leaden cast of his face shocked Todd deeply. He looked like a sick man, a man sick enough to be dying. His eyes were stretched, glazed with weariness and something more; the line of his mouth, healed now, had taken a bitter twist.

Todd found a voice of a kind. "In God's name, Mickey, what's happened? Did you find Wylie?"

Flynn's voice was deeper than always, hollow, bitter-edged. "I found him."

Todd thought he understood. "It was him?"

Flynn shook his head, just once. "Michael knew nothing about it. And, knowing nothing, went straight to the obvious heart of the matter." He saw Donnelly then and acknowledged him with a faint nod. "So now, Superintendent, I can tell you who put the bomb on Flight 98, and when, and how, and why."

Donnelly's eyes never left Flynn's face, watching him as if everything he needed to know was written there if he could read it. His voice still quiet he said, "Who put the bomb on board?"

Very slightly, perhaps unconsciously, Flynn drew himself up to his full six-foot-two. Heavy lids dropped half-hooding his eyes. His eyes were desolate, his voice bleak. He said, "I did."

6

He had been thinking about it constantly, without respite, all the way from Tangiers. He took a commercial flight—there was no reason not to, no-one was trying to kill him—and let cup after cup of coffee go cold unnoticed in front of him. The stewardess thought he must be a nervous traveller. HM Customs thought he must be on something and searched his scant baggage microscopically. He watched without interest. Of course they found nothing. What was breaking Flynn apart was in his head, not his bloodstream.

Long before then he had pulled from his memory all the pieces he needed to know what the picture on the jigsaw was going to be. There were still big holes in the middle, much of the detail was unclear, but he knew what he was looking at. Todd had been near enough right when he thought Flynn was sick.

"It was Laura." He thought he had got the emotion out of his voice by now, the horror and the grief. Perhaps a stranger would have thought so too: the shakes which hit him in the alley below Wylie's office finally left him somewhere over the Bay of Biscay and he seemed calm enough now, if bruised. But Todd knew how superficial that calm was. Beneath it his emotions were in turmoil, a storm neither blown out nor blown over, only battened down, blanketed under layers of determination, nervous energy and pressing immediate need. "She planted the bomb in the bag she bought me, under the clothes she got for me. I didn't even look inside. She knew I wouldn't.

"She didn't know I was flying. She thought I was taking the car. If it had gone off halfway up the M1 I might have taken a couple of people with me, probably not more. The plane took her by surprise—I saw that at the time. I guess she was wondering what to do. Well, we know what she decided. She dropped me at the door and drove away. I thought she didn't want to start crying, but she didn't want to be around if the bomb was discovered. That's why she never called you, Gil. She wasn't afraid I was on Flight 98: she reckoned I had to be, otherwise it wouldn't have blown up."

Todd said softly, "Do you know why?"

Mechanically, Flynn shook his head. "No. But it was always going to end something like that. It's what she was hired for. There must have been something she needed to find, or find out, first or she'd have blown me away the first time we met. She had it all worked out, down to the fine detail." He tried to laugh and the anguish spilled out of his eyes. "I fell in love, Gil; and she was carrying out a contract."

"What about the fire?" asked Donnelly.

Flynn looked at him and looked away. "It wasn't Fahad. Laura set it. Maybe it got out of hand and trapped her, or maybe she had to make it look like that when she saw me coming back early. The fire was real enough, but the intruders weren't. She knew about my problems with the PFLP, must have seen the wanted posters on Fahad. She knew I'd recognise his picture even if no-one else did."

Talking was leaching some of the tension from him. When he had loosened up enough he slumped into a chair. "I think it was my negatives she was after more than my life. She was interested in the darkroom, came in and watched me working. I keep—kept—current negatives in there, she may have thought they were all I had. When I went out she laid a fire in there to destroy them.

"The story about Fahad was to cover her when I came back and found her still there. We should have realised something was wrong when she put together a picture not of the man who held her at gunpoint but the one who disappeared into the darkroom. Anyway, when I recognised the picture it all seemed to fit. That's why she chose Fahad: the built-in motive. She didn't want anyone enquiring too deeply into the reasons for it, at least not until she could check that she'd done what she set out to and then get off-side. She's quite a pro, my Laura.

"So she came back to the apartment with me, and saw me rescue the surviving negatives from the safe under the floor. She even looked through them—to see what they were, if they'd still print, whatever. When I said we'd have to split up she argued—she wanted to stay close to those negatives until she could destroy them. When I insisted, she went out to buy us some gear. That's when she put the bomb in my bag. I don't know if she made it herself or collected it someplace. But since I had damn-all left in the world, she was pretty sure that me, those negatives and that bag would be together for the immediate future.

"She must have set the time fuse when she handed me the thing at Heathrow. There couldn't have been more than half an hour on it: maybe she thought I couldn't be in the air by then. If it had gone off in the terminal it might have killed me, or a baggage handler, maybe a by-stander or two, but nothing like a plane-load of people. I'd like to think that's what she had in mind. If you find her," he said to Donnelly, "will you ask her that for me?"

"We'll find her," Donnelly said with absolute conviction. An astute observer would have seen a quiet savagery in the backs of his eyes, heard it in the quiet resonance of his voice.

"Don't count on it," said Flynn. "She didn't do this because of something I said, or because I was a disappointment in bed. She was doing what she was paid to do, and since it's taken us three weeks to realise it I kind of think she does it rather well. She'll be on the other side of the world by now with a different name, different appearance, different identity. Laura Wade never existed. She's a professional killer. Half the police forces in the civilised world must be looking for her, even if they don't know it. Maybe you can succeed where they've all failed, but you shouldn't stake your pension on it."

Superintendent Donnelly was returning his gaze with an odd mixture of compassion and dislike. He could guess how much this was hurting Flynn, could admire his determination to see it through, to say everything he had to say regardless of what it cost him. At the same time he had any law officer's resentment at being told he had been outsmarted by a criminal. He quelled his instinct to snap back and breathed lightly for a moment. Then he said, almost mildly, "Well, if we can't bring the killer to book, let's have a go at the people who hired her."

Flynn stared. Todd said, "Do we know who hired her?"

"Not yet. But we know a lot about them—maybe enough, now we've got Flynn back on our side. You are back to stay, are you?" he added, not without a hint of sarcasm. "Grand Tour finished for the moment? There's no-one else you'd like to paint a target on your shirt for? Oh good."

There was nothing Donnelly, or someone a lot nastier than Donnelly, could level at him in the way of criticism or abuse that Flynn had not already levelled at himself. Mere words had lost their sting and he had no difficulty ignoring these. It was the other thing Donnelly had said which had captured all his attention. "You think we can get at who did this—who's behind it? How?"

"They've done something else." Already Donnelly was a little ashamed of his small show of phlegm. "At least, I think they have." He explained, for the second time in an hour, about the break-in at Pretext.

Flynn listened in silence. Todd saw him make the connection with the destruction of his negatives in the two earlier incidents. He had no colour left to lose, but it was another kick in the face for him. When the policeman finished he said, "Can I see the list?"

Donnelly passed it to him. "Can't you remember what you sent to Pretext?"

Flynn snorted. "You any idea how many photographs I've taken in the last seven years? How many of them have been published? Greg Miller's had maybe twenty of them. You want me to remember which twenty?"

But the images came back as he scanned down the list. And he stopped at the place where Todd had stopped, and said pretty much what Todd had said. "Jeez, not them again?"

The policeman and the journalist traded a swift, significant glance. Donnelly asked, "Deerings?"

Flynn looked up, startled. "Yeah. Why?"

Donnelly did not answer. "The photograph of Dr. Hehn: why did you send it to Miller?"

"He runs a science magazine. I thought he could use it."

"Did he?"

"Damn right he did." For a moment Flynn sounded indignant, as if his workmanship was being challenged. "First shot of a prize-winning chemist? Of course he used it."

"That was the negative Deerings wanted to buy?"

"Yes. But I don't sell my negatives, not ever. I made them some prints."

"So the Hehn negative was in your flat when the fire occurred, on the aeroplane when it blew up, and a print was in that office until someone stole it."

"There were other negatives at the apartment and in my bag on the plane."

"Any of them on that list of Miller's?"

Flynn read it again. It was not a long list but he wanted to make sure. "These negatives would all have gone in the fire. Except for Hehn."

"Are there any other prints anywhere?"

"Just the ones I sent Deerings."

It could still so easily be a coincidence. No-one knew it better than Donnelly. If he accused an important corporation of complicity in the bombing of an aircraft on no more evidence than this, he would be lucky if he was still a Superintendent at the end of the week. He would be quite lucky if he was still a policeman. "Perhaps they just wanted what they said they wanted, plenty of copies. Perhaps they have nothing to do with the rest of it." He sounded unconvinced.

Flynn stood up, his long body unfolding abruptly. "I can check on that." He picked up the phone, looking at Todd. "Remember I gave their PRO Aiden McNally's number? Let's find out if he used it."

It was not a lengthy call. Flynn was waiting longer for McNally to answer the phone than for him to answer the question. It had been twelve days since he gave McNally's number to the Deering PRO to meet his urgent and excessive need for photographs. But when Flynn put the names of Deering and Hehn and Spalding to him, McNally only answered, "Who?"

"Perhaps they decided they had enough photographs after all," mused Todd. His gaze slid across to meet Donnelly's. "Or perhaps they're satisfied that they now have all the prints that negative is ever going to yield."

Donnelly was nodding slowly. "You think there's something in that picture they don't want people to see?"

Todd raised his shoulders in confusion. "How could there be? The damn thing was published weeks ago—two or three weeks before the fire, even. If there was anything remarkable about it, *somebody'd* have noticed."

Donnelly asked Flynn, *"Was* there anything unusual about it?"

"Christ, I don't know! I didn't even want the picture, it just seemed churlish to refuse. So they stood the guy up in his laboratory, holding his letter of notification and grinning, and I photographed him. Then I sent the print to Greg Miller for *Context* because it was his line and he doesn't get too many first bites of the cherry. The magazine came out and Deerings started deluging me with requests for extra prints."

"And asked to buy the negative."

"I thought they were offering to print it themselves instead of keep asking me."

"So you kept the negative in your flat until after the fire, then transferred it to the case Laura Wade gave you."

"Yeah." Even now he could not talk about her with any degree of detachment. His voice was gruff, his eyes veiled. After a moment he looked away.

Todd said quietly, "And your man at Deerings—Spalding?—kept asking for one more print until you said the negative was gone. After the fire, and after the plane. He was checking to see if the job had been done."

Donnelly said flatly, "I don't believe in that amount of coincidence. That picture is the key to all this."

Flynn sighed. "You mean it was. It's long gone now."

"No," said Donnelly, "it's not. You supplied a lot of prints to Deerings. They're going to need one hell of a good excuse not to be able to find me one when I ask."

"OK, so you get a copy of the print," said Flynn. "What's it going to tell you that the picture in the magazine didn't?"

"God knows," Donnelly said morosely. "Maybe nothing at all. But I'll still be interested to talk to Hehn, and to see your Mr. Spalding's face when I ask for one of his pictures."

It was late evening before Donnelly left for the second time. Todd made some supper and refrained from asking any more questions. Compared with the black torment in his face when he arrived on the doorstep two hours before, Flynn was looking better—more relaxed, more at ease in his body and his mind. If sharing his discovery had hurt, at least it had left the wounds clean.

Now he looked dog-tired. For the last three weeks he had been running on nervous energy, first the rage at what had been done, then the slowly mounting hope that perhaps the worst of it was not because of him after all. Now the rage was gone, and the hope was gone, and even his anxiety about Laura Wade was gone, and half the substance seemed to have gone from his body. Todd sent him to bed. He was asleep before his head hit the pillow, too tired even to dream.

He woke, hours later but still long before dawn, with the memory of a sound he had been sleeping too deeply to hear echoing round the edges of his mind. He rolled onto his back and lay a long time in darkness, listening and hearing nothing. He tried to persuade himself that there was nothing to hear, that what had woken him had been nothing more than one of the middle-ranking civil servants or building society branch managers who formed the bulk of Todd's neighbours coming home well-oiled from a back-stage party at the Royal Opera House and banging his front door.

Noises off were more significant when you lived in an abandoned warehouse in a part of London where the street-lamps were a fond memory and the neighbours were a basement full of winos. Todd lived in a respectable middle-class building with respectable middle-class neighbours, lifts, no graffiti and a uniformed porter. A man could start a reign of terror with a feathered whoopee-whistle in a place like this.

So Flynn lay listening to the silence until the silence became oppressive, staring wide-eyed into the darkness until the darkness crawled, more wakeful with every minute that passed. Finally he gave up trying to sleep, thought he would raid the fridge instead. He pushed the blanket off his legs and padded to the door.

Todd had moved the furniture since he last spent any time here. Aiming for the kitchen on automatic pilot Flynn bumped into the back of an armchair and the sharp edge of the dining table, unseen in the black room, then stumbled over something soft at floor level and went sprawling on his hands and knees on the hearthrug. He had let out a string of virulent expletives before he remembered the reason he had not switched the light on in the first place was that he was trying not to disturb Todd.

Then the light came on anyway. Flynn put up a hand to shield his eyes. At least he had not woken Todd; nor, for the immediate future, was he likely to. The soft thing Flynn had stumbled over was Todd, and he was lying down there because someone had cracked his skull open.

7

Todd lived in a respectable building with responsible neighbours and a porter, not in a derelict warehouse in a part of London's dockland that had gone downhill since Fagin left. So he had never bothered with the extra locks, and indeed extra doors, that were indispensable to the security of Flynn's home, in the days when he had one, and the peace of his mind. The consequence was that Todd's front door had proved laughably easy to broach. But that was not what Flynn had heard.

But Todd, sleeping more lightly than the young man collapsed exhausted in his spare room, did hear something unfamiliar and, thinking it might be Flynn stumbling round the dark flat, pulled his dressing-gown on and went to see. He saw nothing. As he came through his bedroom door with the light behind him, something heavy and hard and swung with force connected with the back of his skull and pitched him into a deeper blackness than that of the curtained room. Blood exploded behind his eyes and he was unconscious before his face hit the rug.

Flynn knelt over the quiet bulk lying face-down on the floor in its paisley dressing-gown, possibilities racing through his mind. In spite of all that had been happening, his first thought was that Todd was not a young man, nor a fit one, and that even normally he led a fairly stressful life, and Flynn was afraid that Todd's heart had given out. He struggled with the body, easing it onto its side, searching anxiously for pulse and respiration.

But before he found them he remembered that the light had come on after he was already falling over the man on the floor, which meant someone else was here with them. He looked up quickly, and now his eyes were sufficiently adjusted to the light to pick up the figure standing by Todd's open door, and to recognise from the distinctive position of its hands that it was armed.

Then Flynn was afraid that the sound that woke him was a gunshot, too worried to realise that such a sound in the confines of a three-room flat would not so much have woken him as projected him bodily out of bed and left him crouched quivering in the tightest corner he could find. His shocked gaze snapped back to Todd and he ran his eyes and hands over the big man looking for wounds.

He stopped when he found one, not a bullet hole but a ragged tear in the scalp behind his right ear. Todd had been not shot but sandbagged. Flynn looked up again with anger in his gaze, a deep resentment at this overspill of violence from his own life into his friend's home.

And only then did he find time to wonder who the intruder was. His mind went first to Laura, but the outline was wrong: shorter and despite that essentially masculine. It was too short for Spalding, too slight for Hehn.

When he spoke, Flynn recognised his voice. There was no chance in the world of Flynn ever forgetting that voice. "In view of everything you've been saying about me, Mr. Flynn," said Jamil Fahad, "I thought we should talk."

The fear and frustration of three weeks, the pain and the grief and the guilt, all came to a head in a quick blaze of fury that paid no heed to the heavy gun in Fahad's hand and the certainty in Flynn's heart that he had come here to use it. Rage snapped in his eyes, cracked in his voice like ice. "You bastard, Fahad! He's an old man. What have you done to him?"

The Arab made a minimal shrug. His lightly accented voice was negligent. "Nothing. I knocked him out, that's all. He's all right."

"All right? Look at him!" Todd had not responded to Flynn's hands. His eyes remained not only shut but still. His broad face was pale, the muscles that animated it flaccid. His head was bleeding freely. Flynn looked round for something to staunch it with. All there was within reach was what he was wearing—a T-shirt and a pair of pyjama trousers Todd found for him. They must have been a Christmas present from someone who knew Todd when his waistline was twenty years younger.

He pulled off the T-shirt, and with Todd propped against his knees wadded the material firmly against the back of his head. Bent there, his scarred back a bony bow, Flynn looked up fiercely at the man with the gun. "What's the matter," he demanded nastily, "they running out of old men you can beat up where you come from?"

Fahad was not a thug, though he had done thuggish things in the pursuit of his cause. Though he had effected and inspired much violence, he was not by nature a violent man. He was a professional soldier, though his services were not for hire as Michael Wylie's were. His career as an officer in the Palestinian Army had been barely hindered by the absence of a Palestinian state. The world was only now recognising the intifada, but Fahad had been fighting it for more than twenty years, since the Six Day War pushed Israel's borders up to the Jordan and hijacked a province of Arabs who, if they had felt like second-class citizens of Jordan, relished still less a future as a religious and ethnic minority in a Jewish state.

In the course of those twenty-odd years he had done things world opinion had not approved of. He had done things he had not much liked himself but which he accepted had been necessary to his cause. Killing Mickey Flynn would have been one such act if the Israel Defence Forces had not broken his operation up at the critical moment three years before. But he had never sought to further that cause by beating up old men and he objected to Flynn's suggestion that he had.

It was a measure of how strongly he felt that this professional soldier, whose calm mind and pragmatic manner allowed him to move freely in a country where his picture hung in police stations and across international borders where the same portrait was available for constant reference, now shifted his gun into his left hand in order to stab the air in Flynn's direction with his right fore-finger.

"Now you *know* that I do not go round beating anybody up for the pleasure of it. I do what I have to do; and last time our paths crossed that old man succeeded in wrecking my operation, closing my camp and putting my team behind bars or in the ground. I am not going to under-estimate him again."

Todd was still bleeding. Flynn looked up from his work only briefly. "Any beef you have is with me. Gil did only what he had to to haul me out of the pit you dug and I walked into."

Fahad's voice was quieter. "I know that. What I don't understand is why."

Flynn did not follow. "What do you mean?"

Fahad's gaze was like a slap in the face. "People stick their necks out for you, Mr. Flynn. Good people, people like him, risk their freedom, their jobs, their health, their lives for you. And I look at you and I don't understand why."

Flynn flushed and made no reply. Made as it was with no venom, only a quiet contempt, the attack cut at the roots of his being. He did not know either why he inspired the kind of friendship that made people crawl out on limbs for him. He thought he did nothing to deserve it, felt ashamed as if Fahad had caught him out in something underhand.

Had Todd been awake he could have explained to both of them that Flynn earned friends like that by being one himself, that the people who at one time or another had stood up to be counted for Mickey Flynn all knew that, as and when needed, Flynn would be up being counted for them.

And so he would. But there was a naive streak in Flynn that failed to recognise that simple truth. He behaved towards people as the fancy took him, unaware that the kinder side of his nature tended to dominate the more cynical one on which his self-image was founded. He thought that the kindness he received in return came out of nowhere and left him in debt. He could not defend himself against an attack he believed was justified, and Todd who would have defended him was still lying deeply unconscious across his knees, bleeding into his T-shirt.

Finally he looked up at Fahad, a flayed look in his eyes. His voice was low. "He needs a doctor. He's losing too much blood. Let me call him a doctor. Then I'll come with you."

"Are you mad?" Fahad raised his head in a scornful gesture inherited from his desert ancestors. He had equipped himself with a beard some time in the last three years, on the Arafat rather than the Khomeini model. "Where should I take you—back to Palestine? I came to talk to you, not to elope with you. For talking, here will do just fine."

"Fahad, please." There was nothing left of the anger, in his face or in his voice. It was a luxury he could no longer afford. "He needs a doctor. He's bleeding, he's unconscious, I think maybe his skull's fractured. I'll do anything you want. But please, let me call him a doctor."

"Begging, Mr. Flynn? I don't remember you begging for your own life."

"Jesus, Fahad!" It came out as a soft explosion of despair. "If you've come here to kill me, do it. But don't just keep talking about it while he's dying. You want my blood?—take it. Something you want to know first?—ask. I'll tell you anything. But for God's sake, make it quick. And get a doctor up here before you leave."

Then Fahad understood how it was Flynn made people care about him. Knelt barefoot on the carpet, the injured man held protectively in his lap, clearly believing that Fahad had sought him out to take a delayed revenge for the Bab el Jihad disaster, Flynn could still spare enough concern to worry about how Todd would get help after he was dead.

Fahad sighed. He was not a vicious man, had no wish to prolong this for the distress it was causing. He had not blamed Flynn for the loss of his camp, any more than he would have blamed a tank or an RPG the Israelis had used against him. He really had come to talk to Flynn, or rather to listen. He said, "I want to know why you're telling people I was responsible for bombing a trans-Atlantic airliner."

Flynn stared at him, literally open-mouthed. "Christ Almighty," he managed, "you're worried about your reputation?"

"I am indeed," Fahad said briskly, ignoring the irony Flynn had failed to keep out of his voice. "Also my credibility, and quite possibly my life. That bombing was the act of a maniac. If there's one thing a cause struggling towards international recognition can do without, it's being associated with madmen.

"It has taken us years to reach the point where Western opinion accepts that there *is* a Palestinian problem, not just a law-and-order problem within Israel; that a solution must recognise the legitimate fears and aspirations of the Palestinian people; and that it must come from the parties involved, the government of Israel and the leaders of the Palestinian resistance.

"The Jews refuse to talk to us on the grounds that we're terrorists. Beyond pointing out that one man's terrorist is another man's freedom fighter, I won't deny the evidence of history. But things are changing: we have them at a disadvantage and we must keep it that way. So direct action is no longer the flavour of the month. It's not easy to constrain people who want to fight for their homes, but we've managed to keep the lid on what you call terrorism and the pressure on the Jews.

"Now this happens. An American plane out of London is bombed and the finger is pointed at us. Specifically, at me. I helped draw up the new strategy, agreed to hold back while the politicians had their chance. Your accusations make a liar of me. I don't like that, Mr. Flynn. I don't like people thinking I can't be trusted. I particularly don't like my General Command thinking that. The policy is working: they'll do what they have to to keep the confidence of our supporters.

If I can't prove that I wasn't responsible for bombing Flight 98, they'll get rid of me, and sooner rather than later. I can't even blame them.

"But I don't have to take it lying down. Why did you tell the police it was my doing? Did you really believe that?"

"I didn't— Well, yes." Flynn took a breath and began again. "I didn't say it was your doing but yes, I thought you were involved. We had a positive ID from someone who saw you. OK, so it turns out the woman who ID'd you was lying, because it was her who planted the bomb. Or rather, it was me."

"You?" Fahad's voice ran up, disbelieving and amused.

"Damn you, Fahad," snarled Flynn, and his voice cracked, "don't you dare smirk at me! Two hundred and twenty people are dead, and if it wasn't exactly my fault it was at least because of me; and I have to tell you, the least of my worries is any stain inadvertently splashed on the character of an Arab terrorist."

Fahad regarded him with almost no expression. But what he was thinking was that Flynn was no easier to dislike now than three years ago. He said, quite patiently, "Tell me what happened." He could just about envisage circumstances in which he too might be prepared to step out of line for the American.

Aware that while time might be on his side it was probably not on Todd's, Flynn recounted the briefest version of events that still contained all the relevant facts.

When he had finished Fahad said, "This woman—Laura Wade— she was living with you?"

"For a few days. Just long enough to do her job."

"Destroy these photographs of yours."

"We think so."

Fahad shook his head and again found it hard to contain his mirth. "What an example you sophisticated Westerners set the rest of the world! So she was prepared to share a stranger's bed for the money she could get for destroying your negatives. What was your excuse?"

Flynn flinched from the good-natured scorn in his voice, let his head bow over Todd's, unconscious in his lap. Not much more than a whisper of a reply escaped him. "I loved her."

Fahad smiled. "Doesn't falling in love with a contract killer come under the category of unsafe sex?"

The Arab was getting ready to leave. First he was looking for something, opening Todd's cupboards and glancing inside while his gun and most of his attention remained on Flynn. He need not have worried: while Todd needed his care and there was no immediate threat to either of them, Flynn was going nowhere.

While he was searching, Fahad was talking. "I could kill you now," he said conversationally. "But that wouldn't do much to impress on my colleagues the virtues of restraint, tolerance, responsibility and humanitarianism which make this allegation against me so manifestly unjust. For now you are worth more to me alive and testifying to the fact that this woman lied about my involvement in order to cover up her own. So it would please me very much to read in a newspaper in the not too distant future that enquiries into the loss of Flight 98 have discounted the possibility of a Palestinian connection."

"Sooner or later the police will charge somebody with something. I guess the reasons will come out then."

"Given the speed at which police investigations proceed," said Fahad, "I could be an unmarked hump in the desert sand by then. I had something swifter in mind. Newspapers are your province: arrange it." Flynn said nothing. His face was stubborn. "You have three days. After that I shall come back, but I shalln't be looking for you." He jerked the gun at Todd. "I'll be looking for him."

Then he found what he was looking for. He lifted from the bottom of the dresser a bottle of whisky, half full, and a glass, and put them on the rug beside Flynn. "Put him down."

Watching him, Flynn said, "You don't give spirits to an unconscious man."

"It's not for him. Put him down."

Carefully Flynn eased him onto his side on the carpet and reached for a cushion to support his head. He risked a peep under the T-shirt. The bleeding had slowed to a trickle. Flynn did not understand about the whisky. "Then—?"

"When I leave here," said Fahad, "I want to get further than half a block before converging police cars bottle me up. So I want to keep you away from a phone. I could tie you up but you're a strong, determined and resourceful young man—you'd find some way of drawing attention to your plight. I could hit you with the gun butt, but as you see it's an imprecise weapon used that way: if you woke too soon I could get caught, and if you never woke at all I could be that hump in the sand by weekend. This is the safest way for all concerned. The whisky isn't for him, Mr. Flynn. It's for you."

"No!" Flynn's face jerked up at him, and if it was not the first time Fahad had seen fear there it was perhaps the first time he had seen panic.

He looked at the label with interest. "I don't know much about it, but I would have thought Mr. Todd a fair judge of a good whisky."

Flynn watched the bottle like a man watching a snake. And indeed, regardless of its merits as whisky, it might as well have been poison. It had all but killed him once before. Todd had hauled him back from the abyss, kicking and screaming, and he had not tasted alcohol from that day to this. Not because he had not wanted it—sometimes, early on, he had wanted it so much that the sweat broke on his brow—but because in the first weeks Todd had watched him like a hawk, and after that he would not risk being put through the same purgatory again.

After seven years he did not know how vulnerable he still was to the lethal seduction of alcohol. He knew that he could not afford to start drinking again. He did not know if what Fahad proposed would tip him over the edge or not. He would have given almost anything to avoid finding out.

His mouth had gone dry. He whispered, "I can't. I'm an alcoholic."

Fahad chuckled softly in his face. "Poor Mickey Flynn. You do make a habit of loving not wisely but too well." Still carefully, because if Flynn was going to do something silly this was probably the time, he leaned forward and poured pale liquid into the tumbler, filling it to the rim. "Drink that, then the same again. Then we'll see."

Flynn's legs had gone to sleep. He had been kneeling on the floor for perhaps twenty minutes, and for most of that time he had had some of Todd's considerable weight on them. If he could have trusted them to work he might have made a lunge for the gun now. He did not think Fahad meant to kill him, and he would as soon risk a bullet as a return to the nightmare waiting in that half bottle of whisky. The cramp robbed him of that chance. It would take him seconds to get to his feet. An old lady with an umbrella could have got the better of him. So he just shook his head. "No."

Fahad frowned, breathing heavily. "You know I can make you, don't you?"

Flynn was scared enough to stick to his guns. His voice came fast and thin. "If you kill me, nobody'll ever believe you didn't bomb Flight 98."

Fahad had already thought of that. The angle of the gun swung smoothly through thirty degrees. "I don't have to kill you. I don't have to touch you. Rather than let me hurt him, you'll do as you're told."

And finally, if it came to that, if there was nowhere else to go, he was right. Flynn was not in the classical sense a brave man. He took endless risks in the course not only of doing his job but also of enjoying his life, but mostly these fell into two categories. Either he was quite sure he was smart enough to get away with something, or he had done it before he had quantified the degree of risk involved. Bravery was the thing that made you do something you did not want to do, that you doubted if you could get away with, when you were fully aware of what the likely consequences would be.

But if he was not a brave man, he was not a coward. He did not let his friends pay his debts. If there was nowhere else to go, he would become a drinker again, with all that followed from that, rather than see Fahad lay another hand on Todd.

But Flynn had not quite reached the point of believing there was nowhere else to go. He let his shoulders slump. "OK." He picked up the tumbler.

Before the pale stream was in mid-air, gleaming in the light of Todd's slightly pretentious chandelier, Fahad knew what he intended. He stepped out of the line of fire, at the same time ranging the gun back on Flynn's chest. Flynn, who had meant to follow the whisky with the heavy glass, now let his fingers part and the tumbler bounced dully on the carpet.

Fahad said nothing. His face was unreadable. Unhurriedly he moved towards Flynn again, stepping over Todd's body still senseless on the floor. Flynn wanted to get up but dared not: he had made his play and failed, he could not find the nerve to try again and anyway there was no more time. Fahad stood over him with the gun. Flynn straightened as best he could. His lungs sucked in a deep breath that made his chest swell to meet the muzzle, its small steel mouth rounded in perpetual surprise.

"Oh Mr. Flynn," sighed Fahad. Then his hand jerked.

There was no sound, at least not of gunfire, so Fahad had not shot the weapon. He had palmed it and swung it in his hand like a pendulum, clapping its length along Flynn's jaw as he flinched away from the sudden movement.

Pain exploded in his face like fireworks. He did not go out, not quite, but he certainly went down, toppling sideways off his cramped knees, too disorientated to save himself with his hands so that first his shoulder crashed with a thud on the carpet and then his head did. His eyes rolled; nausea boiled in his belly. All the nerves on the left side of his face shrieked as if cut; the nerves in his teeth raged. Flashes of light stabbed in his eyes. He could hear nothing over the pounding of his blood. Still he did not quite lose consciousness.

Fahad did not intend that he should. His purpose was not to injure Flynn, or even to punish him, only to knock the fight out of him. He needed both hands for the next bit, which meant putting the gun away. Unlike Flynn, Fahad always thought first and never took chances.

There was enough whisky left in the bottle. Fahad picked it up as he passed. The couch was handy: he sat on its edge and propped Flynn's back against his legs. Flynn's head rolled. Fahad steadied it with one hand, the slightly long brown hair washing over his knuckles, and with the other held the bottle to his lips. "Just the thing for toothache, Mr. Flynn," he murmured gently.

Flynn retained wit enough to know what was happening but not the strength to resist it. Fahad was a much more powerful man than his compact stature suggested, and had no difficulty controlling the random flailing of Flynn's good hand with his left knee, clamping the arm to Flynn's side.

So one hand held Flynn's head and the other fed him the whisky. He choked and some of it ran out of the corner of his mouth, but most of it went down his throat. Fahad stuck to the job patiently, like a farmer's wife feeding an orphan lamb, until the bottle was empty.

CHAPTER 3

Kehama's Reign

1

First thing in the morning, unaware of the man lying unconscious and the other dead drunk in the respectable flat in the respectable building in Kensington, Superintendent Donnelly and his sergeant visited Deering Pharmaceuticals in their tall building overlooking the river. Donnelly asked first for Dr. Hehn. It took a flash of warrant card to persuade the chemist's secretary to make room in the great man's schedule for a quick interview with some policemen.

He saw them in his office, which was divided from the laboratory by a glass partition and a Venetian blind. The blind was three-quarters closed, but Donnelly could tell from the shifting patterns of light that someone was working in there. By sitting down at his desk in his white coat, Hehn suggested quite forcibly that the laboratory was the only proper environment for a scientist and as soon as he could dispose of this interruption he would be back in there too.

Apart from that he was charming. He was a man in his mid-fifties, built to much the same specification as the breeze block—not a curve in his body unless dictated by strict biological necessity, otherwise he was composed entirely of solid rectangular planes. The severity of the basic design was reinforced by the voice, which was deep and gravelly, and by the dark-framed rectangular glasses he wore, but alleviated by the improbable twinkle in the eyes behind them.

In a man of half his years or one growing towards a cuddly old age, it might have seemed mischievous. Men in their fifties with heavy German accents, heads like breeze blocks, rectangular spectacles and wiry dark hair cut in the latest style from the Heinrich Himmler Salon generally find it difficult to express good-natured impishness, but Dr. Dieter Hehn was doing his level best despite the fact that his lab-coat stretched ominously across his square chest and his biceps strained the sleeves.

He said, with ponderous good humour, "What's the problem, Superintendent? Have we let the homunculus escape again?"

Donnelly did his amiable smile. "Not to worry, sir. It'll probably start its own pop group and make you a fortune."

He had not got to be a Detective Superintendent with enough of a track record to be given a job of this magnitude by charging at an enquiry bull-headed, accusations first. Instinct fed by experience told him that Flynn's photograph of this man was the reason why Flynn had been persecuted and, as a consequence of that, why two hundred and twenty people on a trans-Atlantic airliner had been blown out of the sky. That did not necessarily mean that Hehn was to blame for it, or even knew about it; or if he did, that he could be made to talk about it. Softly softly catchee monkey was still an approach with much to recommend it, even in the days of faxed crime sheets and genetic finger-printing.

So he did not ask Dr. Hehn what it was that he was up to that had to be hushed up whatever the cost. He did not ask what it was in Flynn's photograph that threatened to give the game away, or how they had found a professional fixer of Laura Wade's stature to tidy up after them. He said, "Purely routine enquiry, sir. We're trying to reconstruct the contents of the baggage hold of Flight 98."

Hehn frowned and waited a suitable moment before remembering. "The New York flight? The one that crashed?"

"The one that was bombed, that's right. I don't know if you're aware, sir, but negatives of a photograph taken of you were on board."

Again the short pause suggesting the matter was not at the fore-front of his mind. "That's right. That young American who was here, he was on board. But didn't he get off?"

"He did, but his bag—with his negatives in it—stayed on the plane."

The heavy brows drew down on a powerful stare. "My God. Was he the one responsible? The young man who came here—Finn?" It was perfectly possible that Hehn's interest in and recollection of the disaster were no greater than this, that he hardly remembered Flynn and did not much care what happened to either him or his negatives. But Donnelly did not believe it. He believed that the photograph of this man had cost two hundred and twenty lives, and now he had met him he felt Hehn knew all about it.

And he knew that in the absence of incontrovertible proof Hehn might take the secret to his grave. He was a tough, solid man, not easily bullied or panicked, and a mind as agile as his might withstand any amount of quite pointed interrogation.

There are occasions in police work when an investigating officer knows who committed the crime, and how and why, and has the culprit where he can throw at him every shot in the legal armoury, and still, unless he loses his nerve and either confesses or tells demonstrable lies, there is insufficient evidence to try let alone convict him. It was too soon to start panicking, but Donnelly's first impression of Dr. Hehn was that he was precisely the type of strong, self-contained individual who would sit calmly under the hundred-watt bulb—interrogation had been hit by spending cuts like everything else—and deny everything, and challenge Donnelly to prove what he knew. If Hehn was the weakest link in this chain, God help them.

He said, "Mickey Flynn, that's right. But no, we don't think he's responsible. We think he was the target."

"But if he got off—?"

"He had all the luck on the plane that night. Some colleagues of mine tried to arrest him. By the time the misunderstanding was sorted out, the flight had left."

The eyes behind the rectangular lenses were unwinking. "Then who was responsible?"

"I'm working on that," Donnelly said smoothly. "This photograph of you—can you describe it?"

Hehn laughed, a sound like a train leaving a station. "It was me, looking absurdly pleased with myself and rather as if I'd been sniffing my way through the solvents cabinet. I had just received the letter, you understand, about the prize. It was a very pleasant surprise. But surely Flynn told you this."

"Some of it. But he takes a lot of photographs, he can't remember them all in much detail. I'm hoping the pictures will have made a bigger impression on the people in them."

He was keeping the tone casual, but Hehn had not missed the central implication. "You think that something in one of these photographs was the reason for what happened?"

Donnelly feigned a slight helpless shrug. "Dr. Hehn, we don't know. It's a possibility. So—essentially it was a portrait, was it?"

"I have a copy somewhere," Hehn said unexpectedly and started rooting through the drawers of his desk. Donnelly breathed lightly and declined his sergeant's invitation to exchange significant glances. "Yes, here." Hehn pulled out a copy of the magazine *Context* and put it in front of the Superintendent.

The big rectangular head, the bulky rectangular body, the rectangular spectacles and the SS haircut were the same. The only difference was the silly grin beaming out at him from the magazine's cover. Hehn had not exaggerated: he did look to be high on something.

Donnelly smiled. He had seen the magazine before. Then he glanced around the office. "That wasn't taken in here, was it?"

Hehn shook his head, precisely, once. "In the laboratory."

The blind forming the backdrop, then, was the other side of this at the glass partition. There was the corner of a bench on the right-hand side, with glass jars and retorts and a shimmer of distortion probably caused by a Bunsen burner, and the edge of the blackboard on the left. There was nothing else in the photograph, and nothing anyone could have wanted to hide.

"Yes, I see." Donnelly handed it back. He looked expectantly towards the connecting door. "Before I go, could I have a quick look at the laboratory?"

Again the unwinking gaze. "Whatever for?"

Donnelly shrugged carelessly. "The picture was taken there. It might tell me something."

"You don't think it's *this* picture that . . . ?" He spread a large, eloquent hand, the blunt fingers stained with chemicals, the nails ruthlessly manicured.

"I don't know which picture it is. I don't know for sure that it is a picture at the root of this. Police work is an empirical science: you try different things until one of them works." He stood up.

Hehn passed him edge on, opened the door. "This way."

There was the bench—different glassware, same burner—there the blackboard and the blind. Flynn must have been up against if not actually perched on that range of cupboards. The internal wall was covered with graphs and charts, the exterior one was made of glass and looked over intervening roofs to the river. There were two people working here, both in white coats: a young man and a woman. They nodded politely at the visitors although Hehn did not introduce them.

In three minutes Donnelly had learned all he was likely to by looking. "What is it you do here, Dr. Hehn?"

One of Hehn's eyebrows lowered while the other stayed put so that he looked like a coy breeze block. "Our competitors would pay thousands for the answer to that question."

Donnelly smiled. "In lay terms. And on the clear understanding that Sergeant Herriot here is not a spy for Boots."

Hehn returned the smile with a jovial version of his own. "Well, in that case . . . I am searching for new antibiotics. The problem with antibiotics—and don't worry, Sergeant, Boots already knows this—is that the pathogens they are used to combat become resistant with repeated exposure. Since they are exposed not only to those we treat our own ailments with but also to those used to treat livestock reared for food, the problem of obsolescence is continually with us. We have to keep producing new antibiotics to replace those which are losing their effectiveness. Otherwise one day we'll meet some virulent strain of typhoid, say, in a major centre of population and have nothing capable of dealing with it."

"Yes, I see," said Donnelly. "Well, thanks for your help. I don't expect I'll have to trouble you again, but if I do—?"

"I'll be here, Superintendent," promised Dr. Hehn. Donnelly did not doubt it for a moment.

Leah Shimoni had strong teeth, a fact which she attributed to a childhood crammed with sunshine and oranges. Dental checks were swift, uncomplicated occasions for her. This particular morning she had an appointment at nine, was in the chair at five past, left at quarter past and—for no better reason than that she found herself in the area —was ringing Todd's doorbell before half past.

There was no reply. She rang again and waited. His car was outside, and anyway it was too early for him to be out. He was not a morning person. She thought he would be surfacing just about now and could give her some breakfast.

Still no reply. She frowned. The morning papers—four of them, he might as well have declared his profession on a brass plate beside the door—were wedged in the letter-box and the milk had not been taken in, so he had to be in there. Probably they both were. She leaned her thumb on the bell and, very slightly anxious now, kept it there. She knew it was working, could hear its bray like an asthmatic donkey through the door.

After what seemed an age she heard movement within and released the bell. A hand fumbled with the lock and the door swung in. When no invitation was forthcoming she pushed it wide and stepped inside anyway.

The first thing she saw was Mickey Flynn, and the state of him was such that for a moment her mouth dropped open in shock. Then it clamped tight with disgust.

He was just about upright, though the wall could have had something to do with that. He stank of stale whisky. His head hung so that his hair trailed lank in his face, and his eyes would not focus enough to meet hers: it might have been shame, or hangover, or a combination. His face was ashen but for dark moons under both eyes and purple bruising along the angle of his left jaw. He had almost no clothes on and his long body was shuddering with cold.

Shimoni said, in her teeth, "What in God's name happened to you?" and thought she knew. He mumbled something she could not understand. *"What?"*

He dragged his eyes up from the carpet. The whites were muddy, shot with blood. He really did look ill, enough for Shimoni to feel a twinge of conscience. His voice was thick, his breathing too ragged or his brain too fogged to manage a complete sentence. "Gil. See . . ."

So the second thing she saw was Gilbert Todd on the living-room floor, a quiet mound lying on his side with a cushion under his head and his hair thick with congealed blood. She could hear his stertorous breathing from where she stood, and as she stared aghast one hand twitched laxly by his face.

If she did not yet know what had happened, she knew who she blamed. She spun on her heel, her eyes aflame, and struck Flynn once in the face, very hard. Because she was right-handed it was the left side of his face she hit. Because she was five-foot-two and he was six-foot-two she did not expect him to fall over, drunk as he clearly still was. But he did, and lay against the skirting board, long body curled foetally, nursing his face and moaning.

Shimoni lifted the phone and called for an ambulance.

After leaving Dr. Hehn, Donnelly asked for Mr. Spalding of the public relations department. Mr. Spalding was in fact the executive responsible for public relations and his secretary could not say when or even whether Mr. Spalding would arrive at the office today, but just as she was saying it Spalding walked in. He might have walked out again but Donnelly recognised him from Flynn's description and did not give him the chance. He steered him briskly into his own office before his secretary could tell him the policemen had just come from Dr. Hehn's.

Byron Spalding was tall—perhaps as tall as Flynn—and narrow, with long limbs and a long lean face. There the resemblance ended. Spalding dressed with meticulous care and taste. He wore hand-made shoes which he polished, or had polished, to a glorious conker gleam. He bought suits in wonderfully tasteful fabrics, made up with just the right acknowledgement to fashion: twin vents when, and for as long as, appropriate, trouser legs as wide or narrow as they should be. He never matched his tie and his handkerchief and would probably have shot himself rather than wear a shirt with a contrasting collar.

For all that, and the ready smile on his aristocratic face, Byron Spalding was not a superficial man. He was a man who took immense pains to get things right. Donnelly could understand Flynn thinking him no more than a middle-aged trendy getting excited every time he saw Deerings' name in print and sending photographs all over the world in the hope of drumming up a little more glory.

But actually Spalding was a much more substantial character than that. Donnelly supposed that the job of selling a corporate image in a competitive industry required a man to pay ruthless attention to details. He thought that that neat, fussy exterior was probably another of Spalding's creations, and that behind it the man was a consummate professional. In his own way he was as impressive, and as difficult to out-guess, as Hehn.

"Well, Superintendent," he smiled, "how can I help you?"

Donnelly repeated the preamble he had given Hehn. "So I'm looking for one of the prints Flynn sent you."

"Right," Spalding said promptly. His brow creased in thought. "I must have one somewhere. Of course, I sent most of them off to different people. Free advertising, you know, it's the best kind. I'm afraid I was a shocking nuisance to young Flynn, and he only came in to borrow our view." An idea struck him. "I know. Make yourselves comfortable, I'll be right back." He was gone before Donnelly could ask where from.

He returned with a triumphant smile and a print that was identical to the one on *Context*'s cover. "There you are. I kept that one for the house mag. Hold onto it if it's any help, we've made a PMT."

Donnelly accepted it with suitable gratitude. Actually he was disappointed. He had felt sure Spalding would find some reason not to produce it. It was inconceivable that he could have conspired at the bombing of a passenger jet in order to destroy a negative in the baggage hold, then calmly produce a print from that negative at first time of asking. It left Donnelly with almost nothing more to say so he took the print and left, acutely aware that he could still be wrong about this.

By the time the ambulance reached the hospital Todd was showing signs of returning to consciousness, mumbling and searching vaguely with his fingers for the source of the pain in his head, and Flynn was shaking uncontrollably. At the casualty entrance, staff whisked them in two different directions, Todd straight to X-ray, Flynn to a screened cubicle.

Shimoni was left waiting alone on a plastic chair, between a policeman with a bandaged hand and a boy who had glued his fingers, wondering why she always reacted to Flynn with violence—of thought or word, or in this case strong right arm.

A blind man could see he was sick. A man with half a brain would know that Flynn could not have hurt Todd, neither deliberately nor carelessly, sober nor drunk. It was literally incredible; yet she had fallen on that most unlikely explanation for what she found almost with glee, because of the opportunity it gave her to punish Flynn. She did not like what that told her about herself. She rather suspected there was a problem there that she ought to be tackling.

Flynn had tried to tell her what happened. Between his swollen jaw, his concussion and the alcohol still running riot in his bloodstream, he had not made a great deal of sense. But from the way he kept repeating the name, she gathered that Fahad had been there, and that the condition of both men was a consequence of that. She called Donnelly's office and left a message for his return.

A nurse came to reassure her about her two casualties. Todd had a hairline fracture of the skull but there was no displacement and no reason to anticipate lasting damage. He was coming round now, although after five hours' unconsciousness he was inevitably very groggy. He would be in hospital under observation for some days, but there was every reason to hope for an uneventful recovery.

There was not much they could do for Flynn. The poison that could destroy him, that had all but destroyed him once before, was already in his blood and out of the reach of a stomach pump. He had no option but to see it through now.

It might not be as bad as all that. Half a bottle of whisky, especially when he had not fallen off the water-wagon but been thrown off, might not be enough to make a drinker of him again, not after seven dry years. Partly it would depend on his reaction to it, whether he came out of it angry or frightened, ready to fight or already beaten. It would be some little time before he would know, and for that time he would need looking after and even watching. His friends would be invaluable to him now.

Except that, Shimoni thought briefly, with Todd in here and his girl turning out to be the person who tried to kill him, he did not actually have any friends.

Soon after that they let her in to see him. He had a white hospital smock over Todd's pyjama trousers, and a face to match. He looked utterly washed out. When his eyes closed, the lids were almost transparent. They had him propped up on pillows and he made no effort to raise himself from them. He was sober enough now but looked if anything sicker. It might have been the drink, or something the hospital had given him. It might even have been the fact that someone had knocked him down with a deadly accurate blow to his aching jaw just when he had dragged himself back to the land of the living.

"Mickey, I'm sorry," she began.

But Flynn was not interested in her apologies and interrupted, his voice both weak and urgent, mumbling through his swollen jaw. "Is Gil OK? They keep telling me different things. They say he's all right, then they say he's still unconscious. Have you seen him? Is he OK?"

Shimoni laid her hand on top of his, the undamaged one, on the side of the bed. "He's going to be all right, Mickey. They'll keep him in a few days, but he's going to be OK. He's just about waking up now. I expect you'll be able to see him before long."

About then Donnelly arrived in response to her message and Shimoni finally heard a coherent version of the night's events. Partly it was that Flynn was getting his head together, but largely it was due to

Donnelly's skills as interviewer. He had an instinct for when to prompt and when to wait patiently for the tale to find its own way forward. Shimoni was surprised and rather touched by his gentleness.

When he got up to leave, Shimoni walked him down to his car. "When they discharge him," she said, "I'm going to take him back to my place. You have the address. He shouldn't be on his own, and it'll be a while before Gil's up and around again. Also, if Fahad comes back, we might as well make him harder to find."

Donnelly considered for a moment, then nodded. "You have a dog, don't you, Miss Shimoni?"

Shimoni smiled. "Yes. But I think I can protect them both."

She bought herself a fresh coffee, then went back to Flynn.

Flynn was gone, his bed empty. Panic surged in her in the moment before common sense intervened. She knew where he was. She found the room and opened the door quietly.

Todd's head was bandaged and he appeared to be asleep, or nearly so, drowsing like an old man before a fire. She thought he may have seen her come in, though that faint flicker of a smile might have been only a dozing twitch. He looked comfortable, even complacent, under the sheet and not at all like a man at death's door.

Flynn was at the window, looking out over London though Shimoni doubted if he was seeing it, talking to Todd in a low fast urgent monotone. For a moment Shimoni thought he had overestimated the extent of Todd's awareness. Then she realised that Flynn did not know either of them was listening.

"You don't do this to me, Gil," he was saying. The New York accent whined in his voice like the keen of a buzz-saw. "No way; not you. I've already been left by all the people I'm prepared to be left by.

"You got any idea what it's like surviving a plane-crash two hundred and twenty people died in? When it's because of you the plane was blown up anyway? I got to tell you, having a charmed life ain't the greatest feeling in the world. It has you saying too many goodbyes, and too many damned apologies. All those people dead. How the hell do I apologise for that?

"Gil, whatever I've said to you in the past, forget it. I need you. I need your help. I need you to get me through this. I don't know how to handle it. I'm telling you, I can't hack this on my own." A little snort that might have been half laughter, half a sob. "Hell, if you're really lucky you might get to dry me out again. You remember what fun that was!

"So listen to me, old man, wherever it is you've gone to. The pipe and the slippers and the eternal fender and the harp lessons got to wait. You aren't finished here yet. I've kind of lost track whether I owe you or you owe me at the moment, but either way I'm not about to let you quit on me. You die and I got nothing. You die like this, because of me, and I honest to God don't know how I'm going to live with that. I'm lonely and I'm scared right now. A man's got to die some time but please, Gil, for the love of God, wait your turn. Don't leave me alone in this."

Leah Shimoni slipped out of the room as quietly as she had slipped in. That had not been meant for her ears.

It had not actually been meant for Todd's either. But he opened one eye just the same and said, patiently and a shade plaintively, "Mickey, I'm not going anywhere yet."

2

The Forensic Science Laboratory put Donnelly onto a chemist working in that same field of antibiotic research. He took the name he was given round to the address he was given and waited while Dr. Ash was paged. When a lad of about twenty-two in cord jeans and a Fair Isle sweater just odd enough that his mother must have knitted it wandered in, Donnelly assumed he too was looking for the chemist.

But he stood in front of Donnelly with a slightly shy smile and his hands in his pockets and said, "Superintendent Donnelly? I'm Laurie Ash." Donnelly saw then that he was older than he had thought, perhaps by as much as ten years, but still not at all what Donnelly had been expecting. He realised with a twinge of grim humour that he had been expecting another Hehn; possibly without the accent, but essentially another impress from that archetypal mould. As if all policemen looked like George Dixon; as if all photographers looked like Mickey Flynn and none like Cecil Beaton.

"What I need to know, Dr. Ash," he said, "is just how cutthroat a business is pharmaceutical research?"

Ash gave a pensive frown like a swottish schoolboy. "On a scale of one to ten? About minus three."

Oh well, Donnelly thought resignedly, another theory bites the dust.

"No, that's not altogether true," Ash went on mildly. "What I'm working on at the moment, nobody'd walk up two flights of stairs to steal. Not because it isn't important, but because any commercial implications are long term and it's commercial considerations which are to blame when drug companies stop behaving like the benefactors of mankind and start behaving like dogs round a bitch in heat."

"I'd have thought pharmaceuticals was a business like any other: you identify a need, design a product to meet it, market it and hope to make a profit. No?"

"Certainly, in principle. In practice there are certain idiosyncrasies, the main one of which is the size of the R&D budget as a proportion of gross income, and the amount of R&D that will never recoup itself in product sales. It's the nature of the thing. If you sell—say—furniture, you know before you start how to make a bed, or an armchair. You might experiment with different woods, different fabrics, but you know from day one that you'll have a product of some sort at the end.

"Pharmaceuticals isn't like that. Either you start at the consumer end—Mrs. Jones wants something to stop her piles being such a pain in the arse, so you hunt through your lexicon of compounds for something that might ease Mrs. Jones's discomfort without, for example, blowing her left leg off. Or you start at the chemistry end and try to find a useful role in life for a reaction that looks jolly impressive on the bench but might be a long way from adding to the sum of human happiness.

"Either way you waste a lot of time, effort and money. You test a lot of things that don't help Mrs. Jones's piles, or do blow her leg off. And you chase up a lot of blind alleys before you accept that, since turning iodine white or making sulphur smell like tortillas is not in itself a useful accomplishment, this particular reaction is never going to make money."

Donnelly was not sure where this was leading him but he was content to follow it for a while yet. "So how do you develop new products?"

"Occasionally," Ash said succinctly. "Most lines on sale are variations on a fairly limited range of themes. Cough-drops in different flavours. Torpedo-shaped analgesics instead of round ones. Creams instead of lotions, gargles instead of sprays. What you're selling is the same remedy as everyone else in a different package. You won't get rich doing it, there's too much competition, but you won't go broke either."

"Then how do you get rich?"

Ash looked down at his well-worn cords. "You're asking me?" Donnelly grinned obligingly. "You get lucky. You work hard, you do your R&D, and then once in a while you get lucky. You cross a couple of selling-platers and breed Red Rum. You find yourself staring down a microscope at something that's behaving how you want it to behave instead of how it wants to behave. You test it on some lab rats and it doesn't blow any legs off. You get as far as clinical trials, and Mrs. Jones says it makes piles a pleasure. You put it on the market, and people eating off mantelpieces buy it faster than you can turn it out. Your shares go through the roof.

"And then some whey-faced accountant on the third floor who didn't get asked to the celebration party gets out his pocket calculator and works out that the projected five-year profits on Bum-Eez are just enough to cover the cost of all the R&D that came to nothing. So you tidy away the streamers and the champagne corks and get back to work."

"So how," Donnelly said again, "do you get rich?"

Ash shrugged. "I suppose the most reliable way is theft."

"What do you steal?"

"Ideas. Research. Just finding out what doesn't work can save you time and money. If you can actually find out what does work you can be on the market in direct competition with the market leaders without having their costs to offset. Industrial espionage is big business throughout big business, but there can't be many industries where the rewards are so great. Is this being any help, Superintendent?"

"I'm sure it is," said Donnelly.

Ash called his bluff. "How?"

"No idea," admitted the policeman. "But it's R&D I haven't had to pay for so it must be worth something."

Before he left he looked round Ash's laboratory. His first impression was that it was nothing like Dr. Hehn's. Then he realised it was just the same only older. All Ash's equipment was a generation senior to Hehn's, and gathered together piecemeal so that the cabinets did not match. Ash appeared to have cornered the market in other people's rejects. He worked on what might once have been a kitchen table. Even the blackboard was second-hand: it had the letters of the alphabet printed in block capitals down one side and in joined-up writing along the bottom. A girl was scribbling a formula: when it worked out wrong she swore, erased it with her sleeve and began again.

Donnelly said, "What is it you're working on here?"

"Liver fluke."

"Lots of luck," said Donnelly, leaving hurriedly.

Shimoni took Flynn home to the cottage outside Windsor. The dog remembered him, stuck its nose out from under the couch and risked a brief wag of the tail.

During the drive they had hardly spoken, which would not have mattered if they had been comfortable in their silence. But Flynn needed to talk and Shimoni wanted to, and neither of them could find a way of breaking out of the cage that events and their own natures had built around them.

The strain was greater because silence was not a natural element to either of them. Shimoni in her sturdy self-reliance seemed reticent, but she had never before had difficulty saying what she wanted. Flynn by instinct was downright voluble: words ran out of him as fast as, and sometimes faster than, his ideas came to mind. He would talk to anyone about anything, and argue too given half a chance, and argue as passionately for whims that amused him as for beliefs he had held all his adult life.

What stood in the way of communication between them was guilt. Both of them were ashamed.

Though Todd was recovering visibly, Flynn was tortured by the hurt he had brought on him. He felt as if, whatever way he turned, someone else paid the price of his mistakes. A plane-load of strangers dead; a man he cared about in hospital with a fractured skull; the woman he loved turned into some kind of an ocean-striding Nemesis with death on a leash.

In a way he did not understand, he felt as much responsible for Laura Wade's transmutation as for Todd's broken head and the two hundred and twenty broken bodies. He was not thinking very clearly. He felt more like the culprit than another victim. He wished someone would punish him for whatever it was he had done and stop taking it out on his friends. Then he remembered the whisky and supposed he was going to get his wish.

Shimoni was ashamed of her behaviour towards Flynn, going back to but not confined to the night of the plane-crash. She understood her feelings well enough. She had felt jealous of and threatened by this special relationship between Gil Todd and Mickey Flynn, suddenly revived after three years. She had not trusted Todd to take her interests into consideration. Now she felt rather ashamed of that too. She had behaved like a child who thought someone was going to snatch her doll away.

Most of all she regretted that stinging blow she had dealt Flynn's battered face, that had sent him reeling in agony. She knew that, if he remembered it at all, he would not hold it against her. But she did. She knew, as he could not, that the scene which greeted her when Flynn wobbled to open Todd's front door neither explained nor justified her action. She never thought Flynn had attacked Todd. She had been waiting for her chance to hurt Flynn, and this was it. She could have told Todd that and felt the better for it. But she could not explain it to Flynn, and it stood in the way of anything she could have said.

She went to make up the spare room, which was about three inches longer than Flynn if he lay with the crown of his head against one wall. He asked if he could help, she suggested he feed the dog. He found the bowl, and the bag of meal and the cans of meat, but could not find the can-opener. Rather than ask he hunted, and in hunting discovered where she kept her drinks.

If she had spent another thirty seconds wrestling a cover onto the spare bed duvet she would not have returned to the kitchen in time to see him gazing thoughtfully at the green and dark and bright bottles ranged within, for he had closed the cupboard and straightened up before he knew she was there. He said, by way of explanation, "Can-opener?"

She passed it to him and Flynn fed the dog. He said carefully, "In view of what happened to the last guy who gave me a bed for the night, you sure you want me here? It might not be the cleverest move you could make."

Shimoni shrugged. "I grew up with people like Fahad around me. Not just Arabs, there are Jewish Fahads as well. You learn not to let them dictate your life. It's like having snakes in the garden: you take sensible precautions and then you forget about them. You can always be unlucky, but it's better than living your life with one eye over your shoulder. I'm not prepared to be held hostage by a man who may be thousands of miles away by now with no intention of coming back.

Whatever happens next, we'll deal with it. You have a charmed life, remember?"

She found his eyes on her face, his expression ambivalent. "You were there, weren't you? While I was"—his shoulders, and his expression, gave a tiny shrug—"talking to Gil. While he was waking up. I heard the door close. I thought it was a nurse, but it was you."

She saw no point in denying it. "Yes."

His chin came up. "Is that why—?"

"No." Her tone was uncompromising. "Mickey, I'm not sure what the relationship between you and me is going to be, but it'll be founded on something a damn sight more substantial than pity. I don't know if we can really be friends. I'm willing to wait and see. In the meantime, you're Gil Todd's friend and that's enough. I'm on your side, Mickey. I realise it may not always have seemed like it, but you can rely on me.

"And now," she added, turning away, "the sun being over the yard-arm or under the gunter or whatever it is, I think we should split a—"

She stopped as if shot. She glanced at him over her shoulder, horrified. The magnitude of the faux pas stripped her self-confidence away like a skin. Desperation made her inventive. Watching him out of the corner of her eye she murmured, "A tea-bag?"

Flynn began to laugh. He had an inordinately silly laugh, and when it got started it could go on until everyone around him had either joined in or gone looking for a psychiatrist who made house-calls. It started as a low chuckle deep in his throat, served time as a definite giggle, threw in a couple of walrus impressions along the way and finally petered out, when the need to breathe became paramount, in a diminishing volley of snorts like a winded horse.

They ended up on the carpet, back to back, tears streaming down their faces while the dog Flute ran round them excitedly trying to work out if they were dangerous.

Flynn wiped his eyes on his sleeve and sighed. "Listen, we got two ways to handle this. We can play Let's Pretend: you pretend not to be watching me while I pretend not to be watching the cupboard where you keep your hooch. Or we can behave like two mature, sensible adults and pass the time in some intelligent and meaningful way until we see whether this thing's going to have me crawling up the walls."

"What do you have in mind?"

Flynn considered. "We could get a Bugs Bunny video."

They played Scrabble. Todd had taught her, with the idea of extending her English vocabulary. She now had an excellent vocabulary of words with q and z in them. She used them all in a serious attempt to beat Flynn by as wide a margin as possible.

But halfway through the first game she realised that Flynn was playing not to win but to amuse himself. "Gin" and "sling" could have been a coincidence; she was definitely suspicious of "punch," thought she could be over-reacting to "tonic" and was left in no doubt whatever when he added a y to "whisk" which also transformed the word "tips" above it. He was sending her up. When he saw that she knew, he gave her his grin that was sweet and crazy in approximately equal proportions, and for the first time she began to understand the affection Todd bore him which had survived three years in which he had not so much as received a postcard from the wanderer.

Mid-way through the evening Donnelly came round. He had the photograph Spalding had given him, but Shimoni got the impression that he had called not to discuss the picture but to check that they were all right.

The policeman was clearly depressed by his day's investigating. He sat heavily in a chair with his grey raincoat settling round him like a shroud. "At nine this morning I'd have given reasonable odds that we were close to cracking this thing. I reckoned we knew who was behind it, and a bit about why, and that we'd have the rest including signed confessions probably by close of play today.

"Then I talked to Hehn, and getting the signed confessions started to look a bit of a problem. And then Spalding gave me this thing, and the whole idea that the bomb was to destroy the picture suddenly seemed about as feasible as the nuclear aeroplane." He passed the photograph to Flynn in a way that suggested it was rather heavy. "I mean, if this is what it's all about, (a) why give me a copy of it, and (b) and more fundamentally, why worry *who* sees it?"

Flynn took the print and examined it. He looked at the marks on the back. He held it close to his eye to examine the grain in the darkest and lightest regions. He flexed it between his fingers, feeling it bend and reform. He said, "This isn't actually the photo I sent Deerings."

Superintendent Donnelly could not have looked more startled if the improbable nuclear aeroplane had not only taken off but had flown through Leah Shimoni's livingroom window. He was out of his chair as if shot from a gun and peering over Flynn's shoulder, helped by the fact that Flynn remained seated. "What do you mean, it's not the one you sent Deerings?" He ferreted his copy of *Context* from his raincoat pocket and compared the cover with the print minutely. "It *is* the same. What are you talking about?"

"Well yes, it's the same print," said Flynn. "But when I sent it to them it was about half as big again. Look. The full negative included a lot more background than that. I sent it to Greg Miller like that so he could crop it to the shape he wanted, OK? It's pretty standard practice if you're not sure what format the editor's looking for. So Greg, or his picture editor, cut it down to what was basically a vertical-format portrait to fill his cover up to the title.

"So when Spalding came looking for copies, naturally I printed the full negative again. Including the background. For some reason he's cut this one down to the same format that Greg printed in *Context.* I wonder why, that's all."

Donnelly squinted at the print—the cheerily grinning Hehn so different from the block-house of a man he had met—then at Flynn. "So what has he cut off?"

Flynn shrugged. It made no more sense to him than it did to Donnelly. "Nothing. I mean, maybe an inch and a half all round, but nothing in it. Background."

Donnelly was a man with considerable reserves of restraint. He plumbed them deeply now. He said evenly, "You're telling me that the key to this whole business is contained in an inch-and-a-half-wide strip of disposable background trimmed from a photograph? That that's the only difference between a negative worth murdering two hundred and twenty people for and a print the putative murderers are happy to give to the investigating police?"

"Hey, I'm not telling you anything." But Flynn sounded thoughtful. "Still, it would explain why nothing happened after the magazine came out, only after I started sending copies to Deerings. They thought the cropped version was all there was, until they got the first full-negative print. That's when they saw they had a problem."

"Then that's it," said Donnelly, his lips tight. "It's a dead-end. They've got away with it. The negative is gone, and all the original prints from it have either disappeared or been trimmed of whatever evidence they contain. I'll try and trace the other prints you sent Spalding, but I imagine every one of them will have been cropped in the exact same manner. And when I ask him why he'll say, well, that was how it appeared on the magazine cover, that was how he wanted to show it round."

Apropos of nothing Leah Shimoni said, "Rubbish."

The two men looked at her. Somewhat stiffly Donnelly said, "I assure you, Miss Shimoni, Spalding will not have overlooked—"

"No, no," she said, shaking her head vehemently. "Rubbish. Garbage. Waste paper. Photography generates vast quantities of the stuff. Mickey, what did you do with yours?"

Flynn had caught up with her train of thought but he knew it was not taking them anywhere. "I put it in the bin. In the darkroom. You're right, I made a couple of prints that the tone wasn't great on, that I dumped and started again. But even the last ones I made, in the week before the fire, aren't going to be there any more. The darkroom's where the fire started."

"All right, so your rubbish is gone," said Shimoni. "What about the picture editor at *Context*?"

Donnelly had had to sprint for it but he too had caught the train by now. "The magazine with Hehn on the cover was printed the guts of two months ago. Don't you think they might have emptied the waste-paper bin before now?"

"So they might," agreed Shimoni. "And they might incinerate their waste, or have it pulped or something. Or they just might do what other newspapers do, which is bale it and store it and have it picked up when the pile hits the ceiling."

3

Pretext Publications had invested in a waste-paper baler some twelve months previously. Greg Miller had thought it would be the end of his refuse problem. He had not allowed for repeated difficulties in getting the bales collected. Huge and heavy, they lined every wall in the building—much reducing the noise levels on printing days—until the factory inspectors got stroppy, after which they accumulated out of sight in a yard covered by a tarpaulin. Miller suspected that the tarpaulin was a mistake, that the darkness encouraged them to breed.

They stood together in the grimy yard, greasy from the effects of rain on the visiting cards of a hundred generations of pigeons, and eyed the grim towers with doubt and disfavour. The tallest must have been ten feet high. Donnelly, who had a slight mathematical bent, reckoned there had to be a thousand cubic feet of waste paper there, and under pressure at that, constrained by plastic girths. When those were cut it would be like Vesuvius erupting.

He said judiciously, "So that's four months' worth of waste paper, is it?"

Miller, who was standing beside him, looked rueful. "Summer's our quiet time, too."

"And you don't stack them in any particular order. I mean, there's no particular advantage in starting bottom left."

Miller shook his head. He was a slightly plump man of forty in a sweater that Laurie Ash's mother could have knitted, tweed trousers and trainers. Any man over the age of thirty wearing trainers to work is making a statement. Sometimes it is "My God I'm fit, you'll have to be out early in the morning to keep up with me." In this case it was more "No, running a magazine does not mean I'm rich. Sue me for libel and I'll go bankrupt, so see where that gets you."

Miller himself said, "They've been shifted about three times before they end up here. All I can suggest is, look for the dates on the magazines. They're mostly duff ones dumped straight from the presses, so they'd be baled within a week of publication. The photograph could have been handled anywhere in the week before publication."

Donnelly did his sums again. "So the edges trimmed from this photograph should be baled along with copies of the issue prior to the one it appeared in."

"Probably," said Miller, in a voice which conveyed the opinion that there's many a slip twixt the expected and the discovered.

So they began. The search party included two particularly beefy young constables armed with a fork-lift, some police cadets to do the actual picking-through-the-garbage part, and Flynn and Shimoni to go through the remnants of photographs looking for the right one.

It would have been easier if the picture editor had worked with the sharp prints, but he had not. The original print of the Hehn photograph, in its original state and dimensions, had been filed until it was stolen in the break-in. What the picture editor worked with was a photo-mechanical transfer, a rather less sharp image but one which the offset presses could print. The trouble with PMTs is that, like cats at night, they all look grey, and that goes double for bits trimmed from them.

Nor was there any way of knowing whether the margins removed from the Hehn PMT had come away cleanly in one piece, consisted of four strips taken one from each side, or even of a series of narrow ribbons pared as the editor tried out different shapes. After two months he had no recollection. All they could hope to do was find the outside edge of the picture, and then as many strips as were necessary to meet the edges of the portrait on the cover. The searchers each had a photocopy of the cover for reference.

"Well," said Donnelly, "let's do it." He cut the bindings on the first bale a little like the Queen Mother opening a railway station, and multi-coloured paper exploded round him.

Five hours later one of the cadets, whose task was to extract photographic remains from the general waste and pass these on to the experts, paused with his hand halfway to the Hopeful pile, looked again and said, "I think this is it." Three hours before he might have managed a little excitement, but now he was too tired. Five hours is a long time to spend on your hands and knees.

Flynn took it from him. Even before he had worked out just what he was looking at, he recognised his own work. He held it to the photocopy, dog-eared after half a day in and out of his pocket, and was sure. What he had was an L-shaped strip of the Hehn PMT trimmed from the left-hand side and lower edge. Hehn's white coat was a pale area at the bottom, the blackboard a dark area with white scribbles to the left.

"This is it," he said. "It's the right bale. This is about half of what's missing: now we need the top and the right margin. They might be in one piece, like this, or several, but they're in here somewhere."

Other piles were abandoned as everyone turned their attention to the pay-dirt. Within ten minutes the right-hand edge had been found. A minute later Shimoni held up the top strip. Together the three pieces framed exactly the picture which had appeared on the cover of *Context*. Whatever information two hundred and twenty people had died to protect was now before them.

Donnelly took custody of the fragments as if he had been entrusted with the Crown Jewels. He wiped grime off them with his handkerchief then put them carefully into an envelope. Then he tapped Flynn on the shoulder. "You're not finished yet."

A police photographer combined the three pieces of the *Context* PMT with the print supplied by Spalding and made several copies. They lacked the sharpness of the original but were adequate to most purposes. Then he sandwiched the composite in clear film to protect

it, and Donnelly took the composite, the copies and Flynn and
Shimoni back to his office.

"So what is it?" Donnelly gazed down at the pictures laid out on his
desk. "What is it in there that we absolutely did not have to see, that
had to be kept from us at whatever cost?"

They looked in silence, searching the margins for something to
explain the monstrous event which had brought them together. They
saw nothing.

Flynn said, "It didn't have to be kept from me."

"What?"

"They weren't worried about me seeing it, or they wouldn't have
kept asking me to get it out again and print it."

Donnelly nodded slowly. "Right. Well . . . ." He was thinking on
his feet. "Of course, you took the photograph. If this—whatever it is—
had meant anything to you, you'd have said something or done something at the time. When no-one came asking about it, they assumed it
meant nothing to you so it didn't matter how often you looked at it."

"Maybe it's something that would only make sense to another
chemist," offered Flynn. "What happened was this. I'm on their roof
doing something else when the post comes. Hehn gets his letter, goes
round telling everyone, Spalding grabs me and I grab the pic. It's as
spontaneous as that. No preparations, no tidying up, just stand the guy
in the middle of his lab and hit the shutter.

"Well, there's something on view that shouldn't be, but they don't
realise it right away. It isn't there in the *Context* picture. It's only when
I send that first full-negative print to Spalding for his house magazine
that the four-minute warning goes off. I have a negative with a state
secret in the background, and if I sell another copy of it and this one
gets published full-size, the secret is out. Any picture of a chemist is
likely to be seen by other chemists."

"So Spalding tries to buy the negative," said Donnelly, taking up the
narrative. "But you won't sell, so he has to find a way of destroying it.
He hires Laura Wade." If he saw Flynn wince he took no notice. "She
picks you up and moves in with you so she can look for it; when she
can't find it she decides to burn the flat out. It should have worked, it
was sheer luck that particular negative survived. But it did, and she
knew it had.

"She'd have had another go in a day or two, except that you insisted
on splitting up. Once that happened she'd lose track of the negative.

You even told her you might sell prints from it to raise some cash. She had to make sure this time. She bought you the bag and some clothes, and took them somewhere to rig a bomb. You were never going to go over the case with a magnifying glass: you'd open it long enough to put the negatives inside and then you'd go. Wherever you were when the clock ran out, the contents of the case would be destroyed, and probably you with them."

"Afterwards," said Flynn; his mouth felt dusty and the words were a moment coming, "Spalding traced me to Gil's flat. He called asking for another god-damned print. I told him what he wanted to know: that there wouldn't be any more prints, that the negative had been destroyed. I gave him the name of a commercial photographer but he never called him. Why would he?—he didn't want more pictures of Hehn, he just wanted *that* picture of Hehn. To make sure it would never appear any place it could be seen by someone clever enough to understand what he was looking at."

"Another scientist," said Donnelly. "We need a chemist up here." He picked up his phone and called Dr. Ash.

Ash went straight to it. He looked round the three of them as if he thought they were mentally deficient. "It's what he's got written on the blackboard, isn't it?"

And of course it was. The right-hand edge of the blackboard was just visible at the left-hand edge of the picture *Context* printed. But the full print had shown perhaps a third of the board and everything chalked on it. That was what Spalding had seen in the print Flynn had made him: the results of months or years of work, the blueprint for Deerings' next breakthrough, that Hehn had been working on when the post came and that he had forgotten in the heat of the moment.

Flynn breathed softly in the face of revelation. "What is it? What does it say?"

Ash said gently, "I left my microscope at home." And indeed, whatever was written there was very small, a faint white scrawl across a blackboard in the background of a photograph which itself measured only five-and-a-half inches by eight.

"Your darkroom will have a magnifying glass," said Shimoni.

So they all trooped back to the darkroom, four of them now including Ash. The police photographer put the original composite under a big square glass and played with it, jockeying magnification against focus. Then he leaned back. "Try that."

Ash took his place. He moved his head a little back and forth, trying to get his eye in. By degrees the tiny chalk-marks began to resolve as symbols he recognised. He looked away for a moment, perplexed. He took a pen and an envelope from a pocket and jotted down what he could read. He said, with total certainty, "That's not antibiotics."

Startled, Donnelly looked from him to the glass and back. "Are you sure? That's what he got the Sondheim Prize for."

"Well, he wouldn't have got it for this."

Donnelly caught an inflection in his voice that said more than the words. "Why—what is it?"

"Look," Ash said uneasily, "I'm only seeing part of the formula here—not even one section, just the second half of a lot of lines. I'd be guessing if I tried to say what he was working on when he wrote this. But it wasn't antibiotics; and I don't think it was anything he'd have put before the Sondheim committee."

"So guess," said Donnelly firmly.

Ash looked at his notes, at the magnified photograph, at the ceiling, finally at the Superintendent. "It could be a formulation for a synthetic narcotic."

Donnelly was not a scientist. "A drug? We're still talking pharmaceuticals here?"

"Well, yes," agreed Ash. He tapped the end of his pen on a row of symbols sketched on the back of his envelope: $C_{17}H_{21}O_4N$. "But if someone gave me a sample of this, I'd be more inclined to sniff it than inject it into my cow."

"What we have here," Donnelly said slowly—they were back in his office and the other three were trying to work out why he looked so grim when as far as they could see he had just solved the most important case of his career—"is a policeman's nightmare. We have two hundred and twenty bodies. We know who killed them, and how, and now we know why. And I don't know if I can make the case stick.

"We have a limited amount of circumstantial evidence. Part of a formula on a blackboard. If we had the whole formula it still wouldn't incriminate the man who wrote it. He'll say it was just a philosophical exercise, a bit of scientific doodling. A court would want evidence that he took it off the blackboard and tried to put it into production, and in an uncertain world the only thing I am absolutely confident of is that, this long after, Deerings will have been swept to remove any such evidence. Without it, everything we think is mere speculation."

"But surely to God," exclaimed Flynn, "when Hehn knows you know—that you've seen the formula—"

"He'll invite me to show there was ever any intent, on his part or anyone's at Deerings, to use the formula as the basis of a manufacturing process. Because unless they intended making the stuff and selling it, there was no need for secrecy. And Deerings is a respectable company, after all, and Hehn a respectable chemist. The bloody man's won awards. It's like—well, if I want to accuse Wimbledon Fast Eddie of being wheelman on a bank job, I'm most of the way there if I can show he could have been, he wasn't doing anything else that day. If I want to level the same accusation at—say—the Archbishop of Canterbury, I need a different class of evidence entirely. The jury isn't going to exchange knowing looks when he says he was alone in the chantry all afternoon and not even the verger saw him."

Dr. Ash looked thoughtfully at Flynn. "What time of day did you take the photograph?"

"Mid-morning. Why?"

"If the formula was up on the blackboard, without even a cover over it, during office hours when his assistants were in the lab, they must have been in on what he was doing. Any competent chemist reading that formula would have known it was nothing to do with antibiotics, and would have recognised enough elements from it to guess what it might be instead. He wasn't doing secret work by candlelight when nobody was about: that was the project his department was working on. If he won't tell you about it, perhaps someone else there will."

"Oh, I'll give them every encouragement," Donnelly promised grimly. "But Hehn wouldn't have been using anyone he had doubts about, and anyone who started getting twittery after the picture came out will long ago have been moved on and the personnel records altered so we'll never find them. I'll ask the questions, but I doubt I'll get the answers I want. It's so simple for them. They don't need alibis, they don't have to agree on a story, they just deny knowing anything about this"—he tapped the formula in the photograph—"synthetic cocaine, you say? Nobody was working on it. So what if Dr. Hehn did scribble it up? It was a joke. Physicists doodle bombs, chemists doodle drugs. There was no research, there's no product, there's no crime."

While they were talking Flynn had roamed away from the desk, pacing the room with his head down and one hand in his pocket. Twice he paused at the window, the long hunched shape of him silhouetted against the day, but he did not seem to see outside and each time after only a moment he moved on, prowling restlessly. The tension growing in him was filling the room. They were all aware of it, all waiting for the explosion. The atmosphere was like a menagerie three seconds before the bear rips the keeper's arm off.

Flynn too knew what was happening, and what the likely end would be. It was why he kept moving, trying to absorb the frustration building up in him. He did not worry much about his dignity but he did not want to let fly at Donnelly. The man was doing his best in a difficult, complex situation. Flynn knew better than to suppose, even when his nerves were jangling with the lack of progress, that he was the only one who cared what happened to Flight 98. Everyone here wanted justice for the dead and had contributed time and thought and effort to that end. But Flynn wanted more than justice. He wanted vengeance.

So he worked to keep his voice low and did not know it sounded like a tiger growling. "Are you saying you're prepared to let them get away with this?"

Donnelly bridled. He did not need Flynn to tell him about his own shortcomings and those of the system he served. "Now that's not what I said. What I said was, we still have a long way to go to make a case against these people. If we jump the gun we could lose them. What I'm telling you, and what I'll tell my chief when he asks, is that any mistake we make on this one is going to cost us the conviction, and that's why I am going to take all the time I need to stitch it up tight, regardless of whose blood the popular press is clamouring for.

"And that is also the reason, Flynn," he went on, warming to the subject, "why your days of wandering the world like the Flying Dutchman, looking for someone to lift your curse, are over. Such as it is, my case rests on your evidence. As of now you are the only demonstrable connection between Laura Wade and Deering Pharmaceuticals. You're the only witness to the activities of both in the days prior to the explosion. You'll be needed for that photograph to be admitted as evidence: courts like to know where photographs come from, who took them and developed them and whether there was any chance of interference.

"I don't know what the judge at the Old Bailey's going to say when I enter into evidence three fragments of a photograph which has since been stolen, which fragments were discarded and dumped and well on their way to being recycled as fire-lighters and environmentally-aware bog-roll before being recovered from God knows how many tons of assorted rubbish. But if I try to enter them without calling the photographer to swear to them, I'm going to be on points duty in East Grinstead before my feet touch the ground."

The policeman and the photographer glared at one another like a couple of terriers squaring up for a fight.

Shimoni said quietly, "I suppose the people at Deerings will also be aware how much of the case depends on Flynn."

Donnelly disengaged from the confrontation and took a deep breath and nodded. "Oh yes. So far what I've been asking them has been general stuff, there's been no real reason for them to suppose we're onto them. That changes now. When I start asking specifics they'll know that we have the picture; they'll know that I'll have it somewhere they can't get at it; and they'll know that as evidence it won't be worth a damn without Flynn."

"They've already killed two hundred and twenty people to protect their secret."

"Yes," agreed Donnelly.

4

The postcard was addressed to Flynn but it was lying on Todd's hall carpet when Shimoni let herself in. She had been calling by to keep an eye on the place until he should be discharged from the hospital. She was not sure what would happen then, whether he would insist on coming back here or if she could persuade him to come out to Windsor. The cottage was under a certain amount of pressure already with her, Flynn, the dog and the police guard they had been allocated, but she felt that with a bit of juggling they could manage. There was an outbuilding in the yard that a previous owner had used as a kennel. At absolute need, Flynn could move in there.

Shimoni was not afflicted by an over-zealous conscience. She had no reservations about reading Flynn's mail. But what was written on the back of the full-colour photograph of the Djemaa el Fna in Marrakech made no sense to her. She would have to ask Flynn what it meant when she gave it to him.

There was no signature, not even an initial. "It's from Michael Wylie," Flynn said wonderingly. With Shimoni waiting expectantly at one elbow and the policeman at the other there seemed no point in trying to keep it private.

The card read:

"Made some enquiries. British passport—Elizabeth Baron. Works out of Montreal. Word is, she's back in the U.K. again. Don't expect she's visiting relatives.

"Jacquard reckons she's in our line of business and I should be helping her not you. Told him that was why: if I don't stop her killing you this time, nobody'll believe I didn't pay her to do it before."

Donnelly was round rather quicker than you can drive legally from London to Windsor. He read the card twice. "This man Wylie. Do you trust him?"

Flynn smiled very faintly. "With my life." Shimoni was white, Donnelly grim, but Flynn could cope better with this direct threat to himself than with those faced by others on his behalf. "Have you been rattling Deerings' cage?"

"Yes, I've questioned them again. I had to, and I'll have to again, and soon." Then he realised that, since Flynn was not on the attack, he had no need to be defensive. He sighed. "I have to go on with this. You know that."

"Damn right," agreed Flynn. "Whatever it costs, they don't get away with what they've done."

Donnelly appreciated that. He did not do a lot of emoting normally —the last month could hardly be described as normal and he had used up a year's allowance—but his eyes on Flynn warmed. "No," he concurred softly. "OK. So we have to keep her away from you. It would be nice to pick her up, but the lady's a professional, perhaps we shouldn't count on that. We'll step up the security on you instead. Not here. I think we'll put you out of sight somewhere, if she's looking she'll find you here. I'll put you somewhere you have no connection with. You'll be bored, but you'll be safe."

"Boredom has its up side too. When do you want me to go?"

"Tonight. I'll have it fixed up for tonight."

After he had gone Shimoni decided to take the dog for a walk to unwind. Flynn was going to go with her, but the police guard suggested he think again. It was a first taste of what could be months of virtual imprisonment. Flynn found himself thinking about whisky.

Back at his office Donnelly found he had a visitor waiting. The name set him back on his heels. He could not imagine what a man who had long been eliminated from the enquiry could want to see him for. So he thought he had better ask. "Would you show Mr. Loriston in?"

Before Peter Loriston had lowered his classically proportioned posterior into the chair he was offered it was clear that he was deeply unhappy. He moved as if his shirt still had the tailor's pins in it, as if his shoes had been hand-made for somebody else's feet. His tongue, which had made his name as a politician and his living in the altogether tougher world of public relations, seemed unequal to the task of explaining his presence here.

But Donnelly had been in this line of work for a long time, not without his successes, and he recognised the symptoms of conflict in a man doing, or trying to do, something he did not want to do but felt he ought to do. That almost certainly meant that Donnelly would want to hear what Loriston wanted to say, and if it took them a few minutes to get there it would be time well spent.

Donnelly made no attempt to hurry him, nor did he give him any excuse to say something less or other than what he was steeling himself to say. He waited, patient, solemn and still, for Loriston to do what he clearly conceived to be his duty. He was confident that the man's sense of honour would be persuasion enough. It was a compliment Loriston would have appreciated.

Finally he got the words out, chewing them with an expression of distaste like a child eating turnip. "Is it true that you suspect Byron Spalding of Deering Pharmaceuticals of being involved in the bombing of Flight 98?"

Donnelly's voice expressed mild shock underscored by disappointment. "Mr. Loriston, you must know that I cannot discuss with any third party any suspicions I may hypothetically have against Mr. Spalding or anyone else." That was about right: it said everything but "no."

For a moment indignation gained the ascendancy over embarrassment and Loriston's blue eyes glittered. "I don't consider myself a third party, Superintendent. I've already been virtually accused of the crime myself. And Spalding is a member of my club."

Donnelly's natural reticence stood him in good stead. He did not laugh. He did not look as if he was about to laugh. He only said gently, "It's not a relationship as sanctioned by church or state."

Loriston flushed dully. "Perhaps not. But it is relevant. In the normal way of things I would not dream of gossiping about another member's activities. Possibly the only thing that would induce me to do so is the fear of hampering a serious criminal investigation. If Byron Spalding had anything to do with the deaths of two hundred and twenty people, he may not rely for his protection on any relationship he has with me."

Donnelly said levelly, "If you have any information which might assist our enquiries, you should let me have it."

"Do you suspect Spalding?"

Donnelly chewed briefly on the inside of his cheek. "We have had occasion to speak to Mr. Spalding in connection with this investigation."

"Do you suspect him?"

Loriston needed official sanction for breaking his covenant, and perhaps the small victory over Donnelly too, more than Donnelly needed to protect the direction of his enquiry. By now Spalding knew he was under suspicion: there was no real need to keep it from Loriston. "Yes."

"Thank Christ for that," said Loriston, with every sign of meaning it. "I thought perhaps I was wrong."

"About what?"

Loriston took a deep breath and said what he had come to say. "About the black girl he met in the foyer of the National Theatre last night. Because if she wasn't the one that Fleet Street gossip says you're looking for, the man was doing nothing more dreadful than cheating on his wife, in which case it would be the duty of a fellow club member to have seen and heard nothing."

This time Donnelly did not visit Spalding. He had Spalding brought to him. He hoped that raising the stakes might increase the pressure on Spalding to the point where it began to tell. If Laura Wade—or Elizabeth Baron or whoever—was in London and had talked to him, time as a factor was beginning to militate against slow thorough police detection. If Spalding could be induced to waver, it might save a lot of time and Mickey Flynn's life.

He said without preamble, "I have a witness to your conversation last night with Elizabeth Baron."

Donnelly did not expect him to clap his hands to his face, say, "It's a fair cop" and make a full and frank confession, and Spalding did not do so. But if he believed himself inscrutable he was mistaken: there was shock there, in his eyes and the drawn lines of his face and in a certain rigidity of his spine, to be seen and exploited by an astute policeman.

Donnelly had watched very carefully for his response and had the clear impression that Spalding was less appalled at having been seen talking with the woman than by the fact that the police knew her real, or at any event her working, name. A meeting of two people in a crowd could always be explained; but the police had not learned her real name without also learning who she was. Once they knew that, any meeting with her that was not wholly secret was extraordinarily dangerous to him.

So his muscles stiffened and his eyes stretched, and a dew of sweat gathered in the hollows beneath them; and still the man held onto his self-control, betraying himself neither by word nor gesture, challenging Donnelly to prove what he knew. "Was that her name? I don't think she said. A witness?—the entire audience must have been in the foyer about then, plus a small jazz band, a book-stall and a girl selling ear-rings from a tray. Why are you interested in a conversation betweenplaygoers?"

"What did she say?"

"She said she last saw *The Crucible* performed in Toronto and there was a powercut."

Oh you clever bastard, Donnelly thought, wooden-faced. You know we know who she is, so you feed us a conversation she could have had with anyone. He made a note. "And you said—?"

"I said I once saw *Saint Joan* in Dublin when the backdrop fell in on the trial scene."

Another note, then Donnelly flicked some pages back. "Toronto and *Saint Joan*. Was that before or after you said, 'It's essential to both of us that this contract is completed' and she said, 'I'll do it but it's going to cost you'?"

Spalding blinked. It might have been the blink of an innocent man totally mystified by the question. Actually it was the blink of a man seeking a split-second's thought. When he had had it he shook his head deliberately. "Your witness"—he seemed to hold the word at arm's length, as if it smelled—"must have been listening to two other people."

Donnelly nodded mechanically. "I see. So it wasn't you, either, who said, 'This time try and be a bit more discriminating. I don't want him saved by another miracle and half the population of London wiped out.' "

Their eyes met. Donnelly waited for the tell-tale flickering that would be Spalding's defences breaking down. It never came. Spalding's rather prominent eyes slid half closed, and something almost like a smile settled on his lips. "No, that wasn't me either."

After a space Donnelly shook his head. "I don't know what you hope to gain. You must know that, between Flynn and his photograph and the witness to your meeting with Elizabeth Baron, I have all the evidence I need to send you down for a very long time. You must know I've taken measures to prevent you, or anyone on your behalf, from tampering with that evidence. We have you, Spalding, and whether or not we get Baron you're going to pay for murdering two hundred and twenty people.

"About Hehn I'm not sure. There's no direct link at present between him and what was done. Scribbling a formula, even a formula like that one, isn't a crime. We can't show yet that he did anything about it: everything that we know was done came through you. The lengths you went to suggest that it was more than an innocent doodle on the blackboard, but we may not be able to prove it. In which case the court will have to assume that you did what you did without help or encouragement. That may be less than fair to you, but it's how it's going to look."

Spalding was a tall, gracile man and he stretched out long legs towards Donnelly's desk. He said slowly, "I suppose it might look better if I co-operated with you now and helped you to round up those more culpable than myself."

"I'm sure it would."

His eyes came up then, glittering with amusement, and his thin lips broadened in a smile. "Superintendent, you've made a mistake. I had nothing to do with the crash. No-one I know had anything to do with the crash. The formula on the blackboard was a chemist's exercise, nothing more. Dr. Hehn and I have already co-operated as fully as we can. We have nothing to hide and nothing to be ashamed of. If you won't accept that, you must bring that catalogue of coincidence and misapprehension you call evidence in front of a jury and take their word for it. And if you want to discuss it any further you must charge me, because otherwise I have work to do."

Donnelly regarded him for a moment without expression. Then he pushed the telephone across the desk towards him. "Know any good lawyers, Mr. Spalding?"

The dog arrived home first. It scratched at the back door of the cottage and Flynn let it in. The police guard, who was a quiet-spoken, slightly stocky individual with a moustache, sighed as if life had succeeded in disappointing him yet again. His tone was as long-suffering as a missionary's at a cannibal feast. "Mr. Flynn, I really wish you'd let me open any doors that need opening."

Flynn cocked an eyebrow at him. "You think she's going to trick her way in here by scratching at the door and whimpering?" He looked at Flute with new respect. "Man, what a disguise!"

Sergeant Ferris said patiently, "The whole point, Mr. Flynn, is that we don't know what to expect of her. She's a professional, and surprise is how she does her job. And my job is stopping her. If you'll let me do it."

Flynn was magnanimous. "Sure I'll let you do it. I just don't propose being silly about it."

Ferris gave the patient little sigh another airing. "How about a deal? You don't open doors and I won't photograph nude women."

"*I* don't photograph nude women."

Ferris clucked his tongue sadly. "Now I know you're crazy." Flynn grinned.

The dog took a lap at its water, then pattered into the livingroom and inched into its favourite position under the couch. It gave one pant and laid its nose on its silky paws.

The same thought occurred to both men simultaneously. Flynn voiced it. "Where is she?"

Sergeant Ferris called Superintendent Donnelly and was told they were to do nothing—not go out looking for her, either together or separately, not try to leave the cottage, *nothing*—only stay out of sight behind locked doors until reinforcements arrived. Ferris agreed. Then he slammed the phone down and went racing after Flynn who was halfway down the garden path.

He was a solider man than Flynn, and his training involved compelling people to do things they did not want to do, and he had Flynn back in the kitchen and the kitchen door locked before Flynn knew he had been spotted.

Flynn stared at him as if he had gone mad. "What the holy hell do you think you're *doing?*"

The affectation of pedantry was gone as if it had never been. Ferris said briefly, "She's out there."

"Of course she's out there. The dog came back without her. Maybe she's fallen, sprained her ankle—I don't know. She can't be far away. We can't leave her lying there and do nothing."

"We're not doing nothing. I've called for support: they'll be here in fifteen minutes. Until then you do nothing, and I do my job."

"Support?" echoed Flynn. "Shimoni? I don't need help picking her up if she's broken both legs. I can tuck her under one arm. You could get three of her in a coal-sack."

Ferris said tersely, "I didn't mean Shimoni."

Then Flynn understood. The blood drained from his face. "You think—Laura . . . ?" The implications hit him like a train. "Dear God, you think she's got Leah!"

Ferris did not stand to talk about it. He was moving round, checking window catches and drawing curtains, locking doors and pocketing the keys. Mostly he used his left hand. This was not because he was left-handed: a .38 revolver nestled in a shoulder-holster under his left arm. Under his jacket it would not have shown but he was in his shirt-sleeves and it was as obvious as an extra limb. Even the way he moved, cat-footed and slightly sideways, was somehow dictated by the thing. It was impossible to ignore. Its presence filled the house.

Flynn stood numb in the centre of the livingroom pivoting on his heel as he turned to watch Ferris working. His eyes were round and uncomprehending. "What are you doing? We have to find Leah."

"No," said Ferris. His tone left no room for debate. "We stay here, and we stay down, until support arrives. Then we'll find her. We will: not you. Your job is staying alive."

"You really think she's here—out there? Laura?"

"I don't know. In fifteen minutes, once you're safe, I'll go and find out. If I find Miss Shimoni sat on the ground nursing a twisted ankle, so much the better—I don't mind being wrong, believe me. But if your friend is out there, it's for one reason only. Since before she can kill you she has to kill me, I have a vested interest in stopping her."

"But—how would she find me here?"

Ferris looked sceptical. "Your old partner's new partner's house? Even Watson would have found that one elementary."

"So what's she waiting for?"

"She's waiting," the policeman explained patiently, "for one or both of us to go out looking for Shimoni."

Slowly Flynn's stunned wits were beginning to function again. "You shouldn't have pulled the curtains. Now she knows we're onto her, and she'll guess reinforcements are on the way."

"If I hadn't drawn the curtains, sooner or later she'd have got a shot at you through the window."

"So what now?"

"I told you, nothing. We wait."

"Not us, her. What will she do now?"

Ferris looked away. "I don't know."

"Yes you do," snarled Flynn, "because I do and it's not even my frigging job. She'll try to draw us out into the open. She'll use Leah. She'll hurt Leah."

"Fifteen minutes," Ferris said forcibly. "Nearer ten now. That's all the time we have to stick it. Whatever she does, we only have to do nothing for ten minutes."

"You can do a lot of hurting in ten minutes," said Flynn, who knew. "If Leah Shimoni starts screaming, I'm going out there if I have to go head-first through the kitchen window."

"You'd be dead before you hit the ground. She came here to kill you, to complete her contract, and if you give her even the shadow of a chance that's what she'll do."

"I don't care," shouted Flynn. It was not true so he said it again. "Don't you understand? I don't care any more. She's going to get me sometime, it might as well be now. But nobody else is doing my hurting and dying for me. Not any more. Two hundred and twenty people are dead, and Gil Todd's got a fractured skull, and now if Leah Shimoni's going to be hurt too—" He let out a ragged breath. "They can have charmed lives as want them. Honest to Christ, I'd as soon take a bullet right now and goodnight."

"That's not your choice," Ferris insisted. "The people who did these things will get away with them if you don't testify. And sooner or later they're going to find themselves in another tight spot, and they're going to take the same way out. It's easier the second time round. People will be hurt then, people will die, and their deaths will be your fault in a way that nothing which has happened so far has been. Is that what you want?—to let men like rabid dogs go free? You think your conscience is going to be clearer for that?"

Flynn did not believe in an after-life: hell held no fears for him. He shook his head. "I'm sorry. I've done all I can about that. There's nothing more I can do to stop them, or make them pay. All the choice I have now is between trying to save Leah or letting her suffer for me as well. Let me tell you something about guilt: it stinks. I'm not carrying any more of it round with me."

"I'm sorry too," said Ferris, and the gun was in his hand as if it had grown there, the muzzle levelled at Flynn's chest. "This is my job. It is also, thank God, the right thing to do. Sit down, Flynn, you're not going anywhere."

Flynn's eyes recoiled from the gun. But he stayed where he was and kept looking at it, and after long seconds he slowly nodded. "That'll do. If you do it or if she does, it's no odds. As long as she knows. If you kill me, you'll have to tell her. Show her." All the courage in his heart would not have been enough without also the despair in his soul. He went to the kitchen window and opened the curtains, and stood long and still in the square of sunlight.

Ferris could no more shoot Flynn than he could have sawn his head off. He put his weapon aside and tackled him from behind, and the two men crashed to the kitchen floor as the centre of the window-pane sprang an unexpected leak. Fragments of glass showered them. Neither of them noticed.

Ferris had learned the art of subduing a violent man at police college and subsequently on the streets of the capital. But Flynn had learned to street-fight on the New York waterfront, with the advantage that he was not called upon to explain over-enthusiasm. He had fought for fun, for fear and for his life. More than once he had kept fighting with his eyes full of his own blood because he knew if he went down he would be trampled to death. Flynn used his knees and elbows in ways not sanctioned by the police manual.

All the same, the result was still at issue as they rolled, locked together, across Shimoni's kitchen floor, panting hot breath in each other's faces, raining hard blows on each other's ribs, with no enmity between them only a quite different perception of social responsibility.

The turning point came when Flynn, reeling from a telling assault on that side of his face which took all the punishment, remembered he was armed with a weapon Ferris could not take from him. He used it at the first opportunity. Ferris knocked him sprawling against the washing-machine, then yanked him up to hit him again. As they came together the heavy plaster at the end of Flynn's long right arm swung in a powerful trajectory from an unexpected angle and struck Ferris in the temple like a brick.

At once all the fight went out of him. His hands fell away from Flynn, his knees buckled and Flynn, moaning with the pain of his healing hand, caught him as he folded and lowered him carefully to the carpet. Ferris was unconscious before he got there.

Flynn rolled him gently from side to side, emptying his pockets. When he found the key of the kitchen door he fumbled it into the lock and turned it. He paused then, long enough to take a deep breath—maybe deep enough to last him the rest of his life—and then he opened the door and stepped outside.

5

Policemen had been in and out of Deering Pharmaceuticals all day. Detectives, photographers, forensic scientists: if they were not quizzing Mr. Spalding's secretary they were browbeating Dr. Hehn's assistants, and if they were doing neither they were going through the accounts with a magnifying glass or the stores with a fine-tooth comb.

At first the occasional polite visits of Superintendent Donnelly and his sergeant had been accepted at face value, as routine police work aimed at eliminating lines of enquiry. As time went on, though, those with a finger on the pulse of Deerings—people like the commissionaire and the tea-ladies—reckoned that routine enquiry had turned to something more specific, and identified Dr. Hehn's laboratory as the focus of interest. By now even the board of directors knew something was afoot, their senior research chemist was the butt of increasingly impertinent questioning by the police and now their PR executive was assisting with their enquiries instead of liaising with the Sondheim committee in order to get the best mileage out of the imminent prize-giving.

The drama had divided opinion at Deerings. One camp held it a malicious campaign of lies and rumour against a prominent and highly respected scientist, almost certainly prompted by jealous rivals. The other considered it no more than a company might expect which allowed itself to become dominated by foreigners and ex-public school boys. Neither group enjoyed the disruption the police caused to the even tenor of the pharmaceutical season though the latter resented it less than the former.

And neither saw any percentage in trying to obstruct the police. Indeed, the board had sent down an urgent circular that the enquiry was to receive full co-operation from every department; and that being done, retired behind closed doors to find out what had happened, what was happening now, what they should have known about it, what they actually knew about it and what they should admit to knowing about it.

The result was that when another man in a raincoat walked past reception with a nod and the single word "Police," no attempt was made to hinder him or to check the contents of his briefcase. When he asked directions to Dr. Hehn's laboratory he received the fullest co-operation.

Shimoni's back garden was the size of a pocket-handkerchief and filled with lupins and foxgloves and other refugees from a Victorian sampler. A low stone wall surrounded it, broached by a narrow gate opening onto a footpath that ran towards a little spinney a hundred yards from the cottage. It was the obvious place to walk a dog, or set an ambush. Flynn closed the garden gate behind him and turned towards it.

He found himself walking quietly, almost on tip-toe, which was absurd. She knew he was there, she was expecting him. If he was too long coming she might get impatient and take steps to hurry him. He did not want that. He forced a little extra length into his stride. He sucked in some air to whistle with but lacked the control necessary to produce a recognisable tune. All that emerged was the thin piping of a hungry fledgeling, so he stopped. If he could not face death with careless laughter on his lips, at least he need not go out sounding like the village idiot.

He had no idea what to expect: Laura, or a bullet out of the blue that would take him before he knew it. He tried not to think: not about dying, not about the two hundred and twenty people who had already died and whose deaths would now go unavenged, not about the rightness or otherwise of the choice he had made. He made himself believe that Shimoni would be all right now, that Laura—Elizabeth Baron, rather—was too professional to kill someone she was not being paid for. Beyond that his only ambition was to somehow find the nerve, or the determination, or just the hopeless obstinacy to keep putting one foot in front of the other until something came to stop him.

He came to the trees and stepped into their greenly dappled shade. The murmur of air moving gently through the leaves was a susurrus, like voices. It masked the sound of movement, even his own. He stayed on the path, worn by generations of yokel feet, because that would be what she expected, where she would look for him. Mostly he resisted the urge to look for her. If she wanted him to see her, she would ensure that he did; if not, she would blow his head apart before he knew she was there.

He thought she would go for the head shot. It was the professional thing to do. Or she might fell him with a body shot and move in for the coup de grace. He hoped, he believed, that she would not make it longer or harder than it had to be. He just wished now that she would finish it, before his modest impression of a brave man came apart at the seams. If he had known a prayer he might have said it; but the only thing that came to mind was "For what we are about to receive" which did not seem altogether appropriate.

One moment there was the dappled sunlight falling at his feet and the murmur of dryad voices above his head, and the next she was there, in front of him, almost close enough to touch, a long slender figure barring his way with a revolver cupped in her two hands.

Flynn started visibly and had taken a step back before he could conquer the urge to run like hell. He felt the sweat break over him like a fever. He looked at the gun. He was not a connoisseur, could not judge the calibre except that it might have been about the same size as Sergeant Ferris's. She also held it the same way. The muzzle was pointing down but there was never the faintest hope in Flynn's mind that he could do anything faster than she could take her aim and fire.

Her face in the dim place was darkly luminous. Under the partly lowered lids her eyes shone—not with tears, but he thought not with gladness either. She said softly, "Hello, Mickey."

He found it hard to speak. The beauty of her filled him up as it always had. Even now he could not think of her as an evil woman. Amoral, perhaps. He found a voice no-one, except maybe Todd, would have recognised. "Shimoni?"

"She's all right. I had to tie her up. They'll find her when—when they come looking."

"Let me see her."

"There isn't time, Mickey," she said gently. "The police will be here soon. I have to be away by then. She's all right, I promise you."

"You kill—" His voice broke. "You killed two hundred and twenty people. Why?"

She shrugged fractionally, like a tiny shudder running along her shoulders. "It's my job. It's what I do."

"You killed a plane-load of people! I loved you, and you blew a plane out of the sky because you thought I was on it!"

"Because your negatives were on it," she corrected him patiently. "Mickey, I never wanted to hurt you. I was glad you weren't on board. I'd have been happy to leave it like that. But when it turned out that sparing you was going to cost my clients their freedom—well, that didn't leave me much choice, did it? In this line of work, either your first loyalty goes with the fee or the fees stop coming. I'm sorry it has to end like this."

"*Sorry—?!!!*" The word burst from him. She might have been apologising for some minor lapse of fealty, like going to a party with him and leaving with someone else. She was going to kill him, and like a nicely brought-up young woman she was expressing her regrets first. The breath panted in his throat. He felt an hysterical urge to laugh. His eyes on her glowing face were wild; the memory of her strongly yielding body swamped his mind.

Under the lowered lids her eyes held a kindly curiosity. Her finely sculpted head tilted a little to one side. "Are you afraid?"

More than ever he wanted to laugh, but could not or dared not. He had his nerve on the thinnest of leashes: any additional pressure would break it. "What do you think?"

"I won't hurt you," she promised; she seemed quite serious. "It'll be over so quickly you won't know a thing."

She did not ask him to turn round: she moved round him where he stood. He waited. His nerves screamed in the mute stillness of his skin. He screwed his eyes tight and stopped breathing. He waited for his head to explode.

The single gunshot sent every bird in the spinney rocketing into the sky, and the sound of their rising all but swallowed the muffled thump of a body's soft falling.

The man with the briefcase thanked the girl who showed him to Hehn's office, tapped on the door and walked in. He told Hehn's secretary that he was here to speak to the doctor and no, there was no need to bring him in from the laboratory. Seeing the unmistakable monolithic outline against the glass, he let himself in at the connecting door without waiting for an invitation.

By nothing more meaningful than a coincidence he found Hehn working alone. In a way that was convenient, although his business extended also to Hehn's associates. He put his briefcase on a handy worktop, unlatched it and lifted the lid. He was a careful man and so he checked his facts before proceeding. "You are Dr. Dieter Hehn"— he read out an address in Mayfair—"senior research chemist at Deering Pharmaceuticals?"

Hehn stared at him. The accent was surprising: you do not expect English policemen to be anything other than English. But there was no mistaking that liturgy, it was the prelude to an arrest. He drew in a slow breath, using the time to think. He was a big square man with big square lungs and the breath seemed never-ending. The man with the briefcase waited patiently.

Finally Hehn said, "I am. But I would like my lawyer to hear anything else you have to say." He moved towards the telephone extension by the blackboard.

"I'm sure you would, sir," the other man said politely. "But don't worry, he'll know all there is to know very soon."

Hehn looked back at him, puzzled by his words and irritated by his presence but not worried, not yet. He knew his value to Deerings. He knew that those in the upper echelons who had known the nature of his special project, the one that had nothing to do with antibiotics, would mortgage their company cars and stake their pensions to keep him at liberty and at work; and those who had known nothing, quickly realising that their cars and pensions too were on the line, would do the same.

Six months from today Dr. Hehn confidently expected the drama to be over, the threat of prosecution averted by one means or another, the police advised firmly that they had been humoured long enough and should now pursue their enquiries elsewhere. At that point Dr. Hehn expected to be offered a new establishment in a different part of the Deering empire where he could return to the project that had absorbed him these nine months and which he had been on the brink of completing when the exciting, ill-timed news of the Sondheim Prize came through.

Three months after that he confidently expected Deerings—obviously, not under its own name—to have cornered the market with its cheap (but still seriously profitable) cocaine substitute. Once the formula—the one that lived now only in his head, evolving and developing there like a foetus approaching term—once that was right, it could be manufactured on a cottage-industry scale anywhere there was water and electricity. Manufacture close to point-of-sale would eliminate the need for dangerous smuggling. The advantages of local manufacture over the importing of cocaine grown in Central America were, like the potential pay-off, colossal. As a commercial venture, as an achievement of chemistry, it was a breakthrough of global proportions and Hehn was proud of his work.

And from an ethical point of view? No-one had ever paid Dieter Hehn to make moral judgements, and in the absence of such an incentive whatever natural inclination he might once have had to do good in the world withered and died. The prospect of profiting from drug addiction troubled him no more than the human cost of destroying that unfortunate photograph. He had not arranged that, Spalding had, but it had seemed to him a reasonable response to a serious danger. The element of overkill had simply not occurred to him.

Nor had the idea that he would not ultimately be free to continue with his work. He knew it might take a little time. He knew it might cost Deerings something in legal, and other, expenses. But he had thought that all it really needed was for Spalding and himself to hold their tongues in the face of whatever that colourless, clever policeman might throw at them; and he knew he could, and he was pretty sure about Spalding.

That was when he turned back from the phone, puzzled and irritated but still not worried, and saw the gun that the man in the raincoat had drawn from his briefcase.

He had time to notice the curious bulbous sheath on the short barrel. He may have had time to register the soft flat cough that was the only sound to emerge from the silencer. Whether or not, he still looked surprised when he fell over, taking the blackboard with him, and by then he was already dead.

The secretary in the office heard the clatter of the falling board, not the gunshot, and started to her feet. She could not see Hehn for the furniture between them and the blackboard over him, but she could see the man in the raincoat doing something under the lid of his briefcase. Then he closed the lid and came back into the office, leaving the briefcase behind.

He said calmly, almost conversationally, "Dr. Hehn is dead. I've left an incendiary device in the laboratory—no, don't think of touching it, no-one else need get hurt. You've five minutes to clear this floor, a little longer to clear the building. I think you should start now." He pressed a slip of card into her hand. "Give that to—someone," he added vaguely. Then he left.

Someone said, "You can open your eyes now." If he had not known better Flynn would have thought it was Fahad. Fahad as St. Peter?—he hardly thought so. It seemed to suggest he was still alive.

He was not only still alive, he was still vertical. If Laura—he could not think of her by any other name—had shot him in the head, or anywhere else, even if it had not killed him it would have knocked him down. He considered with almost scientific detachment the fact that the great crash of sound which had sent his heart lurching into his rib-cage and a consequent spasm through the length of his body had not been accompanied by the physical shock that a man experienced on being shot. Was it conceivable that, from a range of inches rather than feet, she had missed him?

He cranked one eye open a slit. It was Fahad's voice he had heard. The little Arab was standing in front of him, looking up at him and softly, not unkindly, laughing. It occurred to Flynn, in the last of these surreal moments before his soul properly returned to the body it had half thought itself finished with, that for a man who had caused him fear and pain and tried to take his life, Fahad had always treated him kindly.

He croaked, "What—?"

"—happened?" Fahad smiled, his eyes brilliant with triumph. "A moment before she could shoot you, Mr. Flynn, I shot her."

"Laura?" He lurched round, long legs twisting.

She lay on her back in the leaf-mould, her legs crossed at the knees and her arms flung out as if Fahad's bullet had taken her down spinning. Her gun lay in the litter a few inches beyond her open right hand, the oddly pale palm uppermost. Her eyes were closed, her lips parted on the gleam of white teeth. Blood drenched her left side in a semi-circle as if a shark had bitten at her waist. Pale dapples of light through the canopy played over her still form.

Nothing in Flynn's experience, which had been liberal, equipped him to deal with the violent death of a woman he had loved in the moment she was preparing to kill him. He still went weak in the presence of her beauty. Of course he knew differently, but some part of him was still struggling to believe it had been a misunderstanding, a tragic mistake, that she was still the Laura Wade who had taken possession of him in his heart and in his bed. In spite of everything he needed to hold her. He sank to his knees beside her.

Fahad's iron grip on his arm pulled him to his feet, dragged him back to reality. "The other one needs you more."

"Shimoni?" Unforgivably, Flynn had forgotten about her. "Is she all right?"

"Oh yes. A black eye, a cut lip, maybe rope-burns on her wrists— nothing more. But she'll be anxious to know who's dead and who's alive." Fahad left the track and led the way into the wood.

Still weak-kneed, Flynn could not keep pace with him. He stumbled and Fahad waited patiently for him to pick himself up. But for a moment Flynn stayed where he was, crouching among the tree-roots, looking up at the Palestinian. His eyes held a desperate ache. His voice was low and rough. "I don't understand. How. Or why."

"How?" Fahad showed small white teeth in a vulpine grin. "How was easy. I did what she did: tried your flat, then Mr. Todd's, then Mr. Todd's partner's. Without leaving written directions you could hardly have made it easier."

"The police were going to move me someplace else tonight."

"Tonight would have been too late."

"Ain't that the truth." Flynn got up, dusting leaves and moss from his clothes. For a man who cared little about his appearance, he was aware that he always met Fahad at a sartorial disadvantage. "Then why?"

"I told you. She was getting terrorism a bad name."

The muscles tightened in Flynn's face. "Damn you, Fahad, answer me!"

Fahad took a step back in mock alarm. "Breath of the Prophet, it bites!"

"Why? I have to know."

The Arab relented. "Not for you; not really. I did tell you: she was going to get me killed. My people were being blamed for the bomb on Flight 98, and some of my people were blaming me. It was necessary, if I wished to continue working or indeed living, to prove them wrong. If she had killed you, that proof would have been hard to come by. Also, no-one will say she was working for me now I have killed her. I can go home now."

"You knew she was coming here?"

Fahad shrugged elegantly. "It seemed a safe bet. We move, after all, in interlocking circles: when I learned she was back in London, I guessed why. I found you and waited for her to find you too. There was no certainty of being able to save you—she was, after all, a professional—but even if she killed you, my position would be safeguarded when I killed her. Forgive me, but that was my main consideration. I don't very much care what you people do to one another, but I have a nation to create and your antics were keeping me from doing it. Now I can get back to something that matters."

"You're a bastard, Fahad," Flynn said with certainty.

Fahad sniffed. "You Westerners are so emotional." He turned away, peering into the trees, and nodded. "There."

Shimoni was tied to a tree in the time-honoured manner of romantic fiction heroines. Admittedly, on close inspection there was a degree of bruising, not to mention puffiness, down one side of her face that most leading ladies would have considered unnecessarily authentic, and the handkerchief stuffed in her mouth for a gag was more effective than attractive too.

Still, the comparison just about hung together until Flynn gently eased the gag past her broken lips while Fahad cut her free. Then she issued a string of blasphemy and invective in three languages that surprised and impressed Flynn and actually made Fahad blush.

Mainly it was a way of releasing tension. She had been very frightened, for herself at first, then for Flynn as it became clear that the woman with the gun had no interest in killing her, only using her, and every intention of killing him. She had seemed so professional, so calm and unruffled, almost more mechanical than methodical, that Shimoni could not imagine her being thwarted, at least not by the impetuous emotional hagridden Flynn and the dogged Sergeant Ferris. She knew nothing of Fahad's presence in the spinney. When she heard the shot that sent all the birds clamouring for the sky, she believed as if she knew it that Flynn's soul was soaring with them and his body was just so much bloody rubbish littering the spinney floor.

At that an unexpected grief surged through her, and a bone-shaking rage, and after that an awareness of her own part in his destruction. She could not know that he had left the relative safety of her house in full consciousness of what was waiting for him, an act of sacrifice rather than one of carelessness; but she knew that Ferris would have guessed if Flynn had not, and Ferris would have made sure he understood the likely cost of her redemption. At the shot which she believed ended his life, Shimoni cried out—inaudibly, because of the gag, but from the anguished depths of her spirit. Not the least part of the horror was that she would have to tell Todd how he had died.

When he wandered through the trees towards her, dazed and decorated with leaf-mould yet not only alive but essentially unhurt, relief and disbelief had tried to turn her inside out so that she would have exploded had she not found some outlet for the towering emotions raging within her. So she swore, and she struck at Flynn wildly with her numb fists, and then she collapsed in stormy tears and he gathered her to him as if she were an overwrought child. She spent the worst of her distress against Flynn's chest, with his chin resting on top of her head.

Fahad cleared his throat. "Your police will be here any time: I must be on my way."

Flynn's eyes had cleared a lot in the last few minutes. He shook his head fractionally. "I don't know that I understand it any better now. But, thanks."

Fahad raised a neat hand in salute, smiling impishly. "Stick to photography. You lack the aptitude for intrigue." Chuckling to himself, he turned away and left them and headed back towards the track, a small middle-aged man in a tweed jacket walking with the loose stride of his desert forebears through an English wood.

Thereafter things happened quickly. A sudden snatch of two-tone music beyond the cottage announced the arrival of police cars. Fahad broke his stride and looked up the track and then rapidly back to where Flynn was still standing with Shimoni in the compass of his long arms. He shouted something they could not make out, and dropped into a crouch and was pulling at his pocket when, shockingly close, a shot rang out. It picked Fahad up and flung him momentarily into the air, and then threw him down among the roots like a bundle of old clothes that had never contained a human being.

Then, before Flynn could unfreeze his muscles enough to relax his grip on Shimoni, another figure moved among the trees scant yards to his right, and Laura Wade stepped into the open, her gun cradled carefully in both hands. She said quietly, "I think he was warning you about me."

6

Flynn had thought she was dead and clearly she was not. But he had not imagined the blood. Her clothes were heavy with it all down her left side. It still pumped, thick and slow, from entry and exit wounds at her waist, six inches apart and neatly transected by the side-seam of her shirt. Her eyes under the lowered lids were deep with shock and her skin had lost its roseate glow. Only sheer determination—professionalism—was keeping her on her feet.

Incredibly, Flynn was moved to help her. It had to be his hormones thinking: he knew what she was there for. He started to put Shimoni behind him. "Laura, let me—"

Professionals do not jerk their guns. They do not do anything with them except fire them. Laura's gun remained where it was, rock-steady on the centre of Flynn's face; her eyes flicked at him instead. "Stay where you are, Mickey." The breath was catching in her throat. Cramping pain in her left side kept her from drawing the long, slow, deep breaths she needed. That did not matter with him being so close. She could put the bullet through the pupil of his eye at this range.

Flynn could not believe that she meant to go on with this. "Laura, that's the police. Let me get them. They'll have you in a hospital in ten minutes, you'll be all right."

And Laura Wade could not believe that, after everything that had happened to and around and because of him, he was still such an innocent. She shook her head minutely. Then she said slowly, enunciating clearly, "Mickey, I have to kill you."

He stared at her, still without any real comprehension. He jerked a hand towards the cottage. "They'll be here in a minute. They'll hear the gun. The state you're in, you can't make a run for it. You'll—"

"Go to jail?" She smiled, half amused and half malicious. "Not for killing you I won't. Killing you won't cost me an extra day, not an extra hour. For bombing an airliner with two hundred and twenty people on board they'll give me the maximum they can. You might rate a line on the charge-sheet, in the interests of tidying up, but they can't actually do anything to me for killing you. A line of type is all your life is worth."

Shimoni believed her. "Oh no," she said in a low voice. Then she said it again, and again, and the pitch of her voice rose until she was screaming it in an insane litany while Flynn, shaken, held her by the arms to stop her throwing herself at the woman with the gun. "Oh no, oh no, oh no, oh no, oh no!"

"Leah. Leah!" Flynn bent down to look her in the face. "Listen. I think maybe Laura and I can work this out. If we can just have a bit of time alone. Will you do that for me? Will you find Donnelly and have him keep his distance while we get something sorted? Laura, what do you say—is that OK?"

Wade had moved a little to put a tree at her back and seemed to be leaning on it. Her grip on the gun was unaffected. She shrugged negligently. "Sure. She can go."

"Mickey, she means to kill you!" Shimoni's eyes were wild, not with hysteria but with a very real appreciation of what was happening.

He shook his head to reassure her. "I know what she said. It isn't going to happen. Laura and me— Well, she isn't going to kill me. Unless Donnelly barges in here and forces her hand. Will you stop him?"

She was unconvinced. He had left her no option. She snatched a glance at the older woman, hating her.

Flynn misinterpreted the look. "She won't hurt you. Will you, Laura?" Wade smiled remotely and shook her head. "Go on. Go now." He pushed her firmly towards the track, the shapeless bulk of Fahad's body marking the way. The second step she took alone, hesitantly, looking back. Then she began to run.

When they were alone Wade said, her voice slowing to a drawl, "You don't believe that, do you?—that I'll let you live because we were good in bed. That really would be too naive."

Flynn shrugged. "I don't know what to expect of you any more. I just wanted her away from here."

Lazily she grinned. "Are you in love again, Mickey?"

That stung like a slap in the face, because he had been and plainly she had not, not even for a moment. His jaw came up pugnaciously. "Isn't it female spiders that use their mates and then eat them? The Black Widow—that's where she got her name. Come on then, spider lady, do what you came here for."

Wade's mouth twitched amiably. Her strength was leaching out with the blood coursing down her side. It was sapping her aggression, making her tolerant. Soon she would be too weak to finish the job, complete her last contract. She knew it would be the last contract, and it was important to her—to her self-esteem—to get it right. She had taken money to destroy the photograph that incriminated her clients and more to destroy the photographer.

She held no grudge against Flynn for being the job that killed her— for she had no intention of going to prison, if Fahad's bullet would not rescue her she would save one of her own to do it. But her last contract could not be considered fulfilled until he was dead. It was as simple as that. She could not afford to take a personal view. He was outstanding business to be finished, a loose end to be tied.

She said, "I don't think I can move from this tree. It'll be pleasanter for both of us if you'll turn round."

When there was no answer at the front door Donnelly hurried round the house looking at the curtained windows. But at the kitchen window the curtains had been pulled back and he saw Sergeant Ferris, just beginning to stir on the floor as his wits trickled back from wher- ever Flynn's plaster fist had despatched them. Donnelly went to knock down the back door but found it unlocked and flung it open.

He shouted Flynn's name and Shimoni's without response, checked the bedrooms and found no-one. He tugged Ferris more or less upright against the washing-machine and held a wet towel—he did not know it was the dog's—against his face, and called him back to explain what he knew of what had happened.

Then one of his men called him outside and pointed, and over the low garden wall he saw a figure running towards them out of the margins of the little wood. He knew it was not Flynn; a moment later he recognised Shimoni and hurried to meet her.

Her face was swollen, her eyes red-rimmed. She was panting with distress and effort so that she could hardly speak. There were twigs in her hair and on her clothes. Donnelly caught her by the arms. "What is it? Where's Flynn?"

She thrust a shaking hand back the way she had come. Her hair fell in her face. Her voice surged uncontrollably with the suck of her lungs. "In there. With her. She's going to kill him."

Donnelly's eyes sharpened. "Laura Wade? Is she armed?" It was a foolish question but he needed confirmation.

"She killed Fahad. Fahad shot her, and she killed him. Now she's going to shoot Mickey."

Taken aback, Donnelly blinked. "Fahad's here?"

"Damn Fahad," cried Shimoni. "She's going to kill Mickey! He thinks he can talk her out of it if you'll stay away but he can't. She let me go because I was in the way—she's hurt, she couldn't be sure of covering us both—but she isn't going to let him go whatever he says. She's going to die here—Fahad's bullet or one of yours or maybe her own, I don't know but she's not going to walk away—she'll finish this job because it'll be the last thing she does. For God's sake, do something!"

He stared at her a moment longer. She almost saw cogs spinning in his grey eyes. Then he thrust her into other hands. "Perhaps. Or perhaps I can change her mind." Then, calling for a marksman and, inexplicably, a radio, he started for the spinney at a run.

Flynn would not turn his back. He doubted that it would make much difference to him whether the bullet went through his face or the back of his head, and he was not concerned to make it pleasanter for his murderer.

She was dying on her feet. The blood had soaked all the way down her trouser leg and was pooling in the dirt at her foot. Flynn might have drawn some hope from the certainty that she must soon pass out, except for the other certainty that the last thing she would do as she felt her grip slipping was blow his brain out. She was a professional. She would not leave it a moment longer than she could afford to.

She would also kill him, right away, if anyone else came near them or if he made a move towards her gun. He knew that, close as they were, there was nothing he could do—not reach her, not run or dive for cover—faster than she could send on its way the bullet with his name on it. One would be all it would take, and she would fire at the first sign of interference because she would not be confident of seeing the second.

Flynn did not know if he had any real hope of coming through this, but if he had an ally it was time. There was not much he could do, but he could avoid making it easier for her. Forcing himself to move slowly he folded his long body like a deck-chair and went down cross-legged to the ground. He bridged his arms across his knees and looked up at her. He wondered if she could see that he was trembling. He wondered if she would be pleased or dismayed or indifferent if she knew how sick-to-his-stomach scared of her he was. The Black Widow. But it had been more than mere professionalism she had brought to his bed. It had been pleasure.

He said shakily, "I don't see why you couldn't write me a Dear John like anybody else."

She laughed at that, weakly, but it made her cough and coughing hurt. She wiped her mouth with the hand that did not hold her gun. "I couldn't see us resolving custody of the stuffed parrot." He had won it for her, ironically enough, at a shooting gallery.

They smiled together, almost like friends. Then Flynn said, very quietly, "Oh God, Laura, don't do this."

There was surprise, even disappointment, in her glance. She had not expected him to beg. "Sorry, Mickey. Your life has been bought and paid for."

"Not from anyone with the right to sell it," he retorted. "OK, you're good at your job: I know it, now everybody's going to know it. You don't need my hide on the wall to prove it."

She was getting tired, too tired to want this conversation, too tired to be trying to explain it to him. She thought every moment—so did he—that she would bring it to its inevitable end. But actually she wanted more from him than just his life: she wanted his company as well. She was not afraid to die, but there was loneliness in the waiting. Flynn who had known her, who had cared for her, who said he loved her, was better company for these last minutes than she might have hoped for. If he could not see it out to the end with her, he could stay by her most of the way. She would know when he had come far enough.

So she talked to him instead of killing him, and she knew that her voice was beginning to slur and her eyes to slip out of focus; and she knew too, as surely as if she had it in writing, that the last faculty she would be left with would be her accuracy with the gun. There was time yet.

She said patiently, "It's not a question of proof. It's— Given the choice, you'd go out with a world exclusive in your camera, yes? It's the same thing. They can say I got killed, but as long as you die first they can't ever say I got beaten."

"Neither of us has to die. There are other options."

"Not for me," she said with conviction. "And therefore not for you either."

Donnelly heard them before he saw them, and slowed right down, signalling the marksman away to his left to do the same. Another step or two and he saw Flynn, hunched cross-legged on the ground a little like a thin Buddha and a little like a stick-insect.

Flynn saw him at the same moment and could not keep the mingled hope and fear out of his eyes, and Laura Wade—despite her own dulling senses—saw them and saw the policeman reflected as in a mirror. With startling agility in view of the amount of her blood soaking into the ground, she pushed herself off the tree supporting her, crossed the line of his vision quicker than Donnelly could have reacted even had he been armed, and dropped into a crouch behind Flynn, protected by his body at the front and a hundred-year-old beech bole behind.

Unless she saw him moving the marksman might have drawn a bead on her from the side but it was always going to be a risky shot. It became an impossible one when she fisted her left hand in Flynn's hair and dragged his head back onto her shoulder, and pressed the muzzle of her gun into the gullet behind his jaw. He could not believe how strong she still was. Sweat broke over him in a wave.

"If you kill me stone dead with the first shot," she remarked conversationally, "I'll still blow his head off."

Donnelly froze to the spot where he stood and hoped his marksman would have the sense to do the same. He said, with a nice admixture of calm and urgency, "Miss Baron, there is no need for anyone else to die. More than that, there is no point in anyone else dying—not him, not you. It's over. The secret your clients bought protection for no longer exists. Dr. Hehn is dead. The synthetic cocaine formula he was working on died with him. Even if there was a record of it somewhere, it's almost certainly been destroyed: his office and his laboratory have been gutted. That entire floor of the Deerings building is alight, and the Fire Brigade don't rate their chances of saving the rest of it. You no longer have a client to consider."

"What happened?" So he told her. She shook the cloud of dark hair, disbelieving. "You're lying. You think you can fool me. You think you can save his skin by fooling me." She pushed the muzzle into Flynn's throat sharply enough to cut off his air. "You're wrong."

"It's the truth," Donnelly insisted. "I don't altogether understand it myself, but it is the truth. I can prove it. I brought a radio."

It took him half a minute's increasingly desperate hunting through the airwaves to find a news broadcast, and when he did it was rattling on about the balance of trade and what the Chancellor of the Exchequer said to the Foreign Secretary and what the Foreign Secretary said back. Then there was the momentary hiatus heralding the radio equivalent of a Stop Press, which is when the producer slides an incoming report in front of the news-reader on air.

Then, with the unperturbability under fire characteristic of her kind, she read out the first account of a major fire in progress in the City of London. Early reports from the scene were that the fire at Deering Pharmaceuticals was started deliberately with an incendiary device. Although most employees had escaped, it was believed that there were casualties including Deerings' senior research chemist Dr. Dieter Hehn, recipient of this year's Sondheim Prize for his work on antibiotics.

When the news-reader returned to her schedule with a story about a drunk and disorderly footballer, Donnelly turned the radio off. In the little wood the sounds of the twentieth century had seemed intrusive; now they were gone the silence stretched and crawled.

Donnelly said quietly, "You see? It's all over. There's nothing left for you to do."

"Who did it?" she asked. "A bomb? Who'd bomb Deerings?"

"I don't know. Yet. We're working on it."

"And Hehn's dead? No. You arranged this with the radio-station, to fool me."

Donnelly was aware of her eyes on him, watching for his response. He was deeply impressed by her ability to reason like that in her current state. He shook his head. "That sort of thing takes time to set up. I only knew you were here twenty minutes ago. I didn't know what I'd find here until I arrived just now. I was already on my way when I heard about the fire. Hehn's dead all right. He was shot, and then his laboratory was blown up round him."

"Who else?"

Donnelly did not know what she meant. "Who else what?"

"Who else is dead?" So there were others at Deerings she was pledged to protect, not just the formula and its creator.

Superintendent Donnelly was an honest man. It was why he had been attracted to a career in law enforcement. He believed that honesty was not so much the best as the only policy for an honourable man. He did not fiddle his income tax. He did not speed his car except where demanded by the public interest. He had never in his life attempted to travel free on public transport.

He was, however, perfectly capable of lying like a trooper. He listed, without a flicker of conscience crossing his face, all the people he hoped she might be interested in. "Most of the people who were with him half an hour ago. His secretary, who tried to stop the intruder. Two of his assistants, a man and a woman. The company's PR executive, Byron Spalding—"

Laura Wade let out a breath like a sigh. "I see." She still held Flynn bent like a bow with her knee in his back and her gun in his throat. But slowly some of the tension drained away. She released her grasp of his hair, absent-mindedly patting it back into place more like a mother than a murderer. She lowered the gun so that he could breathe while she was thinking. Finally she pushed him, quite gently, from her.

He fell forward onto his hands and knees, and as quickly as he could he twisted round so that he could see her. He was still not sure if she meant to shoot him.

She smiled at him, quite kindly. "He's right. There's no point going any further with this. I'm not going to kill you to protect dead men's reputations." She looked pensively at the gun she had withdrawn from his gullet. "I suppose you want this." She turned it in her hand and offered it butt first, not to Donnelly who had never been closer than a dozen yards away but to Flynn.

He regarded it for a moment with fear and loathing. Then, reluctantly, still on his knees in front of her, he reached out to take it.

Her smile broadened as if she had played a clever trick on him. " 'Bye, Mickey." As his unencumbered left hand closed on the figured stock her fingers straightened the barrel and one slipped inside the trigger-guard and pushed. Without violence, without haste; with just enough pressure against the resistance of Flynn's hand to do the job. She was looking all the way up the barrel when the hammer fell.

7

Donnelly found time, or rather made time in the flurry of activity that filled the following days, to collect Todd from the hospital. Shimoni would have gone, was looking forward to going, but when the time came she could not leave Flynn. Not that she could do much with him, or for him. She just felt strongly that he should not be left alone.

When they were on their way and Donnelly addressing himself to the London traffic, Todd said quietly, "How is he?"

The policeman kept his eyes on the road. "He's in trouble," he said honestly. "I want him to see a psychiatrist, but he won't and I can't make him. It would be better if he'd done something I could arrest him for, at least then I could make sure he got some help to deal with this, but he hasn't and I can't. Leah's been terrific with him—*she* got over it like a dog shaking rain out of its coat—but it's not enough. God knows he needs his friends, but he needs professional help too. I think without it he's going to fall apart."

"Is he drinking?"

"Oh yes."

It was how he was drinking that chilled Shimoni to the heart. She had seen people go on blinders before, done it a couple of times herself—to dull a hurt or draw a veil over something she wanted to forget. She had not found it much of a solution: when she surfaced the hurt and the memory were still there, still waiting for her to come to terms with them, and her head ached and her skin looked like socks washed in Brand X as well. But if others found a passing comfort in it enough to compensate for consequences as inevitable as a flung stone's falling, Shimoni was not one to object on moral grounds.

But that was the kind of drinking she was familiar with, the kind of drinking Israeli soldiers did after failing to find an honourable way of waging war on Palestinian children directed against them like missiles. She had never seen anyone drink like this before: steadily and savagely, not merely without enjoyment but as if the stuff was creosote, without talking, without pausing, almost without getting drunk, heading resolutely for oblivion. He had been drinking for two days. He had not eaten anything for nearer three.

He had hardly spoken since the ambulance trundled silently away—no need for a siren—with the bodies of Elizabeth Baron, aka Laura Wade, and Jamil Fahad who had never got back to his important job after all. The doctor who pronounced them dead left tranquilizers for Shimoni and Flynn, but neither used them. Shimoni spent a stormy hour crying into Flute's silky fur, and the dog cried too. After that she was on the road to recovery, unloading the horror behind her.

Flynn could not match her resilience. He had of course been much closer to it, and for longer. Once again he had been crucified by paradox, the shine stripped from his improbable survival by the death of the woman he had never got over, in front of his own eyes and at least arguably by his own hand. The charm and the curse had torn him between them to the end.

Shock and horror wrenched a cry from him as her face shattered like the image in a broken mirror. Her finger caught in the trigger-guard and he had not the sense to release the gun until Donnelly pried it out of his grasp and let the limp body with its terrible face fall away from him and find a kind of dignity among the roots and the leaf-mould. Still Flynn knelt there, wide-eyed and open-mouthed, unaware of her blood spattered on his face and shirt, until Donnelly lifted him to his feet almost bodily and steered him up the slope towards the cottage.

The shock Shimoni could understand, and the horror; even the grief, because whatever had happened in between he had loved her and she had died. What she could not understand and did not know how to deal with was this savage bleak despair he waded into like a man wading deliberately into a bog. Even the drink when he started into it was not so much an alcoholic's crutch as a suicide's weapon. When he looked at her at all, which he did not do often, she saw a pit in his soul filled with loathing.

It was not for her: she wished it had been, backlash hostility she could have coped with. As near as she could judge he was sick with hatred for a life bought with too much death. Now he had it safe home he did not know what to do with it. He had no use for it but nor could he give it up without making a mockery of all the sacrifice tied up in it. So he drank, alone in his savage silence, to avenge himself on a life he could neither endure nor abandon.

And Shimoni watched him covertly and wished she could take some of his hurting away. And she watched the clock and wished Todd would get here, and was afraid what would happen when he did.

When she heard the engine she hurried out to the front of the cottage and had her arms most of the way round Todd before he was fully out of the car. Shimoni was not a tall person, consequently her limbs were not long, and all of the way round Todd was a considerable distance. Most of the way was a creditable effort in the circumstances.

To his eternal credit, Todd asked about her before he asked about Flynn. His eyes were concerned. Her bruises were fading now, but not yet as if they had never been. "If I'd known what I was letting you in for, I wouldn't have brought him within ten miles of this place."

She stood on tip-toe and brushed a kiss lightly onto his cheek. He had shaved before leaving the hospital. So far as she could see he was none the worse for his fractured skull. His doctor must have thought so too, because he had raised no objection when Todd said he was leaving. Shimoni said, "Where else would you bring your problems?"

Flynn was in the kitchen, seated at the scrubbed pine table with no company other than an empty bottle, another going the same way and the dog Flute who appeared to have recognised a soul as mournful as his own and had taken to cramming himself under the vegetable rack.

Todd ambled into the kitchen as if he had been no further away than the livingroom all this time, and closed the door behind him. He made no acknowledgement of Flynn's presence. He went to the cupboard and found himself a glass. He pulled out a chair and sat down solidly, facing Flynn; facing the top of Flynn's head, rather, because he was hunched over the table and would not look up.

Todd took the bottle and poured himself a liberal measure. Fortunately it was Scotch, which he liked; he felt it could equally well have been wood alcohol or surgical spirit. He dumped another inch into Flynn's glass, which was not in fact a glass at all but a thick pottery mug which held more.

Tapped together the Tyrone crystal tumbler and the pot mug made a homely clink. Todd proposed as the toast an old Russian saying which had proved apt on divers occasions before today. "Life is hard," he said, "then you die."

That low abdominal rumbling was Flynn chuckling darkly into his mug. "Ain't that a fact." He emptied the mug and filled it again.

Todd drank more slowly but, despite it being good Scotch, with no greater enjoyment. It had been seven years since he had seen Flynn like this, and he had not expected to see it again. Even so there were differences, and not for the better. Flynn at twenty-four drinking himself to death for lack of anything better to do had at least given the impression that there was some glory in the light of a candle burning at both ends. He might have been starving, he might have been cold; his liver might have been on its last legs and his brain too slow for the petty larceny he lived by; but there had been a kind of bravado in his dissolution, a kind of guttering style. Todd looked at him now and saw nothing like that to redeem the bleakness of his intent. Flynn at thirty-one was drinking to make the world go away, and he was drinking fast because he wanted it to go sooner rather than later.

Finally Todd said, "She's dead then—Laura Wade."

Flynn grinned into his mug. But his voice was thick and bitter as gall, so perhaps he was just baring his teeth at it. "Oh yeah. Laura's dead. Fahad's dead. Everybody's bloody dead. Except Flynn. Good old Flynn with his charmed life, he ain't dead yet."

"So what am I," asked Todd, "the ghost of Hamlet's father?"

Flynn looked up at him for the first time. "I thought you were going to die. That bastard Fahad. I thought he'd killed you."

"He gave me a headache, that's all. But nothing to the one you're going to have."

Flynn grinned again. Almost there was a little humour in it this time. "She sent for you, did she? Shimoni? Flynn's drinking again, come and sort him out before his breath strips the wallpaper?"

Todd smiled. "Something like that. Except it's not the wallpaper she's worried about."

"No need to worry about Flynn," he said, heavily confidential. "Flynn's got it cracked. You want to know something?" He leaned forward over the table, peering into Todd's face. Todd nodded. "Do you?"

"Yes, Mickey."

"OK then. When my blood-alcohol level reaches four hundred milligrams of alcohol per hundred millilitres of blood"—he said this very carefully—"some poor sod on the Clapham omnibus will drop dead of alcoholic poisoning." He chuckled bleakly into the whisky.

Todd laughed too, softly, fondly. "Oh Mickey, Mickey." His gaze took in the bottles, the mug cupped in Flynn's hands protectively, as if he thought someone might try to snatch it. "What's this all about?"

Flynn leaned back, leaving his hands on the table. One was whiter than the other. The doctor Donnelly called had removed the wreckage of the plaster for him. It was weak and the scars of surgery livid against the sun-starved skin, but it was a working hand again. He could pour with it.

He lifted his eyes from the scrubbed pine and smiled. It was not something he did very often. Mostly he grinned, and his grin was a live thing, vibrant and wicked, that charmed and exasperated in approximately equal proportions like a fox seen high-tailing it out of a chicken-run with feathers on its nose.

The smile was different: quiet, secret, without artifice, without defences, the sweet smile of a child or a simpleton. It was the shortest distance between his soul and the outside world. Everything that he was had its reflection there. Todd who had seen happiness and hope and kindness and strength in their season was shocked by the depths of pain and sorrow and weakness he found there now.

"What can I tell you, Gil?" he said quietly, the words slurring only partly with the drink. "I think between them they have broken my heart."

Todd's cracked too; but all his instincts warned him that sympathy on his part now would be the unmanning of them both. Besides, Flynn could not afford the indulgence of compassion. "Mickey, I know you're hurting. I'm sorry, I wish there was something I could do about it. But there isn't. I can't help you, and I don't think anyone else can either.

"It's your burden, son. It's not fair, they had no right to dump it on you, but they did and now you've got to find some way to pick it up and carry it. Get drunk if you want to. Shout, cry, throw wild parties, bed a lot of women. But it'll be there waiting for you in the end, and in the end you're going to have to find a way of dealing with it.

"And I don't want to rush you, they say time heals and maybe it does if you're not using it to inflict new damage on yourself, but the clock's still running and the sooner you pull yourself together the better because you have things to do—important things. You're still the main witness in the prosecution of Byron Spalding for conspiracy to murder two hundred and twenty people, and various other crimes. Make no mistake, Hehn or no Hehn he'll fight it all the way. He'll have the best lawyers money can buy. And if there's anything worth more to them than Flynn dead, it's Flynn drunk and maudlin with it."

Flynn seemed barely to be taking in what he said. He mumbled into his mug, "Spalding's dead."

Todd knew he had been told, knew his mind was having trouble absorbing details and even more in recalling them. "No, he's *not* dead. Mickey, try and get your head together. Donnelly only said he died in the explosion to get you off the hook. He wasn't even at Deerings that day, he was already in police custody. Hehn's dead, but Spalding's alive and he's going on trial.

"And he's going to go free, too, unless you get your brain out of that bottle and face up to your responsibilities. Two hundred and twenty people died, Mickey. You are their witness. If you don't testify, their murderer goes free and their deaths unrequited. Is that what you want?"

Flynn's head twisted from side to side; he was not shaking it so much as trying to evade the assault. His emotions had already had all the punishment they could take, and then some; now Todd of all people was turning the screw on him, and turning and turning as if he could not hear him scream and his bones crack. "Gil, I—"

"Is that what you want?"

"No." His voice broke. His eyes travelled round the cornices of the room as if seeking an escape. "But I don't know if— I'm so damn tired."

"I know," said Todd, his tone unyielding. "But you can't rest yet. After the trial; then you can live or die as you choose. But for now you have work to do, and debts to pay."

At last his eyes came back to Todd's. There was no resolve there, only exhaustion and perhaps a little fear. "Oh God, Gil," he whispered, "we're back here again, aren't we?"

Todd understood. "It won't be so bad this time. For one thing you're stronger: I know you don't feel it right now, but you are. For another, it's only a few days' drinking you've got to get on top of, not a few years'. You'll cope. A rough day or two, a couple of bad nights, and you'll be in the clear. And then we make Deerings pay."

Todd sat with him until Flynn went to sleep with his head pillowed on his arms on the table. Then he went looking for Shimoni and a blanket.

Donnelly was still there. He nodded economically at the kitchen door. "Is he going to be all right?"

"Oh yes, I think so," said Todd. "It might take a bit of time. You could leave me the number of that psychiatrist, in case we need him. But Mickey'll come through. He's tougher than he thinks."

Todd saw the policeman out to his car. Pausing at the front gate he said, "There's one thing I don't understand."

"Only one?"

Todd smiled. "One to be going on with. Who bombed Deerings, and killed Hehn, and why?"

"We don't know who he was," said Donnelly, "and it's beginning to look as if he made a clean get-away. He was an American, probably a professional hired for the job. We know who sent him, though. Obregon."

Todd stared. "Tomas Obregon? Mickey's—?" He held his hand out brokenly. "The drug baron? How do you know?"

"He sent his calling card." Donnelly extracted a slip from his wallet. The original was under bond as evidence, but he had had copies made. He passed it to Todd without comment.

On the white card was a simple black line-drawing. It showed a big white car driving away from the smoking ruins of a building, and underneath was the legend "Next time kick the bottom out of somebody else's business."

About the Author

Jo Bannister is a former newspaper editor who lives in Northern Ireland. She has won several awards for journalism in the United Kingdom, and a Royal Society of Arts Bronze Medal. She is the author of nine previous novels; *Death and Other Lovers* is her seventh for the Crime Club.